A Cold Winter's Deathe

Also by Mark Wolfgang

Bedderhoff Dead

Available in print

Watch for these upcoming *Yoopernatural Mysteries*:

Deathe and Taxes

Deathe Warmed Over

A Cold Winter's Deathe

Tales of Life in Deathe

A Yoopernatural Mystery

by

Mark Wolfgang

Copyright © 2012 by Mark Wolfgang
First Edition
ISBN: 978-0-615-58811-7

All rights reserved.

This is a work of fiction. Names, places, brands, media, and incidents are either the product of the author's imagination or are used fictitiously. The author acknowledges the trademarked status and trademark owners of various products referenced in this work of fiction, which have been used without permission. The publication/use of these trademarks is not authorized, associated with, or sponsored by the trademark owners.

All rights reserved. Without limiting the rights under copyright reserved above, no part of this publication may be reproduced, stored in or introduced into a retrieval system, or transmitted, in any form, or by any means (electronic, mechanical, photocopying, recording, or otherwise) without the prior written permission of both the copyright owner and the publisher of this book.

All the characters portrayed herein are fictional. No resemblance to any real person, living, dead, undead, incorporeal, spiritual, metaphysical, unhinged, hinged or otherwise familiar to the reader or writer is purely unintentional. They might, however, be conglomerations of people and traits. If you know the author and think you recognize yourself in one of the characters, you might be right. But probably not.

Front and back cover photographs by Mark Wolfgang
Cover graphics & title work by KnowHow Graphic Design

www.yoopernaturalmysteries.com

Sudden Deathe Press, LLC
P.O. Box 325
Mason MI 48854

Thanks to my wife Kim for putting up with me and team-editing me with Thora Wease of Old School Editing, and Bonnie Gurzenda. Also: to my friends and supporters at Peninsula Writers and the Skaaldic Society; and Sue Howard of KnowHow Graphic Design for her phenomenal work on the front and back covers. They all serve to make me better than I am.

And special thanks to the residents of Deathe, Michigan, for letting me invade their town and their privacy to tell their stories.

Mark Wolfgang
January, 2012

A Cold Winter's Deathe

1

THE INVISIBLE MAN stumbled into the Buck Snort Saloon late on a January evening, materializing like a wraith out of the blizzard that howled through the streets of Deathe.

OK, that must be the wine talking.

Ron Blank held up his glass and peered through it.

It looked a lot like moose urine.

Normally, a newcomer to the Buck Snort at any hour would snag the attention of the regulars. Conversation and card games would pause and suspicious eyes would turn to the door. But this time there had been no reaction at all. Not so much as a glance. No one noticed him.

But the guy couldn't really be invisible, because Ron, maintenance electrician at Deathe's Cavendish Junior College, transplanted apple knocker and frequent, unintentional source of amusement to Tino and the boys of the Buck Snort, did notice.

And he wasn't much of a man, either, Ron thought. More of a boy, dressed in an enormous red plaid hunting coat and at least two or three layers of pants from the look of it, bunched up over unbuckled swampers. And a ratty, over-sized bomber hat that looked like a molting muskrat sitting on his head. It fit him like a bucket and whenever he turned his head the bomber hat was slow to respond. One ear flap was down, but the other stuck out like it was signaling a left turn.

The word *ridonkulous* popped into Ron's head.

OK, *de Invisible Yooper*, Ron thought with a grin.

And he appeared to be carrying a tackle box.

So de Invisible Yooper snagged two long neck beers off the tray carried by Tino, the bartender, and Tino didn't even notice. Tino got through the crowd to the table to make his delivery and discovered his tray was empty. He glared around the room for the joker thief. De Yooper walked past him, unseen, right under Tino's nose, practically brushing his arm. De Yooper just didn't register with Tino. Flashing a crooked grin, de Yooper tipped a bottle in silent salute, and Tino looked right through him.

Ron recognized a kindred spirit. As a mere maintenance guy, Ron was accustomed to being invisible to the faculty, administrators, and assorted academics and staff of the college. No one *ever* noticed him when he was wearing his Gray Uniform of Invisibility. Once he'd gotten over the frustration of it all, he'd discovered the benefits of eavesdropping with impunity.

And Ron was pretty good at seeing things and people that no one else saw. He had had his own personal ghost living with him in Cavendish House, the derelict old mansion in the bush that he'd bought when he'd moved back to Deathe five years earlier. Then there was Pud, the retired unhandy handyman Ron had replaced at the college, who just wouldn't politely go away, even after he died.

The Invisible Yooper wound his way to the cramped little booth tucked under the stairwell. With a slight wave of his hand, the couple sitting there rose and left without a glance toward the stranger. There was no place else to sit, so they had to squeeze in to stand at the bar.

Curious, Ron thought.

The blizzard, the worst of the season so far, rattled the windows, whistled around loose door frames, and howled through the empty room above the bar. Roaring in from Lake Superior, lifting over the ridges to the north and west of White Wolf Lake, it slanted through town, dumping massive loads of snow. There was no traffic on the streets of Deathe. Even the Close Finnish, the town's "inconvenience store," was closed up ahead of the storm, probably sold out of beer. The "Closed Finnish," it was called whenever the beer ran out.

Eventually The Masticator, Deathe's "Snowblower of Death," would clear the streets of the biggest snowdrifts, and most likely a few buried snowmobiles, and possibly a stray dog or two.

Deathe is a bony little village buried deep in Michigan's Upper Peninsula. It huddles in what the locals call the "iron bowl" on the south shore of White Wolf Lake, surrounded by rugged ridges that generate their own peculiar, and often brutal, weather patterns. Such as the storm that bore down on Deathe this Friday evening, blasting in from Lake

A Cold Winter's Deathe

Superior, dumping untold tons of snow and piling it up in drifts five and six feet high.

Buck Snort patrons were still arriving occasionally, on snowmobiles now, greeted with the expected attention of the crowd. Spending a Friday night trapped at the Buck Snort was sometimes preferable to being snowed in at home with a wife and kids.

No snowmobile for Ron. If he really needed one, he could borrow it. He now lived within easy slogging distance of the bar. Well, "easy" when Deathe wasn't in the middle of the worst blizzard of the season. Erin Coe, Ron's newly hired student intern at the CJC maintenance department, lived a couple miles east of town and had just bailed on him and high-tailed it for home after their traditional Friday after-work burgers and drinks (Erin a Coke, Ron a glass of the house wine, or two or three).

Erin's internship was testament to her wit, guile, and clever subterfuge, in deflecting the objections of Ron's boss Ed Posen, the nominal Director of Facilities Maintenance, and by doing end runs around Lucy "Lucifer" Fergusen, the office manager who actually ran the place as her personal totalitarian regime. So far Lucifer hadn't ripped Erin's throat out, and Erin had even somehow managed to steal her way into Ed's good graces.

Ron hadn't even known Ed *had* good graces.

"He wants me to *coblabberate* with him on remodeling the chemistry lab," Erin had confided to Ron earlier. "*Coblabberate*," she intoned. "I don't think he was being ironic."

"First, Ed wouldn't know the meaning of the word 'ironic,'" Ron said. "Second, *coblabberation* is his new *modus operandi*, right after intimidation and verbal abuse. It gives him the opportunity to blame someone else when things go wrong."

Ed had learned this clever new management technique—actually, *collaboration,* of course—from the mandatory seminars ordered by Miriam Afrika, the interim replacement for President Seagal, who was now under indictment on a multitude of fraud and embezzlement charges.

Meet the new boss, same as the old boss.

Erin had also been trying to talk Ron into staying on at CJC.

"How can I be an *intern* if I don't have a *mentor*?"

A few days earlier, in a moment of weakness, Ron had confided to Erin that he was under consideration for another job out of state. Maybe. He didn't want to jinx it by offering details. And he was wary of burning bridges at the college if the offer didn't pan out. To say nothing of how embarrassing that situation would be for him personally. So he swore her to secrecy.

Erin had bolted for home before the blizzard shut down the whole town, her old Jeep bucking the snowdrifts in crawler gear, leaving Ron to sit alone in the back of the bar, listening to the wind hammer the old saloon.

Inside the Buck Snort there was still plenty of high living going on.

Ron was kicked back at his table, watching the rowdy Friday evening crowd while nursing his wine (*Vin du Swill?* Whatever it was, he was sure Tino bought it in 40-gallon steel drums) and considering his future at CJC, or elsewhere, depending on how things worked out. By this time he was about one sip away from being legally impaired, but that was irrelevant, because he'd left his 1988 American Motors Eagle Wagon—another inexhaustible source of amusement to the Yoopers of Deathe—parked at Mrs. Kinderly's boarding house on the west edge of town. That a dumb Loper living in da Yoo Pee would buy a clapped out, decades old AMC station wagon, then proceed to "invest" nearly five times its value in rebuilding, repairing, and repainting the thing, with the misguided idea that it would serve him reliably through the long Deathe winters... Well, that certainly did not earn the respect and admiration of the locals. At least AMC had never offered a Pacer with all wheel drive, or he might have been tempted.

"You replace da silly putty in da transmission?" they would ask. "You gotta replace da silly putty every quarter million miles or so." Solemn faces and universal attitudes of deep concern almost had him. The car had 212,000 miles on the clock when he bought it.

But Ron knew they were kidding. He thought they were kidding. So of course they weren't kidding. Not precisely. As he found out when the transfer case seized up, and he had to rebuild the thing and replace the silly putty.

The Invisible Yooper slid into the booth under the stairs and pulled off his bomber hat, unleashing an explosion of hair that had probably never seen the inside of a barber shop. He sipped his beer and scanned the room, and when his eyes—they looked to be amber in the dim light—wandered Ron's way, Ron met his gaze and lifted his glass to this kindred soul.

De Invisible Yooper jerked and his amber eyes popped with an expression of shock and... *horror?* At being seen?

A Cold Winter's Deathe

And then Ron's view was blocked. Surprised by the kid's reaction, he craned his neck to see around the obstruction when the obstruction suddenly spoke in Beth Atkins' voice.

"Ron Blank, you old cradle robber," she said cheerfully. "You sittin' here wit' all your friends?"

Ron blinked and cringed and looked up to see Beth grinning down at him. She nodded to the empty chairs on either side of him.

An exceptionally tall woman stood at Beth's side, bundled up in a puffy pink parka over a red plaid flannel shirt and camouflage snowpants—belonging to Beth's state cop boyfriend Bill Trevarthan, no doubt. The Amazon glanced sidelong at Beth, then examined Ron with accusing gunmetal blue eyes.

Beth Atkins, elementary teacher at Deathe Consolidated Schools and Ron's best friend in town, stood side by each with Michigan State Police Trooper Alice Louise Dubose, recently assigned to the Upper Peninsula from the Detroit area. At a shade over six feet tall, Alice towered over Beth and Ron and most of the Buck Snort patrons.

"Cradle robber?" Alice Louise growled down at him.

"She's kidding!" Ron protested. He turned to Beth. "Tell her you're kidding!"

"Oh really?" Alice narrowed her steel blue eyes to slits and fixed Ron with a withering glare. "How old was that little chippie that just left a few minutes ago?"

"She's eighteen! At least! Maybe nineteen! You met her in the fall. Remember? Erin Coe. She's my intern now!"

And you've got all her vitals and her fingerprints on file, he thought.

"*Intern?* I see... Barely legal, then? You're sure?"

"Beth!" Ron pleaded to his friend.

"I'm kidding," Beth said. "Al knows you're not a child molester. Right, Al? Right?"

Ron looked back and forth between them.

"Ron." Alice said. "I'm messing with you. I'll take Beth's word on it. You're *probably* not a cradle robber."

"A bit mentally unstable and a wretched host," Beth added, "trying to scare poor Al here with your ghost stories and all. You can't believe how she makes me suffer for sending her to your haunted house for Homecoming week. You prob'ly shouldn't drink dat," Beth said with a nod toward Ron's wine glass. "It might make you go blind."

"Prob'ly not the only t'ing dat might make him go blind," Alice Louise added in an unexpectedly accurate Yooper accent.

Ron's neck and cheeks flared with sudden heat. "Hey!"

The women looked at each other and giggled, and Ron guessed they'd probably started celebrating the end of the work week earlier that evening.

"Oh! Don't say anyt'ing to anyone about Al!" Beth said. "She's incognito tonight."

Ron had noticed. Alice Louise had never dressed like a doofus. Beth looked trim and stylish, as always, in leather jacket and snug jeans tucked into stylish Sorel boots, her silky brown hair haloing her head like a mink pillbox hat out of *Dr. Zhivago*.

Alice Louise Dubose was *way* out of uniform, in her pink parka and camo pants. Her ash blond hair was hidden under one of Beth's old chukes. Hand knit by Beth's arthritic, colorblind grandmother, it was a psychedelic wonder, with gaping holes, uneven ear flaps, and raggedy tassels.

Unlike Ron, Alice Louise Dubose was a true Loper. A flatlander. A troll who lived *under da bridge*. And she was a state cop—*incognito*, Beth had said, as if no one in Deathe would know who she was. She had made quite an impression a couple months earlier, when she'd busted a North Korean murderer, and then nearly put Ron's college out of business by arresting the president, probably just before he could put the college out of business by embezzling everything he and his lawyer could squeeze out of it. And she'd nearly died for her troubles. After ruining Ron's shoes. But she had proved herself to be tough and fair. Solid. And an accidental friend to the locals, when she gave them the opportunity to take back control of Cavendish Junior College.

As a State Trooper, and not a reviled conservation officer from the Department of Natural Resources (or Department of No Results, as the locals called it), everyone gave her a pass. Ron noticed that the bar patrons had even discretely hidden away their cigarettes.

"Good to see you again, Ron." Alice Louise plucked off her chopper and extended her hand, and Ron took it. Her grip was firm.

She hooked her thumb at the blizzard raging outside the front door. "Shouldn't you be getting back to Cavendish House before you get socked in here?"

A Cold Winter's Deathe

"I had to close it up for the winter," he said. "I'm staying at Mrs. Kinderly's Boarding House now."

"What, you took *my* room?" Alice Louise said with mock dismay. After closing the cases on Helen Kim, the terror of Cavendish Junior College, and the college's crooked President Seagal, Ron had suggested she should move into Deathe and live at Mrs. Kinderly's. But she was assigned to a post in the far west end of the Upper Peninsula, and living in Ironwood, as far as Ron knew, and had no intention in the world of ever living in Deathe. In fact, he was kind of surprised to see her here again, and so soon. She never hid her dislike of the town.

"Just temporarily, until we solve some infrastructural issues."

"With Cathy Cadaver's old house?"

Ron cringed at the name given to Ron's old mansion, former home of the legendary Miss Catherine Cavendish. "No. Remember the rickety old iron bridge leading to it?" he said.

"Condemned?"

"Collapsed."

"Ron was driving on it at the time," Beth chirped. "Totaled his Travelall and nearly got himself killed!"

This had been in the late fall. There was no chance of rebuilding the bridge now that it was just a loose pile of twisted iron girders and wooden planks at the bottom of the Stoney Creek ravine. His thoughts of cobbling together some logs to span the deep creek had not been realistic. Once the International Travelall was hooked, reeled in, landed on the back of the Toivo's Towing, Tackle & Live Bait Shop flatbed, and hauled unceremoniously away, Ron had hiked back and forth to Cavendish House four times, shutting down and winterizing the house, and dragging as many of his essential possessions out as he could before winter hit. He'd taken a room at the boarding house. And then he'd bought the AMC Eagle wagon, hoping its primitive all wheel drive would see him through a Deathe winter in style and with some degree of reliability. He was wrong on most counts. But several thousands of dollars later, he thought it looked really great.

"So, what? You can't even get to your house?" Alice Louise asked.

Ron shook his head sadly.

"And he left behind all his nice booze, too. Hey! We need summa dat stimulus money," Beth said. "I got a shovel!"

They all laughed.

The women shifted, and Ron peered between them toward the booth under the stairs. He had forgotten about the Invisible Man. But there was a ghost of a man there. Ron could just make him out in the shadows. He could almost see the face. Then he seemed to fade away again.

"Did you see the guy who just came in a few minutes ago?" Ron asked. He nodded through the crowd toward the booth.

The women turned and squinted through the blue haze of illicit cigarette smoke. Alice Louise was tall enough to see over the heads of most of the revelers.

"In the booth under the stairs," Ron said, but now he couldn't be sure if there was anyone there or not. After a moment all three gave up. Beth gave Ron a confused shrug. Alice Louise regarded him as if he might be a bit drunk. Which, he had to admit, he was.

The Invisible Man had vanished.

"Care to sit with me?" Ron asked the girls.

"No thanks," Beth chirped. "We're going to hit the illegal poker game in the back."

Ron relaxed a little, knowing the pressure was off him, then he stiffened. "You're going to bust the game?"

"Nah," Beth said with a grin. "We're going to clean out the locals."

With a wink, she and Alice Louise headed toward the back room, bumping shoulders and giggling like schoolgirls.

"Hey, Alice!" Ron called after them. "You still owe me a pair of shoes."

"I put it on my expense report," Alice Louise said over her shoulder with a grin. "It was denied."

Ron didn't care. He turned to see the Invisible Yooper pop out of the booth under the stairs and make his way through the crowded bar... toward Ron.

2

"YOU CAN SEE ME?" the kid asked as he dropped into the chair next to Ron.

He looked dumbfounded, and Ron fought to stifle a laugh.

"Of course. I mean... Why not? You're not *really* invisible, you know," Ron said gently.

"Holy Man," the kid said. He tipped back his beer and took half the bottle at a swallow. He stuck his hand out at Ron's face. "How many fingers?" he demanded.

"Four. And a thumb," Ron said, taking the challenge and being precise, but when the kid's hand turned he added, "but just the one extended now. And that isn't polite."

"Hey, no offense, man. But yah, eh, I really am invisible. When I wanna be. Watch dis!" He tipped back in his chair and boldly snagged another beer off the table of four rough and burly outdoorsmen. The type Ron would never dare to mess with.

There was absolutely no reaction, until Tuck Saarinen scowled around the bar with bleary-eyed confusion when he reached for the bottle and it wasn't there, shrugged, and called for another.

"See? Let's go back to my booth. We can talk dere. You prob'ly don't wanna be seen sittin' here mutterin' to yourself." He emptied the bottle and slammed it down on the table.

"Um, no thanks," Ron said, wondering, *why do these odd people always have to find me?* "I'd prefer to stay here." *Where I won't feel trapped,* he thought. "Besides, someone else is in your booth now." He nodded with relief toward the stairs, where another couple had moved in and gotten cozy.

"No problem, man. Dey'll leave. You'll see."

Ron started to protest, but the young Yooper abruptly stood and weaved his way through the crowd, grabbing up bottles of beer as he went, and the couple vacated the booth as promised. Ron found he was sitting in their place, on the bench, in the booth, across from the Invisible Yooper, with a beer in his hand.

"Pretty cool trick, eh?" The kid beamed like he was showing off a shiny new toy.

Ron looked back and saw his table had already filled with half a dozen people, including the couple who'd just left the booth.

"Who in the hell are you?" Ron demanded, and just then a blast of icy wind hit the broad west wall of the bar and sleet pelted the plate glass front window. It bowed ominously. Expecting it to explode inward, Ron cringed.

The kid was unfazed and about to speak, when the front door of the Buck Snort slammed open. Everyone paused, looked up as usual, then cringed, eyes wide, and ducked as Carl Rowley stalked into the bar—hatless, coat open in defiance of the brutal weather. Alligator cowboy boots kicked coats and buckle boots out of the way as Carl came through the entry, trailed by his minions.

The attentions of all the Buck Snort patrons focused instantly inward. Two dozen or so tough and burly Yoopers and their women-folk turned away to contemplate their navels and the long neck beer bottles on their tables or in their hands with Zen-like concentration.

The Deathe Terror Alert level jumped from *Mild* to *Severe*.

Ron had never had the "pleasure" of meeting Carl, which is to say he'd never come into the range of the big bruiser's radar. He'd just known Carl by a reputation that cut a wide swath through Deathe and the surrounding area.

Carl was Trouble, pure and simple. *With a capital T, and that rhymes with C, and that stands for Carl*, Ron thought.

Carl strolled through the quiet bar, followed by his brother Shelby, and Dennis Whitehead, another notorious local lout, and Carl's son Greg, a rail-thin boy of sixteen. The only sound was the wind-whipped snow, the music on the jukebox, and the occasional clink of a glass or bottle. Conversation, what there was of it, was held in muted whispers accompanied by furtive glances.

Carl Rowley fortuitously found three empty stools in the packed saloon when their occupants suddenly melted into the woodwork.

A Cold Winter's Deathe

This was hardly comparable with the stealthy powers of the Yooper kid. These three bar patrons knew exactly who they were giving their stools up to. Even Ron felt the blood drain from his face.

"You look like you seen a ghost," the kid said. He tipped back his bottle and examined Carl with suddenly cold eyes. "So who is dat guy?"

Ron blew out his breath. "Carl Rowley," he said.

"He's some kind of bad news, eh?"

"Oh yah. I used to wonder why no one would stand up to him, but it all came clear pretty fast. Don't get on his bad side. And he doesn't have a good side. He holds a grudge. And he isn't going away." Ron looked at the young Yooper looking at Carl.

"Last summer two of Fred Andersen's heifers disappeared. Fred's the old guy sitting there at the bar," Ron added with a nod in Fred's direction. Fred was shrunken down as small as possible. "Fred's wife Gertie got up on her hind legs and accused Carl, and she was probably right, but that was *not* wise. She pressed Chief Woody, our chief of police, for an investigation. No evidence was found, no charges were filed, but the next day Gertie's sweet old Angora housecat, Boopsie, turned up dead on her porch, her neck snapped."

"Dat's cold, man," the kid said. His eyes were locked on Carl like targeting radar.

"Oh yah. Then a shotgun blast took out the Andersens' front window while they were at church the next Sunday. Then the oil drain plug on Fred's Buick 'fell off,' smoking the engine a half a mile from his house. Chief Woody just happened to drive by Carl's house south of town that evening, and that night the Deathe P.D.'s old Jeep Cherokee caught fire and burned down to the rims. All chalked up to coincidence," Ron added.

Ron knew, as the town knew, there was no such thing as a fair fight unless Carl won.

But Carl was mellow this evening. Silent, head down, settling in quietly at the maplewood bar. Tino quickly racked up three beers, three shots, and one Coke, without a word from Carl.

Hunching over his beer and cigarettes, massive paws relaxed and at rest, claws retracted, Carl was a sullen grizzly in brown Carhartts. Shelby and Dennis sat on either side of him, still wearing their coats. Carl kept his on, and he had not yet told them they could take theirs off. Young Greg clung to a small corner of the counter, sipping the Coke.

Do bears even have retractable claws? Ron wondered. He thought not. Irrelevant. It didn't matter, as long as Carl kept his sheathed.

"But back to the matter at hand," Ron said. "Who are you?"

"You can call me Conrad, eh? I'd shake hands wit' ya, but sometimes that don't work out so well." He sighed and his shoulders slumped with resignation, apparently a personal shortcoming that Ron couldn't fathom.

"*Conrad?*" Ron practically barked with laughter. "I would never take you for a.... hmm"

He sat back in his chair and regarded the kid critically. The young Yooper tightened his lips and squinted back. Ron thought of the kid's tricky little skill at snaking through the crowds unseen, and stealing beers from big Upper Peninsula Finnish bruisers with impunity.

No, he was more like an unkempt sprite. A fairy. *No*, not *that*. Ron ran through a list of fairy tale dwellers in his mind. Goblin? Elf? A dryad? Certainly not a *troll*. Although he could easily be a poltergeist. And maybe not a fairy tale character at all... exactly.

"*Puck!*" Ron exclaimed.

"Hey! Watch your language!" The kid's eyes darted around the room. "Dere might be ladies present!"

"No. I said *Puck*. Like in Shakespeare's *A Midsummer Night's Dream*. Puck. That would be *you*."

Puck leveled a disapproving glare at Ron.

"I t'ink I hearda dat guy. Shakespeare, I mean. But who's dis Puck person?"

Ron explained, to the best of his meager ability, that Puck was a clever and mischievous elf, "shrewd and knavish sprite." A trickster who would "*mislead night wanderers, laughing at their harm.*"

"OK." Puck said, nodding with considered approval as he tried his new name on for size. "Dat sounds like me. I t'ink I like it."

"You have a last name?"

Puck's shoulders slumped. "Not anymore." He stared morosely at the scarred table. "I don't wanna talk about it. So what's your name?" he asked, taking a tug off his purloined beer and peering at Ron over the top of it.

Ron told him.

"Ron *Blank?* Are you serious? *I love dat name!* Maybe I'll take it for myself! What brought *you* to dis corner of de U.P.?"

A Cold Winter's Deathe

Ron told him about first coming to Deathe when he was sixteen, when his father, Jim Blankenship, had packed up Ron and his mother and moved them north to Deathe, his father's newfound favorite vacation spot, thinking he could be a big fish in a small pond and mold Deathe to satisfy his own ego.

Things had not worked out as Jim Blankenship expected. The locals did not appreciate his interference in their town and their business. So after Ron's graduation from Deathe High School, Jim gathered up his small family and fled back to Chicago.

But more than a decade later, Ron had returned with an electrical engineering degree in his pocket and a bundle of carefully husbanded money in his bank account from working at his father's electrical engineering firm. He came back to a place he loved and appreciated more than his father ever could. He changed his name from Orion Clemons Blankenship to just Ron Blank to protect the innocent (himself), and took a job as maintenance electrician at Cavendish Junior College. Ron had renewed his acquaintanceship with strange things—like the haunted mansion of the Upper Peninsula's legendary "Cathy Cadaver," which he bought and moved into, ghost and all. And the Bottomless Pit next door. And Pud, CJC's deceased unhandy handyman, who was not related to the Phantom of the Liberal Studies Building, CJC's annoying poltergeist.

"O-*ree*-un Clemons Blankenship," Puck echoed. "Yah, OK. I can see why you changed your name. So what is dis town? Like, de black heart of all t'ings evil in de U.P.? How come I never heard of it before?"

"That's pretty much exactly what it is," Ron said. "But it's mostly harmless."

Without a word between them, they both turned to stare at the broad back of Carl Rowley.

"And Deathe seems to fly under the radar of pretty much everyone who doesn't live here," Ron added.

After a few minutes of nervous anticipation, the Terror Alert Level in the Buck Snort slipped from *Severe* down to merely *High*. The normal activities of the bar resumed, slowly, tentatively, as the relieved patrons eventually decided the bear wasn't hungry this evening. With Carl, Ron knew, you could never tell. He could seem to be your best friend, or he could be a hand grenade with a loose pin just looking for a place to detonate. And often both at the same time. It was always better to lay low, hang close to the door, and watch for the first signs of trouble.

The bear was lethargic. Almost hibernating. He hadn't spoken a word to anyone, just calling for more beers and shots with a double tap of his massive ring on his empties.

Tino was very attentive. His eyes never rose above the level of Carl's barrel chest.

Much of the town had turned out that night for a few hours of Tino's brown-bottled amnesia, the better to take shelter from the storm. Twenty or thirty men, and half a dozen women, not counting Beth and Alice Louise in the back, all dressed like lumberjacks against the blizzard, crowded the primitive bar that night. Jake the Dog, Ron Borke's Blue Heeler with the glass eye, kept his wary attention on everyone's feet from his station beneath Borke's table.

At the pool table, Borke and Tom Dicksen circled like hungry animals hovering over downed prey, as they studied the lay of the balls and carefully lined up their next shots as though all life in Deathe depended upon the outcome. They were big men with stout bellies, full beards, and intractable long hair. Ron Borke, Ron Blank's next-door neighbor—an unfortunate coincidence, living right next door, sharing the same first name, confusing the neighbors, and especially the postman—wore a grubby fluorescent orange stocking cap. Tom's cap was the more typical Yooper-issue green camouflage, and both wore quilt-lined flannel shirts that made them seem even larger than they were. Big burly guys with third-degree hat-hair.

Someone dropped a quarter in the jukebox and the noise level increased exponentially. Voices were jacked up to compete with the music. Some dancing was attempted without noticeable success. Pool balls clacked and men laughed and women giggled, and Tony Emmons stood on his chair and accompanied Billy Joel in singing "Just the Way You Are" to Clara Andersen. Jake the Dog sat up and joined in for three-part harmony before two guys pulled Tony down to the floor and sat on him, and stuffed ice cubes down his collar until he cried Uncle. They all erupted in fits of laughter.

"So what are you doing here on a night like this?" Ron asked. He nodded to Puck's red plaid hunting jacket. "You're dressed like a hunter, but this certainly isn't hunting season."

Ron heard a yelp and saw Jake the Dog tumbling across the floor. The Blue Heeler came to rest in the corner, a lifeless pile of limp fur. His glass eye had popped out and now ricocheted through the table legs.

Carl Rowley was on his feet, a rheumy-eyed Golem glaring around the bar.

The bear had come out of hibernation.

3

WELL THIS doesn't look good, Alice Louise thought.

She glanced around the table at the four men challenging Beth and her. They were a rough lot, with blood in their eyes. Or maybe just bloodshot eyes. And slurred speech.

Beth had handled the introductions. No one had stood. Alice Louise had learned over the years not to expect it. She overlooked the contraband cigarettes that were discretely hidden away when she'd entered the room.

First came Arno Svensen. Then two biker dudes, Detmar and Smoke. Claimed they rode to the bar on their Harley snowmobiles. Did Harley Davidson make snowmobiles? Then Bill, who looked like he'd just dropped his tools and crawled out of a grease pit in a truck garage, still wearing grimy coveralls. Finally, a hard man who must have been 80 if he was a day, with gnarled hands and craggy brows and a scar just below his left jaw, as if someone had once tried to slit his throat. Beth had said his name, but Alice Louise found it unpronounceable. Part of it sounded like "roach hair."

"We call him Rick for short." Beth leaned in and added in a boozy stage whisper, "the 'P' is silent."

Alice Louise cringed. But "Rick" hooted.

Arno Svensen had a broad, sloppy face. He was exceptionally scruffy, and wall-eyed. Confusing as hell. She was sure he could see around corners, and he was always trying to peek at her cards with one eye while the other distracted her with a baleful glare.

A Cold Winter's Deathe

But maybe that was just the booze clouding her mind. She and Beth had been tippling since four o'clock, when Alice Louise had blown into town just ahead of the big storm, looking forward to a girls' weekend of sisterly bonding and retail therapy. They'd planned to cruise up to Houghton and Hancock, maybe spend the night at the Magnuson Hotel, hit all the bars on both sides of the Portage Canal lift bridge, then maybe take a loop around the Keweenaw Peninsula before the snow got really deep and roads were closed.

"Head 'er for Sagola!" Beth said with an expectant, sidelong glance at Alice Louise. But Alice Louise had left her friend dissatisfied, refusing to rise to the bait and ask for the Finglish to English translation. She later found out it meant to paint the town red. Neither saying made much sense, she decided.

They thought they would explore Calumet and Laurium. Maybe even Copper Harbor, assuming there was anything to see way up there, besides Lake Superior ice floes and the ghost of the *Edmund Fitzgerald*. Which, Beth insisted, had sunk off Whitefish Point, nowhere near the Keweenaw Peninsula. Whatever.

This was Alice's first full weekend off since she'd hit the U.P. in October. Two months, fifteen days, and about... she glanced at her watch, a three-dollar plastic digital she'd bought at the Close Finnish in October when she'd learned that her father's Seiko truly did not work in Deathe. Twenty-one hours. But who was counting?

As the low seniority Trooper at the Ironwood post, she'd not only drawn weekend duty, she'd volunteered for it. What else was there to do? She was still living in a motel room, paying by the week, until she got her footing. She had no idea how long that would take. A year? With any luck she'd be back home in Brighton before she settled.

Thanksgiving had been spent propped on her bed in the motel, watching TV and eating lukewarm broasted chicken take-out. Christmas was worse. She'd been invited to Gray Mackie's house. Her boss, the post commander, had obviously taken pity on her, and she'd reluctantly joined him and his wife Lisa, their two kids, and, as it turned out, a couple dozen of his extended family, friends, and neighbors. In the midst of that crowd, she'd never felt so alone in her life. An orphan. In a strange and unwelcoming place.

She'd gone straight back to the motel and called her mother. They'd talked for an hour, until Alice Louise's cell phone had died. After a quick charge she'd called Beth and they'd conspired to play hookie and hit the roads for a long weekend.

Then, half an hour after she'd pulled into Deathe, the storm had come down like the hammer of God and canceled all their plans. So they'd uncapped a few bottles, and Beth challenged her to play poker with the boys at the Buck Snort Saloon, and here they were.

Alice Louise and Beth held most of the quarters on the table. And most of the bottles, as she counted them. Assuming she wasn't seeing double.

And she was also staring at a fistful of aces and eights.

The proverbial dead man's hand.

She shuddered.

I am no man! she thought defiantly. Hadn't that worked for Eowyn, niece of King Theoden of Rohan, when she tore off her battle helmet and drove a sword straight into the face of the Witch-King of Angmar, the Ringwraith?

Alice Louise glanced at Arno Svensen. He looked like an Orc. She hoped she wouldn't need the healing powers of Aragorn.

Unless maybe Aragorn was good with hangovers.

Svensen's left eye tried to sneak a better look at Alice Louise's hand. She shot him a warning glare and pulled the cards close. She turned to Beth for support, but Beth was staring into space, her face screwed up with confusion.

"Wha–?" Alice Louise didn't finish before Beth shushed her.

She turned to see where Beth was looking—the door that led to the main floor of the saloon. She realized what was wrong. It was quiet out there. No sound but the howl of the wind in the eaves. Then there came a sound of rapping. Thump, thump, thump. Something solid, like a tire iron on wood.

She and Beth exchanged glances. As one, they pushed back from the table. Alice Louise snagged her shoulder bag. It was reassuringly heavy.

A Cold Winter's Deathe

4

EVERYONE KNEW the bear was fully awake now, and all conversation stumbled to a halt. Even Shelby and Dennis Whitehead looked bright-eyed with fearful anticipation. Greg Rowley stayed quiet and low at the end of the bar.

"*If you should happen to encounter a bear in the wild, drop slowly to the ground and curl up into a fetal position to protect your major organs. Do not run. Play dead until the bear leaves.*"

The Deathe Terror Alert Level was now flashing neon red at about 20,000 watts.

Carl appraised the sheep trapped in the pen. His paws hung loose at his sides, but the claws were out now. Even the biggest, toughest bruisers in the place pointedly avoided his gaze and concentrated their attention somewhere—anywhere—else. Tony and his buddies pulled themselves up from the floor and settled meekly into their chairs and studied their cocktail napkins. From the corner of his eye Ron saw three men slip out the back door with the stealth of cat burglars, hugging their coats under their arms until they were safely outside in the blizzard.

Ron Borke sidled over to check on Jake, now shivering and cowering by the front door. Only Carl's eyes followed, dead and cold.

On the jukebox, Billy Joel crooned his finale and a pall fell over the room. Another platter dropped into place and Bonnie Raitt sang of the pain of growing old and then finding love in the "Nick of Time." Her smoky voice carried sweetly throughout the bar, incongruously soft and soothing.

Mark Wolfgang

Carl nudged Dennis and tipped his head toward the jukebox. Dennis swaggered through the crowd and pulled the plug. Tino didn't object. The room fell silent. Outside the wind hissed.

Carl turned and strolled along the bar, his big steel ring going thump, thump, thump on the scuffed maplewood. He clapped old Fred Andersen on the shoulder with the easy familiarity of life-long buddies, and Ron saw Fred flinch under the strength of Carl's grip. Two guys at an exposed table took that opportunity to scoop up their drinks and skulk away to safety at the back of the saloon.

Carl looked down at Borke and Jake. Borke had found Jake's glass eye—really a blue marble—cleaned it with a paper napkin, and successfully plugged it back into the empty socket. Jake kept a wary watch on Carl with his good eye.

"You oughtta take that dog home. He don't look so good."

Borke stared at the floor. His tiny nod of agreement was hard to see.

At the far end of the bar, near the front door where Borke knelt over Jake, Raúl Lopez hunched as though against the cold, staring at his fingernails. Carl took notice, and now clapped a paw on Raúl's shoulder.

"Hey, Tino. Put our drinks on Pedro's tab," he said. "Pedro here'll cover us." He leaned in close to Raúl's ear. "Won't ya? *Pedro?*"

Raúl was a small man with the scruffy shadow of a beard, bundled up against the Michigan winter in a ragged brown canvas coat and coveralls. Ron knew his family. His daughter Maria was in Beth's third grade class at Deathe Consolidated. Ron knew their story. And he knew Raúl couldn't afford the Corona he'd been nursing for the better part of an hour now. That's why Ron had bought it for him. Raúl hunched closer to the bar and examined his hands with single-minded devotion.

Shelby, now at Carl's side, snickered. Time, at least there in the Buck Snort, held its breath.

Carl waved his hand idly at Dennis, who quickly dug into his coat and fished out a cigarette pack and shook out an unfiltered Camel. Carl took it without shifting his gaze from Raúl and waited patiently while Dennis lit it for him.

Raúl swallowed hard and cleared his throat. "Carl, you know I ain't got no money."

A Cold Winter's Deathe

Carl scowled. "*Carl*? Pedro, I don't think you know me well enough to call me Carl. I think you should call me Mr. Rowley. Don't you think so too, Pedro?"

Dennis and Shelby snickered.

"I suppose so. Mr. Rowley." Raúl's voice was very soft. "But...."

Carl took a drag on the cigarette and focused his full attention on poor Raúl. Ron could detect a sense of relief from the crowd around him. Carl had found his target for the evening. It was as though the herd had just left their weakest member to the predator in order to save itself. Ron was suddenly aware that he was clenching his jaw.

"But what, Pedro?" Carl asked. His voice was butter. Kind and concerned. A real teddy bear.

Raúl shrugged. "I don't got no money, Mr. Rowley," he said in a Mexican accent that he would certainly never shed no matter how long he might live in the north of Michigan.

"That's okay, Pedro. Tino'll run a tab for you. Won'tcha, Tino?"

Tino shrugged without comment, then nodded almost imperceptibly.

"See? Tino's a helluva guy, ain't he? Besides, I thought I heard you was coming into some money pretty soon." Carl stepped in close beside Raúl.

"I don't know what you mean, Mr. Rowley."

"Sure you do, Pedro." Carl took a deep drag on the Camel and blew it across Raúl's face. "I heard you got a snowmobile stolen a few weeks ago. I figured you was gonna get some insurance money out of it pretty soon." Carl's voice was soft, but managed to carry to the far corners of the bar. This was a performance, Ron realized, for the benefit of all present.

"I can't afford no insurance," Raúl said with a shrug. Ron saw his eyes dart from side to side, looking for the rest of the herd. It shuffled and coughed nervously just outside the circle of danger.

"Now that's a shame, Pedro. Seems that I just came to own a snowmobile just like yours. Almost exactly like yours. I picked it up pretty cheap, too. Damned reasonable. Thought maybe you and me could cut a deal on it. I guess I'll just have to find somebody else to take it off my hands. That would be a shame, Pedro, you needing a snowmobile and all. But, hey! Business is business. You understand."

Carl's meaning could not be lost on anyone. If anything went missing in Deathe, it vanished out of the county. Carl Rowley did a big business in snowmobiles, chain saws, snowblowers, and lots of other highly portable and virtually untraceable hardware. It didn't pay to ask how he came by it all. People who asked too many questions of Carl's business suffered from extended runs of bad luck. Dogs getting shot. Barns burning down. Tires getting slashed. Things like that. One of Carl's long-running feuds cooled when Toivo Sarinen was shot and wounded in a hunting accident, still unsolved. Mere coincidence, the locals were assured.

Up in the wilderness, especially in Deathe, where the surrounding hills funnel snow with a vengeance, a snowmobile is not an entertaining luxury. When the wind screams around the ridges and the snowdrifts pile up six feet and more in the heart of town, even the biggest, meanest four-wheel drive truck with tractor tires and snow chains might not make it past the end of the driveway. A snowmobile is often the only thing moving. It can literally mean the difference between life and death. To steal a man's snowmobile in the dead of winter is about as low as you can get. Yet somehow Carl Rowley made a good living at it, smuggling them out of the county, and almost certainly out of the U.P., without repercussion.

Ron felt his blood simmering to a boil.

Carl took a deep drag on his Camel, picked a bit of tobacco off his tongue, and examined it minutely before wiping it on Raúl's coat. Turning and leaning back casually, with his elbows on the bar, he hooked the heel of his cowboy boot on the foot rail and surveyed his captive audience.

"Tell me, Pedro," he said finally, and his low, deep voice carried throughout the bar. He flicked his cigarette butt to the floor. It sparked and sizzled in a wet boot print. "What's a wetback like you doing up here in da north country anyway? I mean, don't wetbacks have thin blood? From the Mexican heat? Seems to me you'd be damned cold up here. And maybe a little homesick. It'd have to be especially tough here without any winter transportation. Ain't it? Maybe I should give you a ride back to the border. Kick your greaser ass right across da Rio *Gran-day*. Whaddya think about that idea, Pedro?"

Somewhere far behind him, Ron heard Puck's voice say, "I t'ink you'd better sit down, man."

Ron wasn't even aware he'd left his bench.

A Cold Winter's Deathe

5

RON BLANK had met his fair share of bullies. He suspected that every town in America has a Town Bully. Counties without towns probably have County Bullies, or Township Bullies, and cities that are too big for a single bully have dozens of Neighborhood Bullies. He'd even known a couple of State Bullies, but they were legally elected to their positions. Ed Posen, Ron's boss, was a bully, but he was manageable. He was all noise and bluster. And he wasn't dangerous.

And yet Ron was on his feet, moving inexorably toward Carl Rowley, running on alcohol and indignation, and it was somehow too late to stop.

It was a reflexive response. Ron had no conscious thought in his head.

Carl didn't see him coming. He was facing his victim when Ron suddenly appeared between them. Carl glared down his nose at Ron, slightly confused at first, then bemused. He scrutinized Ron with squinty eyes, studied him up and down for a long time until Ron felt like a bug under a magnifying glass. Ron had had cops do that to him before. Alice Louise Dubose was an expert at it. But this was different. Carl Rowley had never felt constrained by the letter of the law. He would not read you your rights.

Ron swallowed hard and tried to stand up under his scrutiny. He tried even harder to remember exactly how he had come to be under that malevolent glare. He struggled to lock his shaking knees so they wouldn't fold under him.

He'd never seen Carl this close before. There was a lot to see. Ron was of average height, and Carl towered over him like a full-grown grizzly, and he was just as thick as a grizzly through the middle. His face was large. Tiny red veins crazed his nose and hid just beneath the surface of his cheeks, barely visible. His thick black hair was well-oiled and slicked back like a 'fifties biker. His bright blue eyes were jaundiced and bloodshot. Unfiltered Camels since the age of ten, cheap beer, raw whiskey, and no understanding of the term *moderation* could do that.

Carl Rowley pulled himself up to his full height and he was just about the most powerful figure Ron had ever seen. There hadn't been much room between Carl and Raúl to begin with, and now it was dangerously crowded. Ron became painfully aware of the close presence of Dennis Whitehead to his right, as pain emanated from a firm grip on Ron's arm, just above the elbow. Shelby was sidling around behind Carl toward Ron's left.

Ron knew he was in trouble.

"What are you doing here, professor?" Carl asked, obviously curious. He took a pull on his cigarette and blew his smoke and foul breath in Ron's face.

Professor? Confusion conspired with cheap wine to cloud Ron's mind. Carl had some kind of clue who Ron was? He somehow must be associating Ron with the college. It was the wrong association, but the error did Ron no good, and meant that he had indeed come to Carl's attention somehow over the years. Not reassuring at all.

Apparently Carl had never witnessed such foolhardiness before this night. Ron knew the term "professor" was not meant to be respectful.

Ron considered his question for a fluttering heartbeat or two and realized he had no idea what the answer might be.

"I, uh...."

Suicide seemed like the only possible motive at the moment. Ron guessed that his one chance at preservation was that Carl had never been known to physically attack anyone where there were witnesses. He was more the back-stabber type. Ron Blank might not live through the night, but he was reasonably certain that he'd last until he stepped out the front door. Maybe he could vanish into the snowstorm. Like the Invisible Man. Maybe there would be one sheep in the herd that would be willing to watch his back then.

"I think you should leave Raúl alone now," were the words Ron managed to spit out, but even he detected no conviction in them.

Carl flashed a tiny smile which vanished so quickly that Ron wasn't sure if he'd even seen it.

"Are you threatening me, professor? *Me?*" he asked.

He shrugged at Shelby and Dennis, feigning bewilderment, thoroughly confused that a tough, authoritarian figure like *Professor* Ron Blank would pick on anyone as innocent and harmless as Carl Rowley. Legend said he had played this game all through nine grades at Deathe Consolidated Schools: unassuming, misunderstood, often falsely accused, only dimly aware of the vast conspiracies that surrounded him and complicated his life.

And Ron knew he was in *big* trouble, for Carl was nothing if not a professional victim. All his troubles, real or imagined, could always be blamed on others. But he was not one to allow himself to be victimized for long. He did not leave revenge to the Lord. He took it for himself, and felt justified and vindicated in the results.

"No, I'm not threatening you. I'm just suggesting—"

"Well it sure sounded like a threat to me. Didn't it sound like a threat to you, Dennis?"

Ron felt the dull pain flare in his arm where Dennis squeezed a little harder. Shelby elbowed Raúl roughly off his bar stool and pressed himself close to Ron's face. He felt Shelby's breath on his cheek, hot and beery. He could see Dennis nod in affirmation out of the corner of his eye. Carl glowered down at Ron.

Ron's heart hammered like a kettle drum in his chest.

"I was just having a little fun with Pedro, here," Carl said soothingly. Then he barked suddenly, "You make threats at me—" and Ron jumped, as Carl raised his voice for the benefit of all present, declaring himself to be, once again, the innocent victim of unprovoked aggression—"and I'll be forced to *defend* myself."

He was daring Ron to make a move, any move. Ron glanced left and right, quickly, and knew that he was all alone in the world right now. The rest of the flock stayed safely out of range, watching, waiting, playing the numbers, believing in survivability of the fleetest, and hoping that the sacrifice of one guaranteed the safety of the rest.

At least until next time.

Where the hell was Trooper Dubose when he needed her?

It didn't matter in the long run. He was forever on Carl's shit-list now, like it or not. It was already too late to buy his way out of that. Ever. Whatever harmless gesture he offered right now would be interpreted as a physical attack, and any retreat would be a sign of contemptible weakness. Either way, Carl would feel the need to teach the professor a lesson, for the benefit of all present. There would be no walking away without getting hurt. Ron resigned myself to taking his licks, now and maybe forever.

That job in Washington suddenly looked very enticing.

Dennis gripped Ron's right arm, Shelby his left, each of them glaring at the sides of his head with the meanest looks they could muster, their noses almost in Ron's ears. He could feel their breath on his cheeks as he stood facing staunchly forward. Carl regarded him warily, waiting, feet spread slightly for balance, fists working spasmodically at his sides.

There was nothing Ron could do. He tried to raise his hands in an innocent gesture of surrender and supplication, but Carl instantly reacted as though it was a physical attack.

Pain exploded in Ron's spine as Shelby and Dennis racked him back hard against the bar. Carl was in sudden motion, his fist stabbing at Ron's face. Ron ducked and felt Carl's horny knuckles scrape his chin, but then there was the glint of chrome steel and a hunting knife was in Carl's left hand, moving toward Ron's throat, and Ron knew it was all over, prosecution witnesses would fail to materialize, Carl would be acquitted on grounds of self-defense, and nothing would have changed.

Except Ron Blank.

ALICE LOUISE shouldered ahead of Beth and came into the bar first, with Beth close on her heels.

It was like walking into a wax museum. Everyone was flash frozen in their chairs, or on their benches, or standing at the bar, or crouched over the pool table. No one drank. No one ate. No one spoke. One man stood at the pool table, cue in one hand, chalk held motionless on the tip of it with the other. No one seemed to be breathing. No music played on the jukebox. Even the wind had fallen silent.

Time had stopped, and in the far back of her mind Alice Louise thought, *what a strange place this is.*

Tino stood behind the bar, holding the tap handle open over a tumbler. Beer overflowed the glass and poured over his hand and down the drain.

Then she saw that all heads were turned toward a single focal point near the front of the bar, and all eyes converged on a clot of men there. Like iron filings to a magnet. She followed their intense gaze. Her own vision was a bit blurry, and her eyes stung from the smoky blue haze of illicit cigarettes. She thought she could make out Ron Blank surrounded by a small gang of toughs. One, an oily, black-haired

A Cold Winter's Deathe

Neanderthal, towered over Ron like a colossus, glaring down at him with an expression of single-minded malevolence.

She attempted a quick assessment of the situation. Her brain was fuzzy. Some kind of ugly confrontation, which had the undivided, morbid attention of everyone in the whole place. Whatever was going on, Ron Blank appeared to be in big trouble.

Ron Blank? Seriously? *Ron freaking Blank?* Mr. Peepers? Wally Wallflower? The guy with no personality and no detectable passion for anything other than keeping a low profile and staying out of the way?

What. *Ever.*

She would have to get the situation under control first, sort it out later.

Beth snagged the back of Alice Louise's coat, bringing her up short.

"Carl Rowley." she growled under her breath.

"Who?" Beth obviously meant the big bear of a man, the one who looked about ready to pound Ron Blank to a pile of mush.

"Carl Rowley. Da baddest man in the de whole damned town. Al, if you mess with him, you're gonna have to kill him. I'm not kidding, Al. Kill him. I. Am. Not. *Kidding.*"

Beth's voice quavered. Terrified. A glance back at her confirmed it. Beth had gone white, her eyes were wide and locked on the scene that threatened to play out before them.

Adrenaline surged in Alice Louise's veins, pushing aside the alcohol she knew was clouding her judgment. She shouldn't be in this condition. *Stupid.* Off duty, but drinking, slightly tipsy. *Carrying.* But now was not the time to think about it.

She turned back just as the big bruiser threw a tight uppercut at Ron's face with an immense fist. Ron jerked back and somehow Carl Rowley's knuckles barely grazed Ron's chin.

Alice Louise tugged grandma's stupid chuke off her head and flung it away as she plowed forward through the frozen masses.

Then she saw the glint of chrome steel in the bruiser's right hand, coming up toward Ron's throat.

She had already unsnapped her shoulder bag. She reached in deep.

In that same instant a blur of motion swept across the floor, and a gray whirlwind spun up in the middle of the conflict, and then everything changed.

33

RON WAS THROWN aside and somehow both Dennis and Shelby lost their grip on him, and he saw Carl falling away from him as a hand shot in between them. Long fingers splayed across Carl's face like pallid tentacles, catching him in an iron grip and covering his features completely. The knife clattered to the floor. Carl stiffened as though jolted by a massive electric shock and then stood motionless, every muscle suddenly gone rigid. He rocked back, slightly off balance, yet remained on his feet, held upright by the hand that now engulfed his face.

Ron saw that it was the hand of Puck, *de Invisible Yooper*, the harmless looking kid with the wild hair and crooked grin, and he was very close and in sharp focus. His head was tilted back and he stared up at the face beneath his hand with eyes that burned with—anger? No. Intense concentration, perhaps. Ron turned away, and became aware that nothing else moved in the saloon. Shelby and Dennis had folded back against the bar, stunned by the sudden bizarre turn of events, unable to respond. Time stood still, all was silent, and now Ron was part of a bizarre statuary, a grotesque *tableaux vivant*.

Dennis was the first to overcome his shock and surprise. Ron heard him grunt something like "hey," and he took a cautious step toward the Invisible Yooper, Puck.

Ron couldn't believe that Carl was not moving. He thought that at any instant Carl would come to life and throw the frail figure in the bulky plaid hunter's coat clear across the room, then he would turn his fury loose on Ron. On all of them. Kill them all and gut them and stick their heads on pikes and burn the bar down to its foundations.

Yet for long seconds nothing happened. Not a sound was made. Ron watched in morbid fascination as Carl teetered on the edge of balance, rigid, as if cast in cement, doing nothing whatever to fend off this indignity.

Then Dennis was moving, uncoiling from his crouch. His hand snaked out and caught the outstretched arm of the Invisible Yooper. Puck blinked twice as if coming out of a trance. Then Dennis tugged just a little and the hand released Carl's face.

ALL HELL broke loose and Alice Louise jerked to a halt.

The big bruiser, Carl Rowley, for a moment stood on his toes, suspended like a puppet on strings, then suddenly he screamed and it was as though the doors had been flung open and the icy wind and snow

A Cold Winter's Deathe

and sleet shrieked through the bar. Alice Louise leaped back into Beth, startled, her blood suddenly frozen in her veins.

Carl Rowley spun in place, his eyes enormous, staring at nothing, at everything, bellowing like a wounded bear. His hands clawed at the air and he danced as though barefoot on a bed of hot coals; his face had gone as white as the frost on the front window panes.

As she watched, the blood surged up his neck from beneath his collar and blazed red hot under the taut skin of his face. The bellowing stopped and he fell silent.

Then he lashed out and knocked one of his cohorts into the bar. The other one reached for him and Rowley swept his hand aside. His lungs empty, he sucked in huge gasping volumes of air, then flung himself blindly toward the row of booths that lined the brick wall on the east side of the saloon.

People scattered before him and tables toppled in his wake. Bottles and glasses exploded into the air and tumbled across the floor. Rowley dove under a table and wedged himself deep into the corner, forcing himself farther and farther under the low bench. The gasping subsided to a moan, and then he was gasping again, deep, from his stomach. His eyes were wild like an animal's, searching blindly and seeing God-knows-what, his hands clawing at invisible demons. Saliva poured out of his mouth and dribbled on the floorboards. Alice knew what was coming next, and she turned away as vomit, beer, and bile erupted from him and spilled across the floor under the table.

DENNIS AND SHELBY watched in horror. Greg Rowley stood at the front door, stunned and pale. Puck melted again into the shadows, and Ron had to look hard, concentrate like the devil to even see him through the dark veil that seemed to cover his eyes. Puck stood aside, regarding the scene with an expression of detached interest.

All attention was focused on Carl. He was curled up in a near fetal position, wedged deep under the bench, shaking violently, eyes enormous with terror, staring into the distance at something Ron did not dare to imagine, laying in a spreading pool of his own vomit. Ron had to look away and swallow down the bile that rose in his own throat.

Finally, Shelby moved tentatively across the floor toward Carl. Wary. Alert. Frightened. Carl moaned continuously, his eyes squeezed shut. He lay rocking on his side, knees clutched to his chest, his Carhartt coat soaking up the vile mess. Around Ron, people started coming to life again. Moving around. Murmuring softly. Slowly, they gathered to straighten out the saloon and pick up the toppled tables and broken glasses. The front door opened and slammed shut, and Carl's son Greg was gone, running for safety.

Or running in revulsion from the horrible specter of his father in such incredible distress.

Dennis and Shelby crunched across the floor and crouched down beside Carl, then cautiously reached out to touch his arm. He responded to them slowly, like a man coming out of an epileptic seizure, dazed and confused. For a moment, Ron thought that was what he must have witnessed. Somehow it seemed as though his imagination had played tricks on him, and now his memory was clearing, and all he had seen was a simple seizure. He'd seen them before. He knew how to react, what to do. He'd been trained for it. But he had done nothing. And now he wondered why not.

The bar was returning to normal, almost as if nothing unusual had happened. Shelby and Dennis helped Carl out from under the table and walked him, weak and staggering, one on either side, to the front door. Tino had already brought out a bucket and was swirling a mop around the floor.

Then Ron saw Shelby murmur something to Dennis and they both turned and looked at him.

The trio gathered themselves up and followed Greg out, vanishing into the night. The door slammed closed behind them and the swirling snow stilled and fell to the floor and it was almost as if they'd never been.

Epileptic seizure. Happens all the time. Only somehow it didn't quite ring true this time.

Ron was leaning heavily against the bar, his back and arms burning, his knees shaking, his heart pounding.

Then Ron saw Puck amble back to their booth. He slid in under the stairwell, then turned and looked at Ron.

Ron crossed the room toward the booth under the stairs on legs that still quaked with fear and an overdose of adrenalin.

ALICE LOUISE stood frozen in the middle of the bar.

Something had just exploded in front of her, and her beer-muddled brain couldn't even make sense of it. Somehow, in a way she could not comprehend, Ron Blank had flung his nemesis aside like an old dishrag. Sent him sailing into the corner, under a booth table, crying

A Cold Winter's Deathe

and puking like a shell-shocked riot victim, until his buddies had picked him up and walked him out of the bar.

"What de hell just happened?" Beth said.

"I don't know..." Alice Louise muttered. "It looks like your Carl Rowley isn't so tough after all. I think Ron Blank just sent him home with his tail between his legs."

"Ron?" Beth echoed.

The bar was almost back to normal already, and Alice Louise was having trouble remembering what just took place. She shook her head to clear out the fuzzies, but it did no good. The harder she thought about it, the more distant and indistinct the memories became. Like trying to remember a dream. People were moving around now, finding their seats again, sipping their drinks and calling for more. Conversations stuttered back to life, picking up where they'd left off. Before....

Before what?

A platter dropped in the juke box, and Billy Ray started singing, and voices were raised to compete.

Alice Louise felt Beth's hand on her shoulder. "Come on," she said, "we got more money to steal from those losers in the back room."

Whatever had happened, Beth, too, had forgotten already. Whatever it was.

As Alice Louise turned to follow Beth back to the game, she saw Ron Blank cross the room and slide into the small, vacant booth under the stairs.

Ron slid into the booth just before his legs could buckle under him first.

"Was dat cool, or *what?*" Puck exclaimed. "It gives me a rush every time."

The memory of Carl Rowley, quivering and cowering under the bench just a dozen feet behind him crept back into his mind, and he felt cold fingers tickle his spine.

"What in the hell are you?" Ron demanded.

"I was trying to tell you. I'm a vampire hunter."

6

"WELL, WHAT LUCK!" Ron said. "You just slayed the town's biggest vampire! I never thought of him like that, but he's been feeding on the community for years. Good job well done!" Ron lifted off the bench to make his escape. "I guess you can go home now. I'll just be in the back room, playing cards with *Michigan State Police Trooper Alice Louise Dubose*," Ron said, making sure Puck could not miss his point.

"Sit down," Puck said.

Ron found himself sitting down.

"How did you do that?"

"Just some simple mind tricks I learned a few... years ago. Like wit' your buddy Carl dere. I just... *shared a vision* with him. I can pretty much make people do what I want. You want I should make you sit up and bark like a seal?"

"That is *not* funny!"

"You don't believe me, do you?" Puck said with a sad sigh of disappointment. "I get dat a lot."

Suddenly in dire need of another drink, Ron hailed Tino. The bartender came over and glared down at him with his usual expression of contempt.

"I'd like a bowl of tranquilizers and a shot of absinthe," Ron said, "and leave the bottle."

"How about beer instead?"

"Make it two."

Tino grunted and shuffled away.

Raúl Lopez edged over and stood silently at Ron's side, too humble to look Ron directly in the eye. He was engulfed in a ragged

A Cold Winter's Deathe

orange parka that was molting down like a sick goose, and his hands worried nervously in oversized grimy wool mittens.

"Mr. Blank," he said in a voice so low Ron could hardly hear him.

"Please don't call me Mr. Blank, Raúl. Call me Ron. Okay?"

"I just wanted to say *gracias*," he mumbled. His daughter slid up under his arm from behind. Ron hadn't seen her come in. Maria's dark face peeked out from within billowy clouds of worn blue polyester. Her soft black eyes were enormous, staring at Ron unblinking and bright with awe and recognition. Ron was helping Beth organize the annual Founder's Day play at the school. Maria had the lead.

Only Deathe would celebrate Founder's Day in the coldest, most brutal month of the year.

"I mean...." Raúl's voice trailed off and he shrugged helplessly.

"Hey, it was just a beer or two," Ron protested.

"I don't mean the beer. I mean... well..."

"Holy sh–" Ron saw Maria's eyes flash with expectation. "Don't thank me!" he pleaded. "I didn't do anything. Really!"

Raúl swallowed hard and muttered another embarrassed thank you, then edged toward the door. Maria grinned at Ron. Her hand popped out, waved, disappeared. Together they pushed out into the snow, hand in hand.

Neither had cast so much as a glance at Puck. In fact, the only other person who appeared to see Puck was Jake the Dog. He stared intently, either at Ron or Puck, it was hard to tell with that glass eye, from his safe haven under Ron Borke's table.

Puck watched Raúl and Maria until they were gone, his eyes surprisingly narrow and hard, and Ron could sense dark thoughts swirling under the bramble of wild hair. Then he turned back to Ron. The hardness had vanished. He was just a kid again, and Ron wondered if he had imagined it, or had misinterpreted.

"He should have been thanking you," Ron said. "All I did was nearly get myself killed. Carl will probably be waiting outside for us later. With a shotgun." A cold chill ran down Ron's spine at the prospect, not knowing if he'd just touched on a terrible truth. He glanced at the door, but the view through the window was obscured by the thick frost.

"Nah," Puck said with a wave of his hand. The hand that had vanquished Carl Rowley. "I don't t'ink he'll bother you again. At least as long as I'm here."

"Damned small comfort in that," Ron said. "You'll probably be gone tomorrow or the next day. What do I have to do to stay safe, marry you?"

"Dat's a good one. But you're not my type." Puck laughed. Then he turned serious. "I hear dat a man died here recently." Puck glanced up at Ron and offered an apologetic shrug, as if, though embarrassed, he was nevertheless duty-bound to ask.

"Oh *hell no,*" Ron said. "Do *not* go there!"

"I'll take dat as a yes. How?"

"How did he die? *He was old.*"

"Yah. But how did he die? Exactly?"

"You mean was he bitten by a vampire? Are you serious?" Ron laughed, but Puck's expression was sober.

Tino suddenly loomed over the booth. He plopped down the two bottles and one glass in front of Ron and wiped his hands on his apron.

"Tino," Ron said before he could wander off.

"Yah," Tino grunted.

"Sid Francis."

Tino scowled down at Ron. "Dead."

"How?"

"Blowout." He tapped his temple. "In da head."

"Not killed by a vampire?"

Tino considered the possibility for a long moment, frowning with concentration and stroking his chin and looking off into the distance, then shook his head.

"Nah."

Man of few words. He ambled back to the bar. Never cracked a smile, but Ron suspected he'd be howling and pounding the tables as he recounted this exchange with his regulars after Ron had gone home. Ron had grown accustomed to providing cheap amusement for the locals. This one just might be good enough to clear his tab.

"See?" Ron said to Puck. "No vampires. A stroke. Or an aneurysm. I forget which. Or are they the same?"

"I need to see de body." There was a hint of excitement in his voice.

"Somehow, I knew you were going to say that. Too late." Ron tried an end play. Not lying, really. Just playing fast and loose with the truth. "Viewing hours are over," he said.

"So he's been buried?"

A Cold Winter's Deathe

Caught, Ron thought. And he knew he wasn't a good enough liar. "He wasn't buried. The ground is frozen, and the town backhoe is out of commission. He's laid out in the mausoleum until spring. But don't get any funny ideas! The mausoleum is off limits. And locked up tighter than a bank vault."

"ARE WE HERE to play poker, or what?" Beth demanded, jerking Alice Louise out of her reverie. She hiked up her sleeve and glared at her watch. "Or shall we just take our winnings and move to Florida? Whaddaya say, Al?"

Alice Louise looked around the shabby little room, trying to orient herself. She had been trying to remember something. Something that happened recently. Maybe a bad dream.

"You gotta give us a chance to win it back!" Smoke said. "I think my luck is changing."

"Your luck has done run out," Beth said, swooping up Alice Louise's pile of bills and coins to join with her own. She opened her purse at the table's edge and scooped their winnings inside. "Face reality, Smoke. We *smoked* ya!"

Alice Louise felt a hand under her arm, and she allowed herself to be lifted from her chair. She realized Beth was bundling her up like a child about to be sent outdoors to play, snugging a scarf around her neck and pulling grandma's chuke down over her hair.

"Al? Are you OK? You need some coffee or something before we go?"

Alice Louise saw concern in Beth's searching brown eyes. She shook her head.

"Right," Beth said. "Da cold'll bring ya around quick enough. It's gonna be a hike back to da camp. Brutal for a Loper like you. Get your coat on." She helped Alice Louise into her pink parka and zipped it up for her.

Alice Louise felt herself guided out of the back room into the main room of the Buck Snort.

The bar was almost quiet. The crowd had thinned out. Only a handful of hardy drinkers still hung on, including the guy with the dog. But then she saw Ron Blank, sitting alone in the shadows in the booth under the stairs. She resisted Beth's relentless tug toward the front door and made her way to Ron. Ron looked up at her and his expression clouded.

"Alice? Are you all right?" he asked her.

41

"Just a little too much to drink," Beth assured him. "I'm taking her home and putting her to bed now." She gave Alice Louise another firm tug.

Strangely, Ron sat facing the underside of the stairs, his back to the room. There were several empty brown bottles and two glasses on the table in front of him. Alice Louise dropped into the booth facing him. She bolted instantly to her feet, startled by a sensation like bumping into an unseen body in a pitch dark room. She backed away, shuddering and hugging herself, nearly overcome by a sudden wave of apprehension. *Cold.*

"Come on," Beth said, putting her arm around her and guiding her to the door.

"I wanted to ask Ron something."

"Can't it wait? We can call him tomorrow."

She stopped Beth at the door. Turning to look around the old saloon, she said, "Is this place haunted?"

"You have no idea," Beth said. "The whole town is haunted."

RON WATCHED BETH guide Alice Louise out into the cold. He glanced at Puck, who shrugged innocently. The Invisible Yooper. Alice had not even seen him, but had obviously felt his presence on the bench. She had instantly gone white, her eyes wide with confusion.

Another couple bundled from head to toe in down-filled snowmobile suits—probably Tony Emmons and Clara Anderson, but it was impossible to tell—waddled out the front door, and Ron realized that the coat rack was almost empty and the bar was virtually deserted now. Ron Borke and Tom Dickson had sunk their last billiard ball and racked their cues and were now hunched over their drinks at the bar, smoking cigarettes and staring bleary-eyed at the smear of fluorescent colors on the TV screen. Jake the Dog had moved to lie directly under Borke's bar stool, but he still watched Ron and Puck with unwavering vigilance.

"*Guess what!*" Puck exclaimed. "We're goin' to de cemetery!"

"Swell," Ron said. "Tell you what. Come by my house tomorrow. Go south about 500 miles. I just moved back to Chicago fifteen minutes ago."

"Nah. We really need to check out dat body tonight."

"In this storm? We'd never make it there alive." Or back alive, as the case may be.

A Cold Winter's Deathe

"Hey look! De storm has blown itself out," Puck said happily. He waved his hand and the room fell silent. Ron could hear little more than a muffled breath of wind outside.

"*Did you do that?*" Ron demanded, stunned.

"I dunno." Puck examined his hand and looked expectantly at Ron. "Maybe?"

Ron felt the room spin. "I need to go home now."

"I don't t'ink so. We're goin' to da cemetery first."

"No, no, and a thousand times, *no!*"

7

RON SAW that he was surrounded by aged, tilting monoliths and spires. And tombstones. Drowning in a sea of snow and reaching skyward from a surging tide of snowdrifts. Before him stood a pair of black cast iron doors filigreed with wreaths and ornate floral patterns stained brown by rust. The mausoleum, he realized, seeing now the white limestone structure that burrowed back into a low hill in the middle of Fairview Cemetery.

Puck knelt at his feet to examine the massive iron padlock.

Ron had a vague memory of Jake the Dog watching as he bundled up against the cold, pulling on his winter clothing, feeling like a little kid wrapped so tightly by his mother that he could hardly walk.

He now remembered himself trudging along behind Puck, the not-nearly-invisible-enough Yooper vampire hunter, with his *ridonkulous* bomber hat bobbing on his head, beneath a scrim of furtive clouds sparked to pale incandescence by Deathe's feeble streetlights.

Forging east between houses, where he assumed the street to be. Wading through snowdrifts up to his waist. "Measuring the distance with the length of our bodies," a phrase he remembered reading once, which came to mind about the fifth time he fell flat on his face in the snow.

Carrying Puck's remarkably heavy steel tackle box.

Passing under the iron arch that had misspelled "Fairview Cemetary" for a century and a half.

Glimpsing White Wolf Lake between the trees and houses, stretching away north from the edge of town for perhaps half a mile—a desolate, gray plain glowing beneath the light of a pale moon that floated in the blackness of the western sky. Seeing the dark, wet center

A Cold Winter's Deathe

of the lake, where it was not yet fully frozen over. Unheard of for January, according to Beth.

Ron shook his head to clear it. Big mistake.

The dying remains of the storm sighed high in the barren trees, muffled by the dense insulation of fresh snow. Occasional whirlwinds spun down to ground level and whipped the snow in their faces. Tiny ice crystals stung like a million needles on Ron's bare skin, and the cold air burned in his throat and lungs with every breath.

"Gimme dat tackle box," Puck said, and Ron was happy to be relieved of the weight of it.

Puck pried it open and dug around through about forty pounds of loose steel and iron and lead and God knew what all else. There might have been a dead body in there for all Ron knew, considering how heavy it was. But he reassured himself that the box was too small. Puck finally came up with a big ring of rusty keys.

"In dis business ya never know when dese might come in handy," he said, and in a moment the padlock dropped to the ground with a thud. "Holy wah! We're in!"

"*You're* in," Ron said, finally becoming fully alert to the reality of where he was and what was going on. "I think I'll just wait out here." He hugged himself and stamped his feet and shivered against the bitter cold.

"Suit yourself. It's a little nippy out here. I thought you might like to come in where it might be a little bit warmer."

"Maybe I'll just go back to the bar instead."

Ron glanced over his shoulder toward town. He was certain they hadn't been followed, but with the constant rush of the wind in the trees and the sound-deadening blanket of the fresh snow, a bear could have stumbled upon them and eaten them both before they'd heard him coming.

No. Bears hibernate. *Carl Rowley does not.* Somehow Ron had forgotten his fear that Carl and his evil posse might be waiting for him outside the Buck Snort.

"No," Puck said, "I t'ink you'd rather help me push dis door open and come inside."

They were inside the crypt.

Puck had pulled a flashlight out of his tackle box and was thumping it on the palm of his hand and working the switch.

"Damned flashlights," he muttered. "Dey got like one movin' part, and ya just drop 'em one time and dey don't never work right again." Smack, smack, *smack* went the flashlight in his hand. "I mean, a car's got like a million 'n' one moving parts 'n' if even *one* quits, like de cigarette lighter, everybody's bitchin' about what a piece of worthless junk it is, even though there's like a million t'ings dat still work just like dey're supposed to—"

Ron cut him off by flicking on a switch on the wall. Two bare bulbs lit the room.

"Oh. Well. You could always do *dat,* I suppose. You got mystical powers too?"

"Maybe," Ron said. "I'm an electrician. And I'm lazy, so I look for the easy solution."

The bulbs were low wattage and dusty. They gave off a feeble yellow glow that made the shadows pitch black and impenetrable. There was a distressing profusion of shadows.

The mausoleum was much bigger than Ron had expected. The little stone house visible from the outside was but an entry to a larger room. Beyond a cut limestone archway it burrowed back into the hillside some twenty feet deep and perhaps fifteen feet wide. Coarse stone benches stood on either side of the entry. Puck moved past them like a black shadow, silent and stealthy, and into the larger room beyond. Ron followed reluctantly.

The walls were lined with stone shelves holding the stone and cement vaults of the dead, four deep, stacked to the ceiling. Puck finally had the flashlight working. He stabbed it around the room, making the dark shadows jump to life. Ron counted twenty shelves, and thirteen vaults total, including one covered with a green plastic tarp.

"Hey yah. Lookit dis!"

But Puck wasn't interested in the new vault. He peered into a niche in the back of the room.

Hesitantly, Ron went to him.

A brass plate on the old stone vault said, "Emilie Reindhart, 1853-1923."

Puck took the flashlight and aimed it into a narrow space behind the vault. Ron saw something there. Something....

It was a body, wrapped in a rotting burial shroud, mummified with age. It had been stuffed rudely behind the vault. Puck brushed at it with his bare fingers and the gray shroud disintegrated at his touch. The face beneath was black, the skin like charred paper. Fine wisps of white hair, like cobwebs, uncoiled slowly, celebrating their release after perhaps a century of confinement.

A Cold Winter's Deathe

Stars swam before Ron's eyes. He stepped back and sucked in a ragged, gasping breath of musty air.

"Looks like de vampire has been here, eh? Popped dis one right out of its coffin and moved in, I betcha. Might still be livin' here." He frowned. "OK, dat's just a figure of speech, eh? I mean, dey're *undead*, so ya can't call it living, eh? I shoulda just said *sleepin'* here. Yah. Help me pull dis lid off."

"I. Will. *Not*.".

Once they'd pushed aside the heavy stone lid, Puck pried open the coffin.

Ron flinched and jumped back.

Puck leaned in with the flashlight. "What are you so jumpy about, eh? It's empty. You don't know much about vampires, do ya?"

"They don't teach that course at Michigan Tech."

"Don't get me started on de educational system in dis country," Puck groused. "Yah, well, vampires dey sleep during de day, ya know. Dey put some soil from dere homeland in here to make it more comfortable. We just gotta make it less comfortable. Lump up de ol' dirt mattress a little, eh? Den we better finish up and get outta here before morning or ya never know *what* might happen."

"No," Ron said, "and I'd rather not find out."

"Well, den, let's give 'er tarpaper. Hand me dat bottle out of de tackle box."

The only bottle Ron could find was a clear pint whiskey bottle. The liquid inside had a strange amber glow.

Puck took it, unscrewed the cap, and carefully sprinkled it inside the coffin. "I'm kinda hangin' out a no trespassin' sign here, ya know?" he said. "Markin' my territory!"

"Holy water?" Ron asked.

"No, dis is even better, man!" Puck exclaimed. "Works like a charm, cuz I got magical mystical powers. I don't have much chemistry training, but I can sure turn beer into urine!"

"Marking. Your. Territory." Ron stepped back a little farther. "I think I'll go wait outside."

"We gotta put de rightful owner back in here first and close dis up. And den we gotta check out your buddy Sid. Gimme a hand."

"Nope. Won't do it, can't make me."

Emilie Reindhart was light as a pillow, having spent seven decades dehydrating in her tomb, and stiff as cordwood. Now her vault

47

was closed and Sid Francis's was open. The viewing lid was up on his casket, and Ron was looking down on Sid's kindly old face again.

Ron said, "Why don't you just make me sit up and bark like a seal. I think I'd prefer that for a change."

Puck had pulled the muskrat off his head, and he was leaning in and examining Sid closely, with the flashlight in one hand and a knife in the other. He scraped gently at the makeup and mortician's wax on Sid's throat.

"Looking for bite marks? Puncture wounds? Well? Finding any?"

"You better hope not. Dis could get ugly."

"Ugly how?"

"Well, it's different every time, but if he got bit, he's infected, and we'd have to make sure he don't get up and go wanderin' through town, terrorizing people." Puck looked up at Ron. "Hey, you got one of doze guys already, right?"

Ron cringed at the thought of Carl Rowley. "How would you prevent that?"

"De usual way. You know, drive a stake t'ro his heart. Stuff his mouth with garlic and wolfs-bane and stuff. Cut off his head and put it between his feet. Sometimes de old ways work best. Believe me," he said, shaking his head sadly, "it ain't pretty."

Ron's head spun. He'd caught a glimpse of a steel mallet in the tackle box, and small cloth-wrapped bundle that could have been wooden stakes and wicked knives.

"Well, you'll be glad to know dere's nuthin here," Puck said, straightening up. "Let's close dis up, den I'll just sprinkle a little of my magic water around de door frame when we leave. We'll have desecrated de place for de vampire. It won't come back here now."

This time Puck didn't have to use his mind tricks. Ron gladly helped close the casket and vault, then cover it with the green tarp. Ron turned eagerly toward the door to leave and reached for the light switch, but saw that Puck was still standing in the middle of the mausoleum, staring pensively at the green tarp of Sid's vault.

Puck reached deep into a pocket of his hunting coat and pulled out a clear pint bottle full of amber liquid. Opening it, he tipped it to his mouth.

"Good Lord!" Ron exclaimed. "Is that–?"

A Cold Winter's Deathe

"Hey, don't be a dip, man. Dis is moonshine. Good stuff. I gotta cousin in Tennessee. I'm usually pretty careful not to mix up de bottles. Want some?"

Ron shuddered. "No! I just want to get out of here!"

"Tell ya what. You just go ahead on home, OK? I t'ink I just want to stay here and kinda sort t'ings out in my head for a little while, eh? I'll look you up tomorrow."

"You don't know where I live."

"Don't worry. I'll find you."

"Now *that* worries me."

"Tomorrow," Puck repeated, and he held the bottle aloft in a salute. "Dere's still more work to be done."

Ron escaped into the bitter cold night. But he felt uneasy about leaving Puck alone in the crypt. Not that he thought for a minute an actual vampire was going to appear and carry the Yooper off. No. He thought he'd seen something in the Yooper's eyes that he didn't like.

That something had been left undone and still needed to be attended to.

RON TRUDGED HOME through the silent, deserted streets, kicking through thigh high snowdrifts, clambering awkwardly, wearily, over the really big ones.

Snow and ice crystals still powdered the air, carried on gentle sighs of wind. Mother Nature just rearranging her handiwork, tidying up a bit, and making everyone's insignificant lives all the more difficult for it. Black sky appeared between the low scudding clouds, and Ron glimpsed an occasional star peeking through. A single mercury light swayed over Deathe's main intersection, buzzing like a swarm of angry electronic bees; lacy snow flakes danced and soared and glittered delicately in its electric blue glow, pelting his bare face like icy needles.

Darkness cloaked downtown Deathe like an old blanket. It was often joked that the Rural Electrification Administration workers had come through in the 'thirties and put up some street lights—bare incandescent bulbs huddled forlornly under steel reflectors high up on wooden utility poles—and had never returned to finish the job. Or even replace the bulbs. The thin porcelain coating of the reflectors had been chipped away over the decades by time and the stray BBs of young boys' air rifles, and the rusty shells shed precious little light on the streets far below. Only in winter, when dazzling white snow coated the ground, fresh and unspoiled, was it possible to navigate the streets and sidewalks without the aid of a good flashlight.

The Buck Snort Saloon was closed, its windows dark and featureless. Tino had gone home, wherever that was. Ron had never given it any thought before. He seemed a permanent fixture in the bar, like the pool table or the tap handles. Ron had never seen him outside it.

The building itself was a decrepit old square, two-story, brick and cut stone blockhouse of a place, on the corner of Main and Covington Streets. This, along with the Close Finnish across the street, Hoolie's Cafe, the Deathe Police Station/Village Hall/library/volunteer fire department, and half a dozen similar brick buildings in various states of disrepair that crowded the four corners, pretty much comprised downtown Deathe. The old hardware store opposite the Law Offices of Finch and Chip had been closed down and abandoned a few years before.

The town was deserted and dead-quiet, except for the wind sighing high in the trees.

When he finally turned up the sidewalk toward Ruth Kinderly's boarding house, Ron saw that the sign in her front yard advertising rooms to rent was buried in snowdrifts. As he waded by Ruth's darkened parlor window he thought he saw a figure inside. Ruth, he assumed, passing yet another sleepless night in her old rocking chair, gazing out at the still town. He raised his hand to wave, but on second glance he saw no one, and by the dim glow of the bulb hanging by the outside stairwell that led up to his apartment, he could see that her chair was vacant.

Snow filled his boots, icy cold and numbing. Ron slogged toward the stairwell, impatient to get inside and drape himself over the oil space heater. His Eagle wagon sat in the drive, covered with snow and surrounded by chest-high drifts. Yet he could sense something unnatural about it. There were scattered depressions in the snow around it, now nearly filled in and healed over, yet still visible. The car seemed unusually dark in the dim glow of the yellow porch light.

He stumbled closer, and then saw. The windows were gone. Broken out. All of them. Including the windshield and even the backlight. The empty frames yawned like gaping maws, still holding what remained of the white-crazed glass, limp and dangling. There was precious little of that. Snow had drifted in and filled the interior.

There was nothing he could do for it tonight. The damage was done. Carl Rowley had paid him a late-night visit. He supposed he

A Cold Winter's Deathe

should just be thankful he hadn't been home to meet him, or worse, to try to stop him.

In the distance across town he heard the Masticator rumble to life.

8

NIGHTMARES had washed over Alice Louise all night, like black waves, vague and unsettling. But she awoke Saturday morning to the sound of Beth singing in the kitchen and the smell of coffee in her nose, and decided the bad dreams were purely alcohol induced. She would not let that happen again any time soon.

"How can you be so cheerful?" Alice Louise asked as she dropped into a chair and laid her aching head on the kitchen table.

"I'm just naturally perky," Beth chirped as she set down a steaming coffee mug within Alice Louise's reach.

Alice Louise pried open one eye. Beth looked fresh and alert, bright and cheerful. Her face was smooth and her hair was plush and silky. Alice Louise's face felt like an unmade bed, and her hair was snarled and gross. She closed her eye again. "Just leave me here to die."

"Piker," Beth said. "Get dressed. I'm all outta bacon and eggs, and I hate cold cereal after a night of drinking. I just called and Hoolie's Cafe is open. We need to make our way there and get some breakfast in us. You'll feel better in no time."

"After that blizzard last night?" Glancing at the window, she realized she was not looking at a gray, overcast day. The window was blocked with snow from bottom to top. "We'll never get out of the house."

"That little blow? Don't be such a sissy. This is the U.P. We got *sisu*. I already shoveled out the walk and my car. I didn't find yours, but I think I saw the antenna poking up through a drift. I'll tie a red bow on it so we can find it again later. Get used to this. We get something like thirty feet of snow here in an average winter."

A Cold Winter's Deathe

"But not all at once!"

"Al, this was nothing. The Masticator has most of the streets plowed out already, or at least they're passable with one lane."

"The *what?*"

"Deathe's big badass snowblower. Welded together out of cast iron and boiler plate steel in the thirties. I think it might run on coal and steam. Like a locomotive. Got a maw as big as a barn door, and you don't want to get in its way. It ate a Datsun B210 pickup once! But they were kinda tinny and frail," Beth conceded, "so I guess it hardly counts. But snowmobiles don't even stick in its teeth."

Alice Louise had barely finished her coffee before Beth pulled her to her feet and pushed her into the bathroom to shower.

Clean and feeling almost human again, Alice Louise wrapped a towel around her head and stood in the doorway, watching Beth putter in the kitchen.

"What happened at the bar last night?" Alice Louise said.

"Well, we cleaned up at the poker game, and you got pretty well snockered," Beth said. "But you're a lightweight. Why?"

"Was there some kind of fight there?"

Beth considered the question for a moment. "A fight? I don't think so. Seemed like a pretty typical Friday night at the Buck Snort."

Alice Louise churned through her fuzzy memory of the evening. She felt like she was missing something. She fixed Beth with a puzzled stare. Then she sighed with defeat.

"You ever drink so much you had amnesia?"

Beth hooted. "Not that I remember!"

RON BLANK rolled out of bed late, took a long hot shower, then rattled around his apartment for a while, finally settling on a tasteless breakfast of toast and jam with two cups of strong coffee He folded up his unmade sofa-bed, then bundled up and went out into the cold to survey the damage to his poor old Eagle wagon.

The morning sky was clear, washed clean by the winter storm, and excruciatingly bright. He fought his way through powdery virgin snowdrifts to get to the car, squinting against the blinding sunlight, eyes watering, the tears practically freezing on his face.

The damage was no worse than he had suspected, and no better. He shoveled snow away from the doors to get them open, then shoveled and whisked more snow out of the interior. He found an old canvas tarp in the barn behind Mrs. Kinderly's house, lashed it down with a random collection of rope, twine, and wire, and called it good. Monday he would call Toivo's Towing, Tackle & Live Bait to come load it on the flatbed and take it to L'Anse for new glass.

He would have to catch a ride to the college for the next few days, probably with Naomi Borke next door.

He tried not to think about Carl Rowley.

A thought occurred to him, bred by a nagging apprehension, and he found himself climbing over ten foot high snow piles and taking a quick walk to the town hall: a combination of Chief Woody's police station, a small meeting hall, the one-stall volunteer fire station (motto: "Never Lost a Basement"), and his destination, the tiny village library. The main street had been cleaned by the Masticator, after a fashion.

Just as Ron reached the town hall, a green Jeep Cherokee crossed through the intersection. It parked in front of Hoolie's Cafe next to a few random snow tanks, which is what Yoopers call their massive, old, rear-wheel drive winter beaters. The Jeep's doors opened and Beth Atkins and Alice Louise Dubose climbed out. Beth glanced up, saw him, and waved enthusiastically with a mittened hand.

"Ron!" she called across the street. "How ya doin'?"

"Fine," Ron lied. He waved back. Beth looked as perky as always, bundled up in a puffy down-filled parka and red chuke that made her look like a blueberry snow-cone topped with a cherry. Alice Louise appeared more subdued. Beth grinned, but Alice Louise fixed him with a dark and stormy expression that Ron found troubling.

He thought back to his time spent with her in the fall, when she'd investigated Nyleen Bedderhoff's death at the college and ended up spending a few nights with him at Cavendish Manor because it was Homecoming week and there was no place else for her to stay. He'd been alarmed to learn that she, too, could see ghosts. Like Pud, who infuriated her to distraction. So much so that she wanted to kill him, although it was too far late for that. She didn't know, she didn't suspect. She didn't even believe it when she'd found Pud's obituary and dragged Ron to stand over his grave in the cemetery. She still thought he was real.

Something was troubling her now, and Ron suspected it had to do with the Yooper vampire hunter. He remembered how she had popped up out of the booth last night, white and panic-stricken, after she'd nearly sat on the kid without ever seeing him.

She was sensitive to paranormal things, and probably wasn't even aware of it.

A Cold Winter's Deathe

Deathe, he thought now, was no place for her to be hanging out. "Breakfast is on me!" Beth called. "Come and join us!"

"No, thanks," Ron called back, wilting under the force of Alice Louise's dark and suspicious gaze. "I already ate. Got things to do."

Beth studied him for a moment, then shrugged with defeat and waved. She took a step toward the steps of the cafe, but then had to go back to snag Alice Louise by the sleeve and give her a tug toward the door. Still, Alice Louise hesitated, but then allowed herself to be turned to follow Beth, reluctantly, finally throwing another challenging glare at Ron over her shoulder just before disappearing inside.

RON FOUND the library open. It hadn't occurred to him that it wouldn't be, despite the storm of the night before. Undefeatable Yoopers. They have *sisu*—the ability to accomplish almost anything against overwhelming odds. A little snow might slow them down, but it wouldn't stop them.

Ron ducked through the door and headed down the hall toward the library.

The town librarian, Annie Ristimaki, was settled in at her desk, alone, reading a book.

"Don't mind me," Ron said. "I'm just looking around."

"You just take your time, Mr. Blank." She was a stout little woman with slate-gray hair, bright blue eyes, and glasses perched low on her nose. She was twice Ron's age, but as everyone called her Annie, Ron had naturally taken up the habit too. She had probably read every book on the meager shelves at least twice, and Ron had taken a liking to her instantly. Their tastes in books coincided perfectly. "Lookin' for somet'ing in particular, eh?" she asked.

"No. Thanks," Ron said, a bit embarrassed at his needs. "Just browsing. And please, call me Ron."

"No hurry," Annie said. "I'm here till t'ree."

He followed the run of the alphabet in the fiction section until he came to the S's. There weren't many books to choose from: the library was but one room, smaller than the main room of his two-room apartment, but the shelves were crammed. Annie's collection was eclectic and far more interesting than the library at Cavendish Junior College.

"We should be getting in dat new Teddy Roosevelt biography you wanted any day now, Mr. Blank. But I intend to read it first!" she added with a mischievous twinkle in her eye.

Mark Wolfgang

Ron found what he was looking for—a dog-eared paperback, yellowed with age—and plucked it from the shelf. There was one other chair in the room, a small but comfortable armchair. He dropped into it and began skimming the pages.

"AL!" BETH SNAPPED, and Alice Louise tore her eyes away from the snow-clogged town beyond the window, and looked up to see the frumpy waitress standing at her side, holding two platters overflowing with an omelet and sides of bacon, toast, and hash browns, looking for a place to set it all down. Alice Louise pulled her hands off the table and moved her coffee mug and juice glass, clearing a space. Then she looked down at her breakfast, wondering if this was what she'd ordered, having no memory of it. She didn't even like green peppers.

"So what do you think?" Beth said as she bit into a slice of strawberry jam-slathered toast.

"About what?"

"Al! I was talking to you, and you just went away. What is going on with you?"

"I don't know," Alice Louise said as she picked out bits of pepper and pushed them to the side of her plate. "I just... have things on my mind, I guess."

"What things? You weren't like this yesterday." Beth lifted out of her chair and thrust her hand across the table to lay her palm on Alice Louise's forehead. "No temperature." She sat back down. "I suppose it's just a hangover. Eat up. You'll feel better soon." Beth dug her toast into her eggs, stirring everything into a big red and yellow mess. "So seriously, what do you think?"

"About what?"

"Al! About what we were talking about! About how if things work out right, maybe Ron Blank might get a job as an electrician at the freaking White House! I mean, is that insane, or what?"

"Insane," Alice Louise echoed without enthusiasm. Her eyes drifted to the window again. "Snow tanks" littered the street—big, rusty, heavy old beater cars from decades past that were built for pushing through winter's worst. "I really haven't kept track of him, you know. I haven't seen him since October." But that wasn't right, was it? "Till last night, I mean." She watched to see Beth's reaction.

A Cold Winter's Deathe

"Yah. We should have asked him about it then. See if there's any new developments. Too bad he wouldn't come join us for breakfast."

Beth continued talking, rattling on about this and that, but Alice Louise's mind drifted again.

"I suppose the White House is haunted," she interrupted, catching Beth up short.

"Well... yah! About as haunted as Deathe!"

"But you've never actually *seen* a ghost have you?" Alice Louise challenged.

"Well, no. Of course not. Don't be–"

"Or anything else supernatural? Anything at all?"

Beth squirmed in her chair. "Well, you've been to Ron's old mansion. Cathy Cadaver's house. You slept there. You know how creepy it is." Beth shivered.

"Yes, I do. But that doesn't mean it's haunted. How do you know Deathe is haunted, or anyplace else for that matter?"

Beth shook her head with defeat. "Well, I just know. I mean, on an intellectual level. No, that's not right. I just sense it."

"You mean you've heard all the stories. But you've never actually experienced anything really... frightening? Anything that you *really* cannot explain? Anything that scared you half to death?"

Beth sighed. "No," she admitted.

They ate in silence for a while. Beth rambled on about the snow in the U.P., and how brutal winters could be, and how Yoopers endured, and survived and thrived despite it all. When they finished up they settled their bills and went out into the cold. As they opened the doors of the Jeep, Alice Louise looked across the roof into her friend's eyes.

"Who is Carl Rowley?"

Beth looked startled. "He's a bad man, Al. A very bad man. You, as a new State Trooper in the U.P., will probably find that out soon enough."

"Was he at the bar last night?"

"Of course not!" Beth said. "If he had been, we'd'a known it for sure."

"Why do I feel like I know who he is?"

ANNIE CLEARED her throat, and Ron glanced up to see it was three o'clock already.

At the tiny counter he prepared to fill in a check-out form.

"No need of dat," Annie said. "I'll remember, eh?" She stamped the return date on the card inside the back cover, beneath a half dozen other stamps, then turned the book over in her hands and looked at the cover. "*Dracula*. Now dere's one I haven't read in some time. Good book for a long, dark winter night, eh? I got some Stephen King over dere, too, y'know?"

"*Salem's Lot?*" Ron asked uneasily.

"Afraid not. Checked out already," she said without even a glance at the shelves.

Ron felt strangely relieved. The tale in his hands, now more than a century old, and diluted and tamed with the passage of time and the hardening of modern sensibilities, would be sufficient research material for this weekend.

Didn't Puck say something about the old ways working best? Time to study them.

Ron stepped out of the town hall with little on his mind but a long winter's evening curled up in a thick wool blanket with hot tea, the roar of the space heater, and a research book. *Dracula.*

"*Hey, professor!*"

A Cold Winter's Deathe

9

RON RECOGNIZED the voice instantly. He looked up, and across Main Street he saw Carl Rowley slouched against his shiny new gargantuan red four-wheel-drive super duty pickup. Bare-headed, fleece-lined sheepskin jacket open, cigarette dangling easily from his bare fingers. He was flanked by Shelby, and his son Greg, now a sullen, angry kid. They all stared hard at Ron.

Carl glared at Ron. Cold. Malevolent. Evil.

Ron glanced toward where Beth's Jeep had been parked, but it was gone now. The streets were deserted. He already knew the tiny village cop shop in the town hall was closed for the weekend, hung with a sign that said "Need help? Dial 911. Or for quicker service, stand in da middle of da street & holler!" Chief Woody's old Cherokee was nowhere in sight. Ron turned away without comment and trudged west toward home, his heart already pounding as if he'd run a mile.

"I'm talkin' to *you*, professor. I think we got some things to settle here."

"And what might that be, Carl?" Ron kept walking. He didn't dare stop. The door of the truck was open and he'd seen the shotgun in the gun rack in the back window. Not that Ron thought for a minute Carl was stupid enough to use it.

At least not in broad daylight.

"I owe you, *professor*," he said, nodding. "I owe you big time."

"I think you paid me back last night already." Ron stopped and turned to face Carl across the snow covered street. Better to know what might be coming, if anything.

Carl grinned and sucked on his cigarette. His cohorts snickered a little and shuffled their feet.

Mark Wolfgang

"I don't know what you're talkin' about, professor." He turned to Shelby. "Do you know what he's talkin' about, Shel?" Shelby shook his head in mute denial, his eyes locked on Ron. "No, professor. I still owe you. You and your little greaser buddy, Pedro."

"Leave Raúl out of this," he said. "Let's keep it between you and me." And maybe Puck, he thought. He could use a little of the Yooper vampire hunter's magic right about now.

"No can do, teacher. The little wetback's gonna get his, too."

"Let it go, Carl."

Shelby and the boy fidgeted, but Carl remained stock still, leaning with practiced casualness against the box of the truck. Greg stuck to his side.

"I don't like these wetback Mexicans comin' up here," Carl said, "stealing good jobs away from us hard working Americans, you know?"

Now that was funny coming from Carl Rowley—a guy who'd never held a job in his life.

"Stealing jobs?" Ron barked, suddenly blind with fury. "Am I missing something here? I'm sorry, Carl," he shouted, feeling the anger boil up inside him like a swarm of hornets. "Have you and your saplings there been standing in line down at the employment agency in L'Anse, begging for some of those fine jobs? Like bending over and digging potatoes for fourteen hours a day for minimum wage? Or maybe you would rather have Raúl's current job of makin' wood all day for people—by hand, since some miserable, back-stabbing, low-life coward made off with his chain saw last month!"

Carl snapped suddenly to attention and stood ramrod straight, glaring at Ron with seething hatred. He flung his cigarette to the ground.

Throw a rock at a pack of dogs, Ron thought, and the one that yelps is the one that got hit.

Shelby grabbed Carl's arm and whispered in his ear as he took a step into the street.

"Are those the kinds of jobs you want?" Ron demanded. In for a dime, in for a dollar. "How about your boy, there? Is that the kind of fine job you want for him? He gonna put himself through college that way?"

Ron could see Carl's chest heaving under the fleece jacket. Shelby turned and leaned into the cab of the pickup.

"And furthermore!" Ron added... he was on a roll now, plowing ahead, ignoring the danger warnings flashing through his brain like

A Cold Winter's Deathe

lightning, "Raúl's a U.S. citizen. He had to work at it. He had to study and take a test—things you wouldn't know about—and he's damned proud of it, and *he should be*. It wasn't just handed to him as a birthright. It came a lot harder than that. But that's stuff you wouldn't understand."

It occurred to Ron that his mouth was trying to get him killed for some reason. Shelby had pulled the shotgun off the rack, a very impressive double barrel .12 gauge pump action that probably would have cost Ron a month's wages, and slipped it into Carl's hands. Carl rested the butt of it on his right hip—the barrels pointed casually at the sky somewhere high above Ron's head. Shelby scanned the street to the east and west, north and south.

Greg glared at Ron. He whispered something at his father. Ron could hear the rage in the boy's voice.

"Do it, Pa," Ron heard Greg snarl. "Teach da bastard a lesson!"

Ron's heart paused in its furious work.

Carl stood rooted to the snow slick pavement. Shelby stood aside. Greg faded back behind the open door of the pickup.

Ron and Carl Rowley stood panting at each other from opposite sides of the street. Ron felt like he was burning up inside his down vest. Carl's face was bright red, his eyes small and intense. Ron heard the town hall door open and close behind him. He stole a glance over his shoulder and saw Annie Ristimaki in the doorway, warily assessing the situation.

Carl shifted the shotgun to his left hand and reached out and pointed across the street at Ron with two fingers of his right.

"Later, professor," Carl growled. "You and me. Alone. Later."

He tossed the shotgun to Shelby and hoisted his bulk up into the truck. Greg and Shelby scurried around to the other side and jumped in as Carl fired up the V10 and yanked the shifter into drive. The big truck bellowed away in rooster-tails of snow from all four heavily lugged tires.

"You should be more careful of what you say to Carl Rowley, Mr. Blank. There's no good to come of him, eh?" Annie stepped out of the doorway and squinted at Ron in the harsh late afternoon daylight. "It's for your own good. You stay out of his way now, eh?"

A little too late for that now.

"Yes, ma'am," Ron said, panting, feeling his knees turn to rubber as the adrenaline in his bloodstream abandoned him, leaving him weak and quavering. "I will certainly try to do that."

10

RON CLOSED the book.

Darkness had fallen without him even realizing it.

Amazing. He'd seen the movie. Several of them. Even the silent *Nosferatu*, and at least a dozen more, starting with Lugosi and ending with Gary Oldman, which was probably the best of the lot.

But they'd all bastardized the book in ways large and small.

There was really nothing wrong with the original tale, once it was boiled down to the essentials. It even ended with a breath-taking chase through the snowy Carpathian mountains as Jonathon Harker, Quincey (absent from the Lugosi movie), Professor Van Helsing, and Mina face down wolves and gypsies in a desperate race to destroy Dracula before he escapes forever into the sunset. This was accomplished on virtually the last page of the book, as Jonathon slices Dracula's throat with a Kukri knife and Quincey plunges another knife into the vampire's heart. It seemed to be an ending even Hollywood could love, if they could just leave it alone.

Snowy mountains and icy winds.

Sunset.

The world outside had turned dusky and dark. The purple sky faded to black, and it was night in Deathe again, still and moonless. Ron could see nothing beyond his streaked windows.

From downstairs, in Mrs. Kinderly's quarters, Ron could hear a radio playing softly, and the muted sounds of pots rattling, and plates and silverware being laid out for supper. The scent of a roast cooking—and something else—drifted up through warm air registers. He sniffed the air, and smelled a faint, cloying stench of death and decay.

A Cold Winter's Deathe

He wrinkled his nose and sniffed his way around his apartment, trying to determine where it might be coming from. An animal had probably crawled into the walls and died somewhere. Probably just a mouse, and most likely near the kitchen, he decided. He would have to tell Ruth. Hopefully, in these sub-freezing temperatures, it wouldn't get any worse.

He gave up, stood and stretched, then hovered in front of the open refrigerator for a long time, wishing he had a greater selection of meals. He settled on a frozen pasty, a traditional Upper Peninsula specialty, and a can of beef gravy. He popped it in the microwave, and in a few minutes it was steaming and succulent.

He jumped at a sudden banging on his door.

Ron approached with trepidation, his mind suddenly filled with visions of Carl Rowley and his family with guns and tire irons in hand. He was glad he'd pulled the curtains tight against the cold. And him without so much as a baseball bat or a safety chain on the door. He stood to one side and hooked the curtain back a fraction of an inch with his finger.

The door banged open.

"Holy wah! You look like you just seen a ghost!" Puck exclaimed. He pushed past Ron into the small apartment. "You cookin' sumthin'? Dat smells *great!* What're we havin'?"

Ron slammed the door. "*I* am having a pasty," he groused. "You probably smell Mrs. Kinderly's roast downstairs. Maybe you should go down and bother her."

"Nah. I'll share yours wid ya." He was still wearing his hunting gear, and the dead muskrat bomber hat still bobbed on his head. "We got stuff to talk about. You got any beer? I need to make some more magical urine." He threw open the refrigerator and peered inside.

Ron blew out an angry breath, even as he realized it was probably just a release of the tension from half expecting Carl Rowley and a violent and painful death.

"This settles it," Ron said. "I'm moving."

"Is dat your car out dere?" Puck popped a tab and downed half a can of Miller Lite. The bomber hat nearly fell off the back of his head. "What happened? A tree fall on it?"

"A random act of mindless vandalism," Ron said.

"Kids?"

"Don't I wish," Ron said coolly.

Mark Wolfgang

Puck's eyes fell on the library book, resting on the end table by the lone chair in the room. He tossed his muskrat hat on the couch, releasing a spray of wild hair, and picked up the book and thumbed through it.

"*Dracula!*" he said, and glanced up with delight. "Cool! Is dis your homework for the weekend? Learnin' anyt'ing good?"

"It's quite fascinating."

"You shouldn't take all dis too seriously," he said, waving the book offhandedly. He sank down into the chair and got comfortable. He drained the Miller and pitched the empty into the corner. "It's mostly rubbish. Superstitions. Ol' Bram never even went to Transylvania, ya know," he added. "He just read a buncha travel books. An' he got a lot of de vampire stuff wrong."

"Like that, enter 'freely of your own will' stuff?" Ron watched Puck's expression change as he pondered the question.

Puck shook his finger at Ron. "Now you're catchin' on! You t'ink I might have a little touch of de vampire t'ing in me, wid my mind tricks an' stuff! But you really didn't invite me in, did ya?" He sat back, looking smug. "Maybe you don't have to actually say it, ya know? De invitation might be right dere in your mind, where I can *sense it*. You t'ink of *dat?*"

"Oh trust me," Ron huffed. "That was *not* what was in my mind!"

"Well dere ya go, den. Yup. Dat invitation stuff is *solid*. You can stand dere just inside your door and t'row insults at 'em all night and dey can't do nuthin about it. But den I guess you'd never want to leave de house again, except in daylight."

Puck went back to the refrigerator and grabbed another Miller Lite.

"Help yourself to another free beer," Ron snarled.

"Hey, dat's my favorite kind of beer!" Puck said. "*Free* beer!" He slugged it down.

Ron edged to the bookcase and was careful to block Puck's view with his body as he pulled a book from the bottom shelf.

"Here's another book you might be interested in," Ron said. His heart pounded a little and he prepared to sprint for the door as he tossed Puck the book. Puck caught it easily and turned it over to examine it.

"A Holy Bible," he said. He grinned at Ron, holding the Bible loosely in his hand. "Are you, like, one of dose holy roller guys?"

A Cold Winter's Deathe

"You mean, am I religious?" Ron had never really considered the question. He did now. "I guess you could say... I *choose* to believe."

"Good enough for me," Puck said with a grin. "Not dat it matters much. You know what *my* holy water is." He waggled his eyebrows, drained the can, and pitched it at the sink. Then he handed the Bible back to Ron to put away. "So you were, like, testing me?"

"Yah. Yah, I guess I was."

"So what do you t'ink? Did I pass your test?"

"Damned if I know. You tell me."

"You choose to believe in God. Maybe you gotta choose to believe in vampires, too, eh?"

This was getting ridiculous. The guy was insane. And now he knew where Ron lived. And so did Carl. This town was getting too crowded.

"I'm just saying, I don't know you. I've never seen you in the daylight. I know you have some kind of bizarre influence over me, and the rest of the town. I have no idea what in the hell you were doing in that tomb last night after I left. You might have consecrated Sid's body, or desecrated it, or you might not have done anything to it at all, for all I know. And how do I know that it wasn't you who went into the tomb earlier and removed Emily Reindhart's body? You had a key!" Ron was working himself up into a lather. He stood before Puck, or whatever his name was, fists flexing, glaring at him accusingly.

"But do you believe in vampires?"

Ron was ready now. "There is only one kind of vampire—the Carl Rowleys of the world. Those who are mean, evil, and despicable and violent, and feed like vampires on their victims. But they aren't undead, and they don't drink the blood they spill."

"Well, you're wrong about vampires. Dey're as real as you and me."

Ron weighed that in his mind. He knew *he* was real, but Puck? Ha! This was like hearing Ed Posen, his boss, the frustrated electrical engineer, whose daily command was "Do it my way and make it work!" You just couldn't have it both ways at once.

He pulled two more beers out of his refrigerator and tossed one to Puck. He plopped down on the sofa bed and studied the Yooper. The guy actually seemed to believe. And Ron could almost feel himself buying into the insanity. Assuming that wasn't Puck's mind games again, but he honestly didn't think it was. This time.

Mark Wolfgang

"This vampire..." Ron ventured. "You really think he's in Deathe?"

"*It* is close by!. Don't anthro.... anthropomorph.... OK, don't try to make dis t'ing sound human. It ain't! Oh, it can mimic humans and human activities and even human emotions. But it ain't human. It's a vampire and it's real and it's undead! In de most basic sense of de word, sorta like what you read about in that book. But dat's a fable, a story based on reality, OK? De truth is worse. *It* is an animal dat preys on the living. A dog, or even a wolf, is more human than dis beast. Do not be fooled by appearances!"

Puck's eyes burned with passion. He truly believed. Ron was sure of it now, whether Ron believed or not. And for the first time, Ron actually felt afraid of the guy. And he felt sorry for him.

Ron felt a strange sense of connection. So maybe the guy was a little eccentric. Perhaps even a bit insane. Ron had just spent too many years living all alone in a haunted mansion in this tiny outpost of quasi-civilization, feeling isolated and unchallenged. In Deathe, one day was pretty much like the day before, until now they all seemed to meld together—days into weeks, weeks into months, months into years. And now Ron was over thirty, waking up in the same bed, going to the same job, seeing the same faces, saying the same things and hearing the same responses. The peace and quiet and serenity of the northern wilderness had its price, and that price was cultural deprivation, monotony.... eccentricity.

To say nothing of a deprivation of female companionship. Generally speaking.

The rest of the long winter stretched before him, disheartening and interminable.

Yet in only one day his life had been enlivened beyond all imagining as it intersected with both Puck the Yooper vampire hunter and Carl Rowley. In comparison, Puck seemed quite harmless. And Ron knew he had a power that could keep Carl at bay. That, as much as anything, interested Ron immensely.

"Okay," Ron said. "Let's assume that vampires are real. Where do you fit in? What's so special about this one guy you're chasing? Is he the only one?"

Puck turned his face away, and Ron couldn't see the expression in his eyes. "It's de only one dat concerns me," he said. He drained his third can of beer.

"Why?"

A Cold Winter's Deathe

"Not today," he said. "Maybe sometime. But not today, eh?" Ron waited, but Puck made no effort to fill the silence. He got up and trudged to the refrigerator again.

"You might want to go easy on that," Ron said. "The Shopko is probably closed for the night." *And Carl Rowley might be waiting out there in the street.* He tried to shake off the feeling of dread with more pleasant thoughts. "Well, if you won't tell me about your vampire, then tell me about vampires in general. Is it true you can't see their reflection in a mirror?"

"No. Of course not." Puck tossed a can to Ron and opened his own. "Dese t'ings are not simply spirits or apparitions, ya know. Dey're corpses animated with unholy life and an unquenchable thirst for blood!" He turned to look at Ron again finally, his eyes brightening with his enthusiasm for the subject. "And dey have strong mental powers. Dey can hypnotize and mesmerize–"

"Like you?"

That stopped him short. He glared at Ron for an instant, then looked away.

"Yah. Like me. Don't take offense, eh? I wouldn't really make you sit up and bark like a seal, ya know. But vampires, dey can influence your perception of 'em to alter dere appearance. But dey have trouble with mirrors, eh? In a mirror you can see de vampire for what it really is: an ugly, vile beast. An animated corpse! Dat's why dey avoid mirrors."

"Do they turn into bats or wolves?"

"Of course not! But dey can trick you into believing dey can!"

"What about becoming like smoke? In *Dracula* the three ghostly women materialize out of nebulous dust motes–"

"Are you serious, man? Dat's crazy. It's just anudder illusion!" Puck barked angrily. "Are you payin' attention? Dis stuff is important here."

So now he thinks I'm crazy, Ron thought, and laughed out loud. He decided to change tack.

"OK, so what the hell is a vampire doing this far north in Deathe? Make me believe that, and I'll believe anything. Won't he freeze solid up here?"

"You know what Deathe is," Puck said. "Dere's supernatural stuff dat goes on here. You've seen ghosts. I can tell. I got supernatural powers, too, ya know."

Ron had not mentioned his ghosts to anyone in nearly five years, when he'd realized that he was the only one who saw them. And believed. Except Alice Louise Dubose. She had even seen, but she still didn't believe. Erin Coe had seen and never even suspected. And yet, somehow, Puck knew Ron's secret.

"It probably t'inks it'll be safe here. It can stand the cold. Even better den I can. It can sleep t'rough the whole winter, like a bear in hibernation, biding its time. Sleep for years even. Decades. Maybe centuries, for all I know, even till I grow old and feeble, and maybe even if I die. It could happen," he said with a shrug. "It can outlast me and you. It's *eternal*." He looked up at Ron, his eyes sharp, and Ron saw something familiar in them. "It don't feel de passage of time. It don't grow older, but *stronger*. I gotta end dis soon."

"This is about revenge."

"Yah, well... I suppose dere's always dat, too." Puck's eyes turned away, and he heaved a sigh.

"So you need help. My help. Why me?"

"Hey, you can see me! And you faced up to dat Carl guy when no one else would. You do dat, you can face anyt'ing!"

"Last night I was just being headstrong and stupid! And drunk. Believe me, I'd never do it again."

"Yah you would. And you know it."

"No, I really don't. Not unless you can teach me your... *thing*." Ron waggled his fingers at Puck's face.

"Yah sure," Puck said with a dismissive wave of his hand. "Dat's easy. Nuthin' to it."

Ron suspected a bit of deception here. "But?"

"But first ya gotta help me tomorrow."

"Oooh Kayy... What happens tomorrow?" Ron asked, now very suspicious.

"Tomorrow we gotta go visit yer buddy Sid Francis's camp." He avoided Ron's eyes.

"And why would we do that?"

"Hey! T'ink our pasty's done!" Puck popped out of his chair and dove for the kitchen. "What kind of pasty is it? Hey, I know! My favorite kind! A *free* pasty! You got any gravy to put on it? You gotta have gravy to put on it, eh?"

"Puck, or whoever the hell you are, just what," Ron said. "are you expecting to find at Sid's camp?"

A Cold Winter's Deathe

"Well, I expect to find de lair of my vampire, maybe even with de vampire sleepin' in its coffin. And I expect to *kill it*, eh?"

WHEN PUCK WAS finally gone, Ron was too drained, physically, mentally, and emotionally, to clean up the mess of dirty dishes and empty beer cans left in Puck's wake. He sorted through the sad little collection of videos he'd brought with him from Cavendish House, looking for something he hadn't seen in a while. It would be nice to have cable, he thought. Radio, cell phone, and TV signals could not penetrate the ridges that surrounded White Wolf Lake and Deathe, and Mrs. Kinderly was half blind and had no use for TV, so no cable had ever been run to the boarding house. Besides, she could never afford the installation. She found her entertainment in gossip, and her boarders, and the town, and that was sufficient for her.

Now Ron heard her voice calling up through the warm air register in his kitchen.

"Mr. Blank?" she called faintly. "Are you up there?"

There could be no secrets in this house, Ron thought as he bent to the register to reply. Who needed phones or intercoms?

11

RON MOVED into the kitchen and knelt by the register. "Why are you whispering?"

"You come down here for a bit, eh?"

Ron could picture her huddled in the corner under the vent in her kitchen ceiling.

"Is there something wrong?" he asked softly.

"Oh, no no no. I have someone here who wants to meet you."

"Meet me? Now?"

"Yah sure. You come down, eh?"

Ron glanced at his cheap digital wristwatch.

"Ruth, it's almost ten o'clock. I've had a full day."

"I can tell time! You come down now anyway. I made a coffee cake, and I want you to meet my new boarder, eh?"

New boarder?

"Yah sure," Ron said with a sigh of resignation. "I mean, okay. I'll be right down."

He went to the closet for a coat. He was wearing grubby blue jeans and an old sweatshirt, but he was damned if he was going to change out of them this late at night. The reek of the dead rodent he'd noticed earlier that evening was stronger now, the cloying stench a bit more distinct in the closet. There was nothing to be done about it. Eventually the smell would go away. He pulled on a jacket and left the closet door open to air out, then trundled outside and down the stairwell to Ruth's front door.

The night was clear, the temperature hovering near zero. Apparently Friday night's storm marked the end of the mild weather, now a true Upper Peninsula winter was setting in with a vengeance.

A Cold Winter's Deathe

He'd shoveled off the walkways around the house earlier, when he'd cleaned out his car, but the thin frosting of snow that still remained squawked in protest under his every footstep.

Ron had never felt quite comfortable walking into someone's house without knocking, but the lights were off in the parlor and it was only marginally brighter back in the dining room and kitchen, and since he'd just been invited, he eased the door open and crept into the warm and humid comfort of the old house.

The smell of the dead animal was much stronger here, and he decided maybe it was not a mouse after all, but something bigger—a squirrel, perhaps, maybe down in the cellar. He also detected the odor of wood smoke overlaying the carrion smell.

Mrs. Kinderly lived in outdated comfort. The house and everything in it was old, from the threadbare Persian carpets to the dusty, ornate brass chandeliers; from the faded, textured wallpaper to the heavy blue velvet drapes. Ceramic figurines, knick-knacks, and other collectibles, tiny framed portraits and antique silver spoons, thimbles and dried flowers, covered every horizontal surface. She generally dusted around them without disturbing anything very much. All of the furniture was old, purchased before her husband died, and that was long ago.

Ron eased the door closed and stepped around Ruth's favorite easy chair toward the light.

Then he saw her. Not Ruth, but the person who supposedly wanted to meet him. She sat at the table with her back to Ron, absolutely still.

And Ron thought with dismay that Ruth had taken in a homeless woman.

He could only see her in shadows, silhouetted by the kitchen light beyond, but at first glance she looked infirm, perhaps ill. Unkempt. Her dress was a muddy burgundy, threadbare and shabby, hanging loose over thin shoulders that were all bone and hard angles, and shrink-wrapped in thin, pallid flesh. He rusty blond hair was matted and pulled loosely back with a dingy ribbon, barely constraining the chaotic snarls.

She watched Mrs. Kinderly, motionless, not even breathing, as the older woman fussed in the buffet, selecting antique silverware, tea cups, and dessert plates. Like a statue, Ron thought, except now he saw that her head swayed slightly, as if precariously balanced on her too-thin neck.

Or perhaps she was dizzy.

Or more likely: drugged.

Ron took a couple silent steps toward the dining room, then stood in awkward silence.

Ruth hummed merrily to herself as she set the good china on a silver serving platter. Her slate gray hair was pulled back in a tight little bun and she wore a long flowered apron of pastel pinks and yellows. On the buffet was a homemade coffee cake, still steaming and fresh from the oven, but Ron couldn't smell it over the pungent odor of the dead rodent. All this he saw in a glance, but mostly his attention was on the vagrant woman in the chair before him.

He cleared his throat, and Ruth looked up and beamed at him.

"There you are, Mr. Blank," she said.

The woman rose from her chair and turned to face him in a single fluid motion, as graceful as a dancer. And the shock nearly floored him.

She was, in fact, beautiful. Stunning. Her face was a delicate heart, smooth and pure as fine porcelain and almost as translucent, with lush, full lips, and bottomless dark eyes. What he'd thought was a rat's nest of dingy hair was in fact a halo of coppery blond that flowed like corn silk over her plush, wine-red, velour dress.

So it must have all been a cruel trick of light and shadows.

When she saw Ron her eyes flashed black, as though the pupils had instantly dilated fully wide with anticipation. Like a cat's when it first sees the fingers moving under the blanket.

"This is Julianna," Mrs. Kinderly was saying. It took a few seconds for the information to register, Ron was so instantly captivated. "Julianna, this is Ron Blank."

The angel stepped forward, very close, and extended her hand to Ron, not to be shaken but to be kissed. And, God help him, he kissed it. *There's a first time for everything.* Her fingers were cold in his, but warmed instantly with his touch. The flesh of her hand was sweet and fragrant, and soft as velvet. Her face was mere inches from Ron's as she gazed up at him. The pupils of her eyes were enormous, like black wells, yet he could see that they were a marvelous shade of blue-green, almost turquoise.

"So *you* are the David," Julianna said with a coy smile.

"I'm sorry?"

"The David who slew Goliath." Her voice was light, almost laughing. Her eyes sparkled.

"I'm afraid I don't know what you mean," Ron said.

A Cold Winter's Deathe

"I heard of an altercation in a local establishment last night."

"How did you hear about that?" Ron found at times he could barely remember it himself, and thanks to Puck's wave of the hand, no one else had seemed to remember it at all.

"I have my sources." She flashed a mysterious smile; her dark turquoise eyes blinked languorously. Her teeth were perfect and dazzling.

Ron looked at Ruth.

She shrugged.

He still held her fingers in his, reluctant to let them go. She wore no jewelry whatsoever—unusual in a young woman, even in the U.P. She could have been as young as nineteen, or as old as thirty. Ron split the difference and guessed her age at twenty-three. Her complexion was flawless with youth and good health, but she carried herself with the composure and self-assurance of an older woman. Her trim, dark, wine-red jacket and knit blouse were exquisite. The jacket hugged her waist, embraced her slim hips, and formed two delightful mounds over her breasts. The matching skirt fell to below her knees, full and loose. Crinkly black leather boots hid her legs completely. Ron stood before her wearing his old winter coat over an old Michigan Tech sweatshirt and too-short blue jeans displaying his sparklers. Feeling slightly ridiculous, but yet not really caring in the least.

He realized he was staring at her shamelessly in those first few moments.

"Julianna was confused," Ruth said. Julianna shot her a sharp glance. "It seems she knew about Ron Borke next door. She was quite surprised to hear about you living upstairs."

"Really? Do you know Ron?"

"No," she said. "Perhaps I'd heard the name, is all. It must be confusing, though. To have two Rons living side by side."

"Not really. We can tell us apart!" he said. "Besides, everyone calls him Ron, but most people call me Mr. Blank."

"Oh pshaw," Ruth said. "Julianna has taken the Blue Room, Mr. Blank." Ron grinned at her. She didn't know why. All of Ruth's rooms and apartments were named after rooms in the White House. "She's just moved into town," Ruth said. "She's staying here while she looks for someplace more permanent."

"Julianna." Ron tasted the name on his tongue. "Do you have a last name?"

"When it suits me," she replied with a coy blink of her dark eyes.

"It's Pritchard," Mrs. Kinderly said.

"Pre-*sharr*." Julianna purred, with a flicker of annoyance at Ruth so fleeting Ron wasn't sure he'd seen it.

"I thought you two kids should get to know each other," Ruth interjected. "You seem to be about the same ages, and you're both single...."

"Oh, Ruth," Ron said. He knew he could easily be half again as old as this waif. But damned if he was going to mention it. And then to Julianna: "You'll have to be patient with her. She's taken quite an active interest in my relationships for some reason."

"What relationships?" Ruth snapped. "You don't even have any friends in town."

"There's Beth," Ron said, and instantly thought better of it.

"*That woman!*" Ruth snapped.

Beth had become "that woman" when she'd dropped the F-bomb in front of Ruth years ago. Ruth didn't approve of such language. Ron didn't either, usually, but Beth always seemed able to pull it off with such delightful exuberance that he had to forgive her every time. She wouldn't just drop an F-bomb, she'd spike it.

"Now come to the table, both of you," Ruth said, taking Ron's coat and hanging it on an old coat rack. "I have cake and coffee for us, eh? We'll all get to know each other better."

"I'm sure we will," Julianna said. She slipped her fingers out of Ron's. He hadn't realized he was still holding her hand, and when it was gone his hand felt empty. She drifted to the table, smiling at him over her shoulder, and perched delicately in her chair, and Ron felt an old, vaguely familiar stirring in his loins.

"Why is it so dark in here?" he asked. The old brass chandelier had been dimmed to perhaps half brightness. "Can't we turn up some lights?"

"Julianna's sensitive to the light. We'll keep them down for her, eh?" Ruth smiled at Julianna, who beamed back at her in return.

"I wanted to mention the dead animal," Ron said. He sniffed the air. "Hmm. But now I don't smell it." In fact, all he could smell was a fresh, delicious citrus scent that seemed to emanate from Julianna. Oranges. Lemons. Luscious fruits ripe for the picking.

Ruth frowned at him in confusion. "What dead animal?"

A Cold Winter's Deathe

"Sorry. I thought maybe something had died in my walls," he said. "I can't smell it now, but when I first came in..."

"Well, never mind that now. I'll call someone Monday morning. Sit, sit."

Ron sat. Ruth had arranged the chairs expertly around the oval table. He was forced to sit beside Julianna.

While Ruth cut the cake and placed it on gilt-edged china before them, and then poured the coffee from an elegant silver pot, Julianna watched with a bemused smile, her posture perfect, her hands again folded demurely in her lap.

"Please," Julianna said as Ruth set the cake and coffee before her, "I've just dined, and I really can't eat another bite."

"Oh, you're such a tiny thing. You'll try some of this, okay? Sure and you're not watching your weight, eh?"

"I couldn't. Really. Ron?" Julianna looked to him for help, her turquoise eyes pleading. Her hand floated out of her lap and she rested her warm fingertips on the back of his hand. Her hand was small and fine, her nails smooth and clear, long and perfect.

"Now, Ruth," Ron said. "Let's not force Julianna–"

"Oh, pshaw," Ruth said. "It'll do her good. Here. Eat. I just made it tonight."

"Looks wonderful," Ron said, and as Ruth turned toward the buffet to find napkins he snatched up his fork and sliced off a bite of Julianna's coffee cake and stuffed it in his mouth. He gave her a wink, and she grinned with delight. "It is wonderful," he said around the mouthful of cake, then crammed in a quick bite of his own. Ruth dealt out the napkins and never saw a thing.

"There," she beamed at the sight of plundered cake. "Wasn't that good?"

"Excellent," Julianna said with a sidelong smile at Ron

Ruth sat across from the couple. She and Ron sipped their coffee and ate their cake, a cinnamon glazed confection dotted with bright red cherries. Julianna politely poked at her cake with her fork and pushed it around her plate a little. Occasionally she lifted the teacup and touched the coffee to her lips delicately.

"What brings you to Deathe in the dead of winter, Julianna?" Ron asked, enjoying the taste of her name on his tongue.

"I was looking for a quiet, restful place. I would like some peace and solitude for a while. Rest." She seemed about to say something, then reconsidered. "A long, long rest.."

"I've tried that, and it's not quite all it's cracked up to be. Besides, Deathe isn't always that quiet."

"Julianna is looking for work," Ruth said.

"There's no work in Deathe," Ron said. "And darned little in the whole Upper Peninsula."

"I am patient. I have nothing but time. There are many other things I desire, so much more than work," she said, casting a significant look at Ron. A vague enticing smile passed over her face, and he felt a thrill of adrenaline surge through his body. "I am comfortable. I have little need for work. I come from *old money,*" she added.

"Still and all," Ruth said, "she spent all day looking, didn't you, dear? She just checked in very early this morning, before sunrise, and she was gone all day today. Any luck yet?"

"No... luck," Julianna said. "At least, not in finding a job."

Again she smiled coyly at Ron. Her hand drifted out and plucked at an invisible something on his shoulder, lingering there for a moment, one finger stroking lightly at the cloth of his sweatshirt before withdrawing, and Ron felt the blood stirring within him.

He'd never believed in the power of pheromones to affect human desires. Those subtle scent molecules that communicated sexual attraction among moths, sometimes for many miles, had no bearing on human relations. Or so he'd thought. For Ron Blank, they were no more than a dry topic in biology class. But now he found himself changing that opinion. This girl must have had them in great abundance, and if she didn't turn them off soon he was afraid he wouldn't be able to stand up from the table without embarrassing himself.

"What of you, Mr. Ron Blank?" she said. "What do you do... with yourself?"

He cleared his throat and tugged at his collar. It seemed tight for a baggy sweatshirt, and Ruth's house was unusually warm. He was loathe to talk about his job at the college—a job that was like eternally pushing boulders up a hill. It also seemed petty and meaningless right now, sitting beside Julianna, and after all he'd been through this weekend.

He gave her a short version.

Somewhere in the back of his head he heard the faint sound of alarms going off, shouting at him that here was a woman in a desperate search for a husband, a family, a life of suffocating closeness and commitment. Only this time the alarm was distant, and muted by the nearer music of Julianna's voice. Her smoky eyes clouded his vision.

A Cold Winter's Deathe

He shook his head to clear it.

"Are you all right, Mr. Blank?" Ruth asked. "You looked a little flushed."

"Fine," he lied. He forced a smile. "Just a little woozy. It's been a heck of week in Deathe, ain't it?" he said conversationally. "Sid Francis died, then his camp burned down, and now we have two newcomers in one week. Almost more excitement than I can take."

"We have two visitors?" Ruth said in surprise. "Who else besides Julianna?"

"Some crazy Yooper looking for a vampire," Ron said before he could stop himself.

He looked from Ruth to Julianna, cringing. Ruth's eyes were wide with amused surprise. Julianna was staring at him, darkly solemn.

"Where is he now?" she asked softly. She seemed to suppress a shudder.

Ron shrugged. "I don't know. I guess I hadn't thought about where he was staying."

"Did he find a... *vampire?*" Julianna asked, eyes unreadable.

There had certainly been no vampire in the Fairview mausoleum last night. Just a recently deceased Sid Francis, and a displaced corpse. Which he didn't want to think about, and had no intention of mentioning.

"No." Ron forced a laugh. "Of course not!"

"Are you sure?"

"Julianna, there's no such thing as vampires. Trust me. That's insane. The guy is insane."

"Well," Ruth said sharply, "I don't know where he would be staying if he doesn't have any relatives here. I have the only rooms to rent in this town."

Julianna stood suddenly, gracefully, and extended her hand to Ron. "I'm sorry," she said with a sad smile. "I find all this talk of vampires and death and insanity distressing."

"I didn't mean to say he was insane–" Ron rose and stood beside Julianna. She rested her hand on his arm for support, and he covered her hand with his own. "Are you okay?"

"I believe I should like to go lie down," she said. She slipped her hand out from under his and glided away toward the Blue Room.

"No. Wait," Ron protested. "You have to tell me how you knew about last night. The altercation at the bar."

Julianna shook her head. Her coppery blond hair shimmered and waved under the dull lights. "I'd heard of a man named Ron who confronted a wicked man who preys on the weak. And vanquished him. As David slew Goliath."

"That wasn't me," he confessed. "I nearly got myself beaten to a pulp. The real David was that Yooper vampire hunter kid."

Julianna stared. "He interceded on your behalf?"

Ron smiled at her choice of words.

"Yes, I guess you could say he 'interceded on my behalf'. But nobody has slayed Goliath. Carl was perfectly healthy the last time I saw him. Believe me, he's still just as big and mean and dangerous— and as frightening—as a rabid grizzly bear."

"In truth? You fear him? This... *Carl*?"

"Oh yah. I fear him," Ron said, trying to suppress a shudder. "I fear him *a lot*."

"He resides in the area?"

"Unfortunately. Just south of town. Way too close. Why?"

"I will want to be cautious of him, no?"

Curious, Ron thought, this sudden sense of fear in Julianna.

Ruth was up now, bustling around, collecting their plates and teacups. She stepped through the doorway in the kitchen, and Ron was suddenly alone with Julianna as Ruth drew water to wash the dishes. Julianna cast a glance at her, then leaned close to Ron. He held his breath as she turned to him, her full lips nearly brushing his ear.

"I am fleeing a... I believe you would call him... a *stalker*. A dangerous man, a distressing man, who is obsessed with me for some reason. He frightens me. I would prefer not to burden Mrs. Kinderly with that knowledge," she said with a glance at Ruth. "She seems too fragile, so delicate."

Julianna leaned away from Ron and regarded him with solemn eyes. "Besides, I await my personal assistant. I expect him to follow along soon. I will feel much safer when he arrives."

"You have a personal assistant?" Ron felt a bit envious. And intimidated. He'd never known anyone with a personal assistant. Not even his mother.

"I do. But there's always an opening for one more." She fluttered her aquamarine eyes at him.

Personal assistant to Julianna. Ron rolled that over in his mind.

"How will I know him to avoid this... Carl?" she asked.

A Cold Winter's Deathe

"You'll know. Big, mean, and, well... *big*. And *mean*. Watch out for a big red pickup and stay out of his way. Julianna, will I see you again?"

"I don't know. Perhaps you will. If you wish it."

"What can I do to persuade you?"

A minute smile glimmered in her eyes. "There is much you can do to persuade me."

He felt a breathless thrill. "When?"

"Soon," she said. Her eyes were dark. The bright glint of turquoise was gone, replaced with a deep aquamarine.

She looked up at him and smiled again, and to his surprise she stepped close and kissed him on the lips. Then she turned and walked with a dancer's grace to her bedroom without looking back, and she was gone.

Ron stood staring at the empty doorway for several seconds, his heart racing in his chest. Then, reluctantly, he turned and found his own way out, forgetting to thank Ruth or even say goodnight.

HE DREAMED of Julianna that night.

Of course.

He dreamed that he was awake, and he heard her calling to him—not with her voice, but with her mind, her will. She spoke directly to his soul. He rose from his sofa bed, went to the window and looked out. He saw her staring in at him, beckoning to him to join her, to come out and play in the snow. She drifted and swayed in the moonlight just outside Ron's second story window, perfectly natural, perfectly lovely.

No, he said. He invited her to come to him. Please. Come into my house and visit with me. She smiled at him, a warm and knowing smile.

12

ALICE LOUISE awoke to the sounds of Beth puttering in the kitchen. She rolled out of bed, pulled on her bathrobe, and was headed into the kitchen when she heard Beth say "Holy wah," with a hint of amusement.

"What?" Alice Louise said.

Beth was turning away from the kitchen window, wiping her hands on a dish towel, when the font door jumped under the pounding of a heavy fist.

Beth pulled the door open and Alice Louise slumped at the sight of the doorway filled with the hulking figure of Woodrow W. Wood, Deathe's own Chief Woody. He wore a blue bomber hat with black fur trim and the Deathe P.D. patch on the front, and an immense blue Carhartt coat. His badge was pinned on crooked, and Alice Louise was distressed to see that a gun bulged under his coat on his right hip.

Alice Louise's heart sank. Hoping she hadn't been seen, she eased back into the darkened bedroom.

"Hey, Bev!" Chief Woody rumbled to Beth in a barely subdued bellow. "How's mah favorite teacher gal?" He planted a quick noisy kiss on her cheek and Alice Louise winced.

"What's up, Chief? What brings you here so early on a Sunday morning?"

"Well, I am truly sorry, but this ain't just a social call. I heard your gal friend Thelma Louise Dubose was here, and I kindly wanted to talk to her for a minute. Cop to cop, if'n ya know what I mean. Dis is official police bidness," he added with a stern nod.

"Yah sure, Chief. Come on in." Beth wore a serious expression which fell apart as she turned toward Alice Louise hiding in the

A Cold Winter's Deathe

shadows. "Thelma!" she called, beaming, eyes dancing with amusement. "Come on in here. Chief Woody needs a word."

Alice Louise snugged up her terrycloth bathrobe and tightened the belt. She pulled in a deep steadying breath, and forged her way out into the living room.

"Chief Wood," she said, "what a pleasant surprise. How did you know I was here?" She shot Beth an accusing glance.

The Chief pulled off his choppers and engulfed Alice Louise's hand in his immense mitt.

"Trooper Dubose," he said formally. "Ain't too many secrets in Deathe. And I make it my bidness to know everything that goes on in my town. Now," he continued, "I don't like imposing upon you, ekspecially on a Sunday morning like dis, but we had us a little incident last night, and I was wondering if you might be available to give us a hand dis morning. I promise I'll try not to take up too much of your time, I'm sure you're enjoyin' your weekend off with Bev here. But I called your boss in Ironwood and he said you'd be happy to share your expertise with us."

She decided she would have to thank her boss, Gray Mackie, as soon as she got back to her post. And give him a firm piece of her mind.

"Well, it's like dis. There was a fire out on the other side of the lake. Nobody was hurt, but de camp burned down, and it looks kindly suspicious. I just wanted to have a report on file with the State Police, against future need, if you know what I mean."

"I'm not a trained fire investigator," Alice Louise protested. "I really doubt I could add anything to your investigation. Don't you have someone who's qualified?"

"Not here dis weekend," the Chief said. "And the road out of town is closed after that big storm Friday night. We got twelve foot drifts and some trees down out past the trestle, and it might be a day or two afore we get de mess cleaned up. Besides," he added, "dere's sumthin else goin' on dere I'd like you to take a look at."

Alice Louise's heart sank another fathom or two. The road was closed? And her car was still buried under about six feet of snow. She hadn't felt this trapped since she'd worn an engagement ring for three long days a few years ago. She looked to Beth for support, but her alleged friend just smiled at her distress. Alice Louise shot her a sour look and turned back to the Chief with a sigh.

"Sure, Chief. Just let me have some breakfast and get dressed. How about if you pick me up in half an hour or so?"

"Yah sure. You'd better dress warm. It's a long, cold ride."

She didn't like the sound of that.

"The heater doesn't work in your cruiser?" she asked, not really expecting an answer she wanted to hear.

"Oh, yah. But we can't drive there. All the roads north of town are buried." He looked at Beth. "I was hopin' Bev here would run you out there on her snowmobile."

Of course, Beth ignored the panic in Alice Louise's eyes and nodded enthusiastically.

A Cold Winter's Deathe

13

"HEY, I T'INK we picked up a tail!"

"What are you talking about?" Ron shouted over the whine of the snowmobile's engine and the frigid wind.

This was not going at all as he'd expected.

Puck had showed up late in the morning, in broad daylight, or as broad as daylight was going to get beneath the gray overcast sky. Ron had gone next door to borrow Ron Borke's Arctic Cat for the ride to Sid Fancis's camp, but Borke was obviously hungover, surly and uncooperative. He looked as bad as Ron felt. Or maybe they were both coming down with the latest flu bug.

"No one touches de Cat," Borke had grumbled, to Ron's great relief.

Great!

He was still looking for a way out of Puck's mad scheme, and encouraged that if Borke wouldn't lend him his snowmobile, well, without transportation the whole thing would come crashing down. What could he do? He might be able to convince Puck that no one else in town would lend him a snowmobile, and that was mostly true. But then Borke had tossed him the key to his fifteen-year-old Ski-Doo, a dull yellow hunk of cracked fiberglass and rusty metal, and recited a long list of instructions and warnings.

By the time they'd hit the village limit they'd broken or ignored every one of them.

Puck had insisted on driving. Ron reluctantly hung on for dear life behind him, bundled in every article of winter clothing he owned.

Puck peered into the mirror that shook wildly on the left handlebar.

"Take a look. Are dese some friends of yours comin' up behind us?"

Ron twisted around to look, but his coat hood billowed behind his head, blocking his view. He took a risk and eased his grip on Puck, freeing a hand to pull the hood aside so he could see.

An enormous red pickup with a gleaming chrome grill the size of the Masticator's maw was maybe fifty yards behind them and gaining fast, skewing wildly on the snow-covered road. It accelerated hard and roostertails of snow shot up from all four tires.

"*Holy man!*" Ron said, his heart suddenly in his throat, adrenaline burning in his veins. "*Hit it!*"

Puck twisted the throttle, but not much happened. They were going maybe thirty miles an hour on the open road, and if that's all the Ski-Doo had, they were in serious trouble. Ron looked ahead and saw they were coming to the curve at the edge of town, where the old railroad trestle crossed over at an angle, choking the road down to a single narrow lane and curling it into a nasty, dangerous twist and dip beneath.

"Get under the bridge, then hang a quick left!" Ron shouted. With luck the old logging trail that led north around the east side of the lake would be impassable for Carl's truck.

The trestle suddenly loomed directly in front of them, all cut limestone and ancient brick, scarred with the impacts of hundreds of vehicles over the decades. Puck jerked the handlebars to follow the twist, but the road dropped and the skis took some air, and the snowmobile didn't respond. Ron saw the solid wall coming straight at their faces. Then the Ski-Doo hit hard, the skis bit, and they skimmed past the corner of the trestle, the right sleeve of Ron's coat brushing a limestone block.

They dove through the short dark tunnel at an angle, and Ron tucked in his left arm as they skimmed past the brick and stone again on the far side. The snowmobile hit a drift and jerked back into the middle of the road. It shuddered and for a panicked second Ron thought it might stall. He risked a look back and caught a glimpse of red as the pickup slid sideways in tremendous sprays of snow on the far side of the trestle.

"Left!" Ron shouted. "Go left! *Now!*"

Puck turned into the fire break that cut through the forest. They raced between rows of pines and poplars. With luck they could disappear into the woods where Carl's truck couldn't follow. Thankfully the snow was deep, at least two or three feet. He looked back and saw the truck was on their side of the trestle now and a door was open. Over the roar of the Ski-Doo's engine he heard the boom of a shotgun, then another, and above them the trees exploded with snow. Pine boughs plunged to the ground in their path.

Ron ducked, pushing Puck into the handlebars.

"*Hey!*"

The Ski-Doo skewed and Puck lost his grip on the throttle and the engine dropped to an idle. Another *boom*, and the trunk of a big pine tree less than ten feet away exploded at head level, spraying them with bark and splinters. Puck twisted the throttle and the machine surged ahead again.

ALICE LOUISE stood hugging herself and shivering violently in Bill Trevarthan's snowmobile suit and boots. Beth and Chief Woody stood on either side of her, both staring at the burned out hulk of what was once a shabby tarpaper and asphalt shingle covered hunting shack. Sid Francis's "camp," which, Alice Louise now knew, was the term used for a man's hunting getaway in the "bush." Chief Wood's deputy, a big farm kid, paced at the edge of the destruction, peering into the one corner of the the shack that still had standing walls and what was left of the roof, now collapsed across the bare, scorched plank floorboards.

Looking for clues, Alice Louise guessed.

The acrid stench of wet, burned wood stung her nose. The only sound was the ticking of the three snowmobile engines as they cooled and contracted in the single-digit air temperatures. Alice Louise had panicked when Beth, the Chief and the kid had shut them off. *What if they didn't start again!* They'd all die out here in the middle of nowhere! Beth had reassured her that no good Yooper would ever let that happen. Snowmobiles were precious commodities, and always kept in excellent repair. To prove it she'd hit the button and gunned the engine once before shutting it down again.

"What am I supposed to be doing here, Chief?" Alice Louise asked.

"Donnie!" Woody bellowed to the deputy, as if he couldn't hear from ten feet away. But bellowing seemed to be Chief Woody's normal tone of voice. "Show her what you found."

Deputy Don, Alice Louise thought with a crooked smile. She'd met him when she'd arrested Helen Kim and ruined Ron's shoes, but she'd somehow never caught his name.

Deputy Don looked a little green around the gills, but he motioned her over. Alice Louise followed as he stepped up onto the foundation of the house and edged his way past a corner where the floorboards had collapsed into the crawl space below.

The place reeked of the fire—the pungent, sickening stink of burned wood, now cold and wet. Don tested the strength of the floor with each footstep. It creaked ominously, yet seemed sufficiently solid as it sloped down toward the dirt floor of what looked to be a root cellar.

"It's OK, eh?" Don said. "I was out here early dis morning, after we got de call about the smoke. It'd only be a short fall, no big deal, but just stay in my footsteps."

Alice Louise could see a trap door, but there was a larger opening near what must have been the bedroom, where the beams and planks had burned through and crashed down to the dirt below. They worked their way toward it, Alice Louise following behind at a respectful distance.

Deputy Don sat on the edge of the gaping hole, dangled his feet for a second, and dropped down. He stood aside, and she could see the cellar was less than six feet deep. He looked up at Alice Louise.

Crap. She sat down and dropped in beside him.

"This way," he said, stabbing the beam of a powerful flashlight in the direction of a big cabinet that stood against the south cellar wall. She could barely see it, as though it was at the far end of a low, dark cave.

Alice Louise crouched down and entered the "cave," following Deputy Don. The reek of burnt wood was stifling. Cobwebs and filth hung from the floor beams overhead. They crabwalked over to the cabinet.

It was only singed, but almost all of the jars of canned foods inside had exploded from the heat. Surprisingly, no wild animals seemed to have found this manna yet.

Alice Louise looked around.

"So what?" she asked.

Don nodded to the cabinet. "Behind."

She saw a low square doorway knocked through the stone wall behind the cabinet. It was dreadfully dark back there. Don crouched down and stepped through. Alice Louise followed.

The room was round, perhaps ten feet in diameter and five feet high. Sand floor, concrete walls and roof. It was crowded with small crates and boxes of Sid's stuff stacked against the walls.

A Cold Winter's Deathe

And one coffin.

Alice Louise jumped back and her heart thumped hard.

"What the hell?" she breathed. She was suddenly aware of the cloying scent of death and decay.

"Yah, I know," said Deputy Don. "You gotta take a look at dis."

I don't damned well think *so*, she thought, but he was already beside the coffin and pulling a small pry bar out of his pocket. Against all common sense, she edged a bit closer.

It had to be a coffin. It was impossible to think it wasn't. The length and width and height of it were perfectly proportional to hold a body. There was the classic, almost stereotypical shape of it—narrow at both ends, wider in the shoulder area. Plain boards, old beyond imagining, fitted together with dovetail joints at the corners and big, rusty iron screws.

And the smell.

She cringed back.

"It's OK, eh?" He wedged the pry bar into the seam under the lid. It lifted easily and he slid it aside. A stench of death rolled out like a wave and Alice Louise turned away. "Look in here," Don said, shining his flashlight into the blackness of the oblong box.

Alice Louise stepped away, took a shallow breath, and, after a second to blank her mind, leaned in to look.

THE OLD SKI-DOO did its modest best. Chunks of snow spun out lazily behind them as Puck and Ron bent low and rode it into the woods as fast as it would go. They bucked drifts, hammered through shallow ravines, and bounced over fallen trees and buried boulders.

When he was finally convinced they were safe and out of sight, Ron insisted that Puck pull over and stop. He fell off the machine into a snowdrift. Getting his rubbery legs locked under him, he stumbled over to lean against a thick pine tree to catch his breath. He bent over, hands on knees, panting.

"Wow! Dat was wild!" Puck exclaimed. "Whatta dose guys got against you?"

"*Me?* You're the one who sent Carl screaming under that bench!" Ron barked. "I'm just an innocent bystander here! We always get hurt," he added bitterly.

"Oh. Dat guy. Well, I'm sure he didn't really mean to kill ya. Just scare ya a little."

"*Mission freaking accomplished!*" Ron snapped. He sucked in a huge ragged breath and let it out.

He stomped around in the snow for a while, breathing hard, until his pounding heart settled a little. Puck sat on the idling Ski-Doo and watched.

"Hey, if you're ready, we need to give 'er tarpaper." He glanced up at the leaden sky. "It gets dark early, an' we really don't wanna be out here unprepared. I mean *really*. Tick tock, eh?"

Ron took several deep breaths while peering back toward the road. All was quiet. Even Carl's big truck couldn't get through on this trail, and he *surely* wouldn't come on foot. They had put at least half a mile between themselves and Carl Rowley.

Right now five hundred miles wouldn't feel like nearly enough.

He wondered what he should do about this. Tell Chief Woody? What good would that do? Woody had never been able to make a dent in Carl's enterprises in the past. Ron knew that Chief Woody was as afraid of Carl as everybody else in town was.

Tell Alice Louise Dubose? Get the State Police involved? Would that make things better? Or worse? Carl, Ron feared, was untouchable. Even if he wasn't, could anyone do anything to him before he finally really killed someone?

Ron did not want to be the one who pushed *that* envelope.

He looked at Puck. The Invisible Yooper. He shook his head with resignation and defeat.

Even if he wanted to file a report, he suspected he would not have a witness to back up his tale. No proof of anything. Puck would probably melt into the shadows, and, even if anyone believed him, Ron would be made to look deranged and delusional on the witness stand.

Assuming he lived to give testimony in a court of law.

Carl Rowley had a way of making witnesses recant. Or disappear.

"At least let me drive," he said, pulling himself together and squeezing onto the saddle in front of the Yooper.

ALICE LOUISE peered into the blackness.

Don played his light over the bottom of the coffin, and she saw... dirt?

"Dirt," Deputy Don said, as if reading her mind. "A couple inches thick. But look at this. You look really close an' you can see how it's depressed. There's the outline of a body."

A Cold Winter's Deathe

Alice Louise's head spun. The cloying stench filled her nose, even though she was holding her breath. Her eyes watered. She could see the shallow depressions, and they did indeed have the shape of a body. She could see the deeper areas where there would be a head, shoulders, buttocks. Even the heels of the feet. In the few moments she could stand to hold her face over the fetid dirt, she estimated that this was a small body, quite likely a female.

She pulled back, turned away, and took a tentative, shallow breath.

"Is this all, deputy?"

"Not quite," he said, and her heart sank.

"Don't worry, the rest is outside."

She beat a hasty retreat for daylight with Don at her heels. Once they were back out in the fresh air she followed Don and Chief Woody as they walked gingerly around the shack. Beth followed at a distance, looking more timid than Alice Louise ever would have guessed her friend could be.

"Here. And here." Don pointed out footprints in the snow.

"You were out here alone earlier?"

"Yah. I was alone. I seen these then. I tried to avoid 'em and preserve 'em."

The footprints were small. Female-sized, Alice Louise guessed. A six, maybe?

"Anybody have a camera?"

"I do," Don said, and pulled a compact digital out of a pocket.

"Snap some pix," Alice Louise said. "Be sure to get some scale on them. Are these your footprints, then? Try to get a little of everything for a good relative comparison."

Don surprised her by pulling out a ruler, too, and he set to work documenting the scene.

Chief Woody, Beth, and Alice Louise stood in the deep, all encompassing silence of a windless forest, in the middle of nowhere, in the dead of winter, watching Deputy Don circle the scene, snapping pictures.

"So give me your thoughts here, Chief. What do you think was going on?"

Chief Woody stood with his hands on his hips, looking dour. Humble.

"Sid died last week. Monday or Tuesday, I think. A neighbor found him, we hauled him out on a trailer behind a snow machine.

Mark Wolfgang

Shipped him off to the funeral home in L'Anse. Brought him back Friday. Laid him out in the mausoleum at the cemetery. Then the same neighbor called in the fire late yesterday afternoon. There wasn't nuthin' we could do but let it burn itself out. No way we could get a truck back here. It was gettin' dark, we didn't have enough lights, so I sent Donnie back here dis morning to check it out. Sid was known to keep money hidden all through the camp; Donnie didn't find any, so we kindly figgered it was kids cleaned it out, maybe set the fire by accident. But then he went down in the root cellar."

Alice Louise blew out her breath. Beth kept quiet, watching and listening with eyes wide.

"Got any theories about that, chief?" Alice Louise said, just to try to move things forward.

Chief Woody dug his hand under his blue P.D. bomber hat and scratched his head.

"I got nuthin."

"Where do you think the, um, body... is?"

Beth's eyes popped even wider.

"No idea. Honestly? I was hopin' you'd think of something. Or maybe a clue would fall in our laps."

They all turned toward the sound of a snowmobile approaching from the south.

14

HOLY WAH. *This is just not my day,* Ron thought as he pulled up to Sid's camp.

Alice Louise Dubose, Chief Woody, Beth Atkins and Deputy Don all stood like stone statues, watching his approach with unreadable eyes.

He'd already been seen. There was no turning back. He pulled up beside their three snow machines and killed the engine. The sudden silence roared in his ears. Behind him, Puck jumped off the Ski-Doo and scurried up to the burned out shell of the old camp. No one noticed a thing. All eyes remained locked on Ron.

"Hey, guys," Ron said. He eased off the saddle and strolled up to them. "What's up?"

Good Lord. If he had a gun he'd like to shoot himself.

The woods were heavy with the silence. To the west, White Wolf Lake was almost blinding, even under the leaden sky. Blue white and frozen out a hundred yards or so, but dark in the center where the ice was still forming, thin and dangerous.

"What are you doing here?" Alice Louise queried. At least she didn't sound outraged. Suspicious, maybe. Obviously.

So much for the beauty of the day.

He wished he had a prepared statement. Maybe some kind of little script he could pull out of his pocket and read to the audience. His mind was blank. He looked around at the destruction of the old shack.

Puck scrabbled around, scampering over fallen timbers and piles of debris burned beyond recognition, opening and peeking into charred cabinets and drawers. He pulled a beer can out of the blackened refrigerator and, grinning, held it up for Ron's appreciation. He popped the tab and tasted it, made a face, shook it off, shrugged, and downed it in a long gulp.

Puck. Oh yah. That fit.

Ron wilted under the unwavering stares of his accusers.

"I heard there was a fire out here. Thought I'd come and have a look. Was that wrong?" He winced.

Puck dropped out of sight into a crawlspace under the floor.

"This is a crime scene here now," Chief Woody said. He added, "If you have anything you'd like to tell us, we're all ears."

"No..." Ron said, shaking his head slowly, trying to at least appear to give the question a lot of deep thought. "Nope. I can't think of a thing."

They all stood silent as he glanced from Beth to Alice Louise to Chief Woody to Deputy Don.

Puck's head popped out of the floor, his face beaming with exhilaration. He pointed down, *here here here*, head nodding and bobbing under his big ratty bomber hat. Then he dove under the floorboards again.

Ron heaved a sigh.

Alice Louise was in sudden angry motion, charging him, grabbing him by the elbow and dragging him, stumbling to keep up, out of earshot of the others.

"Ron, what *in the hell* are you doing out here?"

Ron drew in a deep, calming breath. It didn't work so well. "I... can't really say."

"Really? You really can't? Well give it a shot!" She glared down at him from her height advantage. Her eyes bore into his, cold as the blue ice of the lake.

"There are things going on here you can't understand," he said, sounding lame even to himself.

"Try me."

He heaved a sigh. "Would you believe me if I told you there's a guy crawling all over the wreckage of Sid's house behind you, right now, as we speak?"

She didn't dignify that by turning to look.

"And there might be a vampire in the root cellar?"

Alice Louise went suddenly pale. The blood drained from her face and he could see something in her eyes that unsettled him. Fear.

And now he was afraid, too.

"What do you know about that?" she demanded.

A Cold Winter's Deathe

Ron jerked back. "What do *you* know about it?"

She regrouped and regained her composure. "There is no... *vampire*... in the root cellar," she snarled, but he saw a lie in her eyes. There was certainly *something* in the root cellar.

Puck popped out of the floorboards again, almost dancing with excitement. He scurried around the house, nose to the ground like a bloodhound trying to pick up a scent. He froze and practically took a point, facing southeast. Toward...?

Ron tried to orient himself, forming a topographical map in his mind, placing Sid's camp in relation to the trestle, the town, the lake, and....

Cavendish House?

Ron turned back to Alice Louise. She was still in his face, up close and dangerous, filling his vision, challenging him to offer some kind of reasonable explanation.

"*What did you find down there?*" he asked, his voice low to be sure the others couldn't hear.

15

By the time they'd extricated themselves from the woods it was getting late in the afternoon. Puck had done a magical wave of his hand, and before Ron knew it they were on their snow machines, heading south through the fire break to the main road.

After his initial excitement at discovering what he'd thought was his vampire's lair, Puck had finally come up out of the crawlspace sullen. He'd hardly spoken, except to say that the vampire was gone. It had either set fire to its lair and abandoned it, he said, or possibly been driven out by the fire set by kids accidentally—or by vandals on purpose—not knowing what was in the crawlspace. He needed to form a strategy against his "eternal foe."

Ron tried to grill him some more, but had met only stony silence and evasion, until, fearing he would find himself on the four corners of Deathe barking like a seal, he had given up.

Carl Rowley's gleaming red pickup was parked front and center at the Buck Snort. Ron ducked low and averted his face as he eased past, his hand light on the throttle, keeping the old Ski-Doo as quiet as possible. They turned the corner and parked in front of Hoolie's Café.

Ron looked around and Puck was gone. Beth and Chief Woody shut off their snow machines, but Ron kept his idling in case he needed to make a quick getaway. Chief Woody and Deputy Don wandered into Hoolie's, shambling off under Puck's spell like confused zombies. Beth and Alice Louise seemed distracted, their eyes glazed. Already, they were forgetting everything that had happened out in the woods.

Snow floated down from the iron sky, fat and lazy.

Ron begged off joining them in Hoolie's. He needed to get away from them before their senses returned and they started asking

A Cold Winter's Deathe

more questions that he couldn't answer. He also needed to get away from the Buck Snort and Carl... from everyone. He missed his solitude at Cavendish House. There were about 500 too many people crammed into this town. He felt like he was truly becoming a Yooper.

He returned the Ski-Doo to Ron Borke's garage. He thanked Naomi and handed her the key. "Ron's not feeling well," she said of her husband. "He's been sleeping most of the day."

Ron Blank wasn't feeling so well either, so he could sympathize.

Snow was falling thick and fast as he climbed the stairs to his apartment. The old, established drifts were fluffed up and smoothed over, all the hard edges now soft. But once again his American Eagle wagon was covered. He could only see a tiny bit of one corner of the blue tarp. Even if Toivo's Towing could haul it out in the morning, with the county road closed there would be no place they could tow it to.

He collapsed on the couch and immediately fell into a deep sleep.

RON AWOKE to the sound of a steady rumbling somewhere out on the street. He wondered if the Masticator was out, churning through town and flinging fresh snow over the rooftops. The sun had set, twilight was fading fast. He gained his feet, stumbled to the window, and pulled aside the curtain.

Carl Rowley's big red pickup sat in front of Ruth's, backed up to the barricade that blocked the dead end street. Only the parking lights were on. The muffler pipes were open. The exhaust thumped and growled like an restive beast. The deeply tinted passenger side window was open a crack. Ron saw the muzzle of the shotgun sticking out, pointing toward the sky above his apartment.

The shotgun boomed.

Ron hit the floor.

The engine roared with rage, rattling the windows, and the truck thundered away toward downtown until the driver eased off the gas, and the disturbance faded with distance.

Ron's heart pounded in his chest. After several moments he raised up enough to peek out over the windowsill. The street was empty except for the trenches in the fresh snow dug out by the big tires.

He yanked the curtains closed and made his way into the kitchen, opened a beer, draining it in one continuous pull. Wishing he had something stronger. He opened another.

When his heart finally settled down, and his knees firmed up, he forced his mind to other thoughts. Carl was probably done for the day, he convinced himself. He was tempted to call the police department and file a report.

But that, he decided, could be his death sentence. He couldn't think about that just now.

Kneeling over the warm air duct, he listened breathlessly for the sound of voices. One voice in particular. He heard nothing.

He could still smell the faint, lingering odor of the dead animal. It must be in the walls of the main house, downstairs.

He found a frozen pizza and popped it into the oven. Then he checked the curtains, dimmed all the lights, selected an old favorite from his video collection and queued it up in the player. He watched previews of decade-old movies while he waited. When the oven timer dinged, he pulled out the pizza. And popped another beer.

Ron jumped at a sudden knock on the door.

But Carl wouldn't knock. Carl would bust the door down. Julianna? No, that would be too much to hope for.

He smelled the pizza and looked at the beer in his hand, and he suddenly knew who it was.

Damn that Yooper kid! Ron thought. *What a remarkable sense of timing!*

He slammed the beer down on the counter and stalked to the door to give Puck a piece of his mind. Ron had to admit, he found the guy's radar for free beer and pizza remarkable, *the freeloading little twerp.* He yanked the door open and thrust his finger into–

ALICE LOUISE Dubose said, "Get that thing out of my face or I'll bite it off."

Ron dropped his hand and leaned out to look down the stairs as if he were expecting someone else.

"Are you going to let me freeze out here?" She glanced over her shoulder to see if she'd been followed. "Or maybe invite me in?" she prompted when he didn't move.

He motioned her in and closed the door against the bitter cold. But he continued to peer out the window.

"I don't know how you people live up here," she griped as she unwound Beth's woolen scarf and tugged off the ridiculous psychedelic knit chuke.

A Cold Winter's Deathe

"Lots of antifreeze," Ron muttered, still looking out the window. "Mostly alcohol-based."

She sniffed the air and wrinkled her nose.

"What's that smell?"

"Pizza. You're just in time."

"No. Not that." She looked at Ron with suspicion. "Did something die in here?"

"Well, yah, maybe. I think an animal died in the walls somewhere. Probably a mouse."

"It smells a lot bigger than that." In fact, it smelled a lot like the fetid coffin under Sid Francis's cabin. Her stomach did a slow roll. But it seemed to dissipate quickly, overwhelmed by the heavenly scent of the pizza.

She gazed around at the tiny apartment as she shucked out of her parka. One room, plus an adjacent kitchen to the left with a small table and two chairs, apartment-sized range and refrigerator. A small bathroom and tiny closet to the right. Furnishings were sparse—an old couch that probably folded out into some semblance of a bed; one small armchair that didn't match; a floor lamp; a television and video player on a bookcase; a coffee table that would have to be pushed aside to make room for the bed. And boxes. Stacks of cardboard boxes and plastic storage bins, probably full of Ron's possessions salvaged from Cavendish House when he'd had to abandon it for the winter.

"What? No phone?" she asked the back of his head. She'd tried to call first, but got a recording that his phone had been disconnected.

"People might call me and I'd have to talk to them," he mumbled, continuing to peer through the curtains.

She stuffed her hat, scarf and gloves into the sleeves of her parka.

"What are you looking for?" she asked as she hooked her coat on the coat rack.

He pulled back from the window and closed the curtains. But he didn't turn toward her.

Her grin faded.

"Are you expecting someone?"

"No. I just thought you were someone else," he said, distracted.

She waited, but he offered no further explanation. "Obviously," she snapped.

Then he shook himself and turned to her, blinking.

"Alice!" he said, as if noticing her for the first time. "Oh. Hi. You want some pizza? I've got plenty. How about a beer?"

He bustled around the kitchen, fully *there* now, setting out plates and flatware and plucking a lite beer out of the refrigerator and popping it open for her. She sat at the tiny table. The two of them filled up the kitchen. There was barely room for them, and the table and chairs and apartment-sized refrigerator. She thanked him for the beer and took a pull as he dished slices of pizza onto gaudy plastic plates.

"Is this from Wu Fang's Mexican Bistro?" she asked.

"No ma'am. He's closed for the season. John spends winters in North Carolina."

"John? That's Wu Fang's real name?" Ron had dragged her to Wu Fang's in October: her low expectations were fulfilled by the old quonset hut papered with lurid posters of stereotypical "Oriental" villains, but the surprising reality was pizza so good she'd forgotten that Homecoming gridlock made her abandon her car there for the night.

"His American name, yah."

"Not nearly as good," she said, biting into a slice. But plenty good enough.

"What happened to your car?" she asked, with a nod over her shoulder.

"Oh. That. I forgot to get the optional windows."

She pursed her lips at him and waited for a coherent response, but he ignored her. OK then. They ate and drank in silence for several moments.

"You know why I'm here," she said.

"Yah," he said with a grimace. "Tell you what. You give me something, I'll give you something."

"This Monty Hall *Let's Make a Deal* crap ain't gonna fly here. I'll ask the questions, you supply the answers." She fixed him with a cold glare.

He paused with a slice halfway to his gaping mouth, properly intimidated.

"OK. What do you want to know?"

"Everything. Starting with what happened at the bar Friday night."

Ron set down his pizza, grabbed a couple more beers out of the fridge and downed half of his. He took a deep breath.

And let it all out in a rush of words.

A Cold Winter's Deathe

He told her a wild story about some Jeff-Daniels-*Escanaba-in-da-Moonlight* invisible *(invisible!)* Yooper kid coming into the Buck Snort Friday night and stealing beers and standing up to Carl Rowley when Ron had found himself on the verge of getting beaten senseless and sending Carl cowering and puking under a table and then this Yooper kid said he was a *vampire hunter* and then the storm had died and somehow they'd ended up in the cemetery mausoleum disinterring Sid Francis and re-interring some woman named Emilie Reindhart and then Ron had left him (this *vampire hunter!*) and walked home and left the kid to do *God-knows-what* in the mausoleum and he'd found his car vandalized no-doubt-by-Rowley and then Saturday he'd had a confrontation with Carl and his evil family on the main street of Deathe and then Sunday they had gone to check out Sid's camp and Carl had chased them down and *fired a by-God loaded shotgun at them–*

"Ron! Take a breath!" Alice Louise said.

Ron sucked in a noisy lungful of air and panted while Alice Louise sat stunned, attempting to process this smashup of nonsense.

Nonsense? She already knew about the confrontation on Main Street, as the librarian had told it to Chief Woody. Her version of events matched Ron's. Alice Louise and Beth had probably missed it by minutes after their lunch at Hoolie's Café. But Ron and Carl nearly coming to blows at the bar? And Carl Rowley, humiliated and puking under a bench? She knew that *something* had happened there, but no one she'd talked to, not Beth, nor Tino, nor the boozers she'd met at the bar with Chief Woody earlier in the day, recalled anything happening out of the ordinary. And from everything Chief Woody had told her at Hoolie's, anyone besting Carl Rowley was so far out of the ordinary as to be impossible.

She herself still had no clear recollection of Friday night at the Buck Snort, just a vague memory, like a half-remembered dream. And she too had been there.

And I was about to step into the middle of the fray, she suddenly realized with a start.

"Explain... *invisible*," she said.

"He's like an illusionist or something," Ron said. "He's not *really* invisible, obviously, but he has some kind of mass mind control thing going. I know, I didn't believe it either, but you just have to take my word for it. He was there at Sid's camp today, and you couldn't see him. None of you could."

Mark Wolfgang

Alice Louise shuddered at the mention of Sid's camp, her mind going back to the coffin in the crawlspace, stinking of death and decay. The outline of a small body depressed into the fetid layer of dirt on the bottom. The stench of it all still clung in her nose.

There were too many common denominators. Ron. Carl. This Yooper vampire hunter. And an empty coffin in a crawlspace.

Unless it was all some kind of elaborate joke.

She looked deep into Ron's eyes. Scared, confused. Gullible? Quite likely. But either way, she believed that *he* believed what he was saying. So, at the very least, maybe there was something to this *mind control* thing.

She became aware that Ron was studying her as closely as she was studying him.

"I know what you found in Sid's root cellar," he murmured.

She started. She had sworn Chief Woody, Deputy Dan, and Beth to silence. No one else could possibly know. She fixed him with a challenging glare. "What did we find?"

"A coffin," he said. "Lined with rancid dirt. Smelling of death."

Her breath left her. "Who told you that?"

"Puck. The vampire hunter. Seriously, he was in the cellar. While you were giving me the third degree."

"That wasn't the third degree, buddy. When I give you the third degree, you'll know it." She studied his face, his eyes, looking for a "tell," some subtle hint that he was having her on, and he knew it, and he was enjoying it. But his expression was earnest, his blue eyes sincere.

"There was no body in it," he said. "There had been, though."

She was thinking about the depressions in the dirt. Small, like a woman. And the same for the footprints around Sid Francis's cabin

"And what kind of body did your friend think had been in it?"

Ron sighed. "He's not my friend. And I don't know. He didn't tell me. He said he had to go home and plan some kind of strategy."

"Home? Where is that?"

"Again, I don't know. But..."

She waited. But not patiently, and not for long. "But what?" He avoided her eyes and she sensed he was holding back.

"I'm not sure. I haven't seen him today. I figured it was him when you came knocking on my door. Can I get back to you on that?"

"You do understand that this guy could be dangerous–"

"Tell me about it," Ron grumbled.

A Cold Winter's Deathe

"It sounds like he's quite probably mentally disturbed, almost certainly delusional, and if he's that far gone he could be planning some kind of violent action against someone. Maybe you."

Vampire? Ron had to be kidding, Alice Louise thought. Someone was kidding.

"How about if I let you know the minute I see him again? You're still staying at Beth's?"

"You don't even have a phone. How are you going to get hold of me?"

"Well, he might even come by tonight, I don't know. He was who I was expecting when you dropped in. You want to wait here for a while and see?"

She considered the offer. The pizza was gone. "You got more beer? I suppose I need some Yooper antifreeze before I go back to Beth's, anyway."

"I have a movie queued up," he said as they settled onto the little sofa with their beers. "*Bull Durham.* Ever seen it?"

Alice Louise jumped as though jolted.

"Whoa! No way! With *you?* Not in *this* lifetime!"

Ron examined her with wide-eyed surprise.

"I will not stay here and watch *that* movie with *you!*" She stood and snatched up her coat, dug her hat, scarf and gloves out of the sleeves.

"You don't like baseball movies?"

"You really think *Bull Durham* is a *baseball* movie?" She tugged on her coat.

"Um..." Ron said. "*Bull Durham.* The Durham Bulls. Triple-A baseball. Yah, I'm guessing it's a baseball movie."

"You poor, clueless man. *Bull Durham* is not *just* a baseball movie." It was, in her opinion, and the opinion of Beth and 'most every woman she knew, one of the most blatantly romantic—and *hottest*—movies ever made. The first time she had seen it, it had been with her boyfriend du-jour, and eventual fiancée, Alan. It had raised her temperature and her libido, clouded her mind, and had a marvelous, unexpected effect on her.

Two days later, Alan had sprung an engagement ring on her.

She hadn't seen that one coming, and she didn't want to see it again any time soon.

She reached for the door knob, then paused, reconsidered, and turned to face Ron. She thrust her gloved hand out to him. "On second thought... give me the movie. Maybe I'll watch it later."

He hesitated, but got up and ejected the movie..

"Who's gonna risk going blind now?" he mumbled as he handed it to her.

She gave him her sternest look and bolted out of his apartment.

DAMN, RON THOUGHT, *I should have hung onto that. Maybe Julianna would enjoy a baseball movie.*

16

RON KNELT at the heating duct and listened. He heard Mrs. Kinderly's voice drifting up, and another voice that could only have been Julianna.

His heart jumped. He bounced into the living room, pulled on some boots, and straightened up his wrinkled clothes, while his mind searched for some innocuous but urgent excuse for going downstairs. He went into the kitchen and rummaged through the cupboards for a measuring cup. To borrow a cup of sugar is the oldest ruse in the book, but it was the best he had at the moment. He didn't find a measuring cup. He grabbed a coffee mug, pulled on his coat and hat and bolted out the door.

Ruth answered the doorbell. He held out the cup like a peace offering.

"Hi, Ruth, I–"

"Come in, come in!" Ruth said. She grabbed Ron's arm, took the cup from him and dragged him inside. "We were just talking about you."

He let himself be pulled into the sweet warmth of the parlor. Julianna stood in the archway between the parlor and the dining room, smiling at him, her eyes darkly luminous. His body responded automatically to the sight of her, adrenaline jolting him with chemical energy. She was dressed in a dark olive green sweater tonight, and a loose matching skirt that reached to mid-calf. He didn't know whether to drown in the depths of her dark eyes, or allow his gaze to steal down and linger on the soft mounds of her breasts beneath the sweater.

"You would like some coffee?" Ruth said. "I still have some of my good coffee cake."

Mark Wolfgang

He opened his mouth to say yes, but Julianna stepped forward with a dancer's grace and placed her hand on Ruth's shoulder.

"Please, no," she said. "We're not hungry." She gave him a significant look. "Are we?"

"No," he responded automatically.

"We should like to go for a walk instead. Will you walk with me, Ron Blank?"

She enveloped him with her dark eyes. His voice nearly caught in his throat. "Of course," he breathed.

"You'll catch your death out there tonight," Ruth chided. "It's too cold."

"It's not that bad," Ron said. "Warmer than last night."

By about half a degree, he thought, which *might* put the temperature above ten.

Julianna stepped around Ruth and linked her arm through Ron's.

She smelled of fresh apples and springtime.

"This poor creature doesn't have proper clothes," Ruth said to him. "You should see how she dresses."

"I do see," Ron said with an appreciative smile.

"I'm fine," Julianna said as she tugged him toward the door.

Yes, you are, he thought.

"You'll wear a proper coat," Ruth commanded. "And a hat."

She trundled off to her bedroom. Julianna smiled up at Ron, and he shrugged.

"She's right," he said. "You can't go out like that."

Julianna turned and moved in close to him. Face to face, looking up, deeply, into his eyes. She rested her hands on his shoulders. Her smile faded as she pulled his jacket open and pressed her face to his neck. Startled, Ron tried to pull back, but Julianna held him firmly. He heard her soft intake of air.

"You have been with another woman," she whispered. She looked up at him with furrowed brows, and her eyes held his, dark and accusing. She leaned in and sniffed again, gently. "Perhaps two."

Ruth came back with a long, heavy, gray, cloth coat, and Julianna was suddenly at Ron's side again, beaming at Ruth. Ron studied Julianna, perplexed, but she seemed oblivious to his confusion.

Ruth helped Julianna into the coat, snugged it up and buttoned it for her as Julianna stood patiently. Then she snapped open a knitted brown chuke and pulled it down on Julianna's head, over her ears,

A Cold Winter's Deathe

taking care to smooth her coppery blond hair so that it flowed over the coat collar and down her back. She stood back to admire her work.

"There," she said. "Now put on your gloves–" they both did– "and don't stay out too late. And don't go too far, eh? Stay on the main roads and look out for traffic–"

"There isn't any traffic in Deathe tonight," he said. "Don't worry, Ruth."

"Well, you two kids be careful."

Julianna took Ruth's chin in her fingertips, tipped her head slightly, and kissed her sweetly on the cheek. Then she turned to Ron and pulled him out into the cold night.

They walked along Main Street, their boots squeaking on the snow. He wanted to ask her how she could possibly know about Alice Louise and Beth. He hadn't touched either of them. Was Julianna actually jealous? But she made no further mention of it. And he hesitated to bring it up. Who could know what's in the mind of a young woman? He hadn't been faced with such mysteries in ages. He wasn't sure he wanted to face them now.

Julianna locked her arm in Ron's. Her body pressed close against him. Her graceful stride was in perfect time with his. So like a dancer, he thought. The frigid breeze rushed in the treetops high above them, but down at street level it was still and quiet. Vaguely luminous clouds marched purposefully across the obsidian sky, ignited by the cold glow of the moon now high overhead. Stars burned almost painfully bright between the clouds.

"What do you see?" Julianna whispered. She looked up at him with intense curiosity.

"Sometimes, like now," he said, his breath clouding before them, "I see an ancient sky. Just as our ancestors saw it thousands of years ago. I see the night sky as a black bowl, the stars just needle-pricks in the bowl, tiny windows into the fiery universe beyond, the brilliant glow of heaven on the other side of the bowl." He swept his hand across the sky. "Up here, where the air is so clear and the nights are so dark, it's easy to see how our ancestors came to think this way. The stars are like sunshine, leaking through the bowl like water through a sieve. Sometimes it's so easy to get turned around by the illusion that I can't even think of the stars as being distant suns scattered throughout the universe." He pulled his eyes away from the sky and looked down at Julianna. She was gazing up at him, her face white in the moonlight, an

ashen portrait of intense concentration. He felt ridiculous, going on like that. "Can you understand that?"
"I think so." She beamed at him and his heart did a flip.
"What do *you* see?"
They turned left and walked slowly down the gentle incline of Lake Street, toward White Wolf Lake on the edge of town, past houses that were already dark and sleeping. Occasionally they saw a light in a window, behind drawn curtains, but for the most part the town seemed deserted. They seemed to be the only ones left alive in the world.
"I see the stars and the moon and the sky," she said. "Nothing more."
"Nothing? Really? I thought you had the soul of an artist."
She smiled—a sly, secret smile. "Soul.... the soul of an artist? No," she said with a shake of her head. "I think not."
He was guiding them toward downtown. He gravitated toward the Buck Snort, thinking how impressed, and bemused, Tino would be, to see Ron Blank stroll into the bar with Julianna on his arm, to order two hot buttered rums.
But when the Buck Snort came into view, Julianna stopped dead in her tracks. She held back, staring darkly at the bar. Ron found he couldn't budge her.
"What's wrong?"
"I... don't approve of... drinking. *Alcohol*," she clarified.
Ron looked up the street and saw Carl Rowley's super duty pickup lurking in the shadows beside the Buck Snort, its chrome grill catching the light of the neon *OPEN* sign and flashing an evil grin.
"Just as well!" Ron said, pulling them to the left, into the shadows and toward the lake, hoping that Julianna had not seen the pickup and made the connection.
He veered onto the side streets, away from the timid street lights, and she followed along.
At the end of Lake Street was the turnaround for the boat launch. A single bulb shone down on the small parking area from high up on the wooden utility pole. Docks along the shoreline had been pulled in for the winter and sat forlornly on the snow covered lawns, under thick drifts that looked like beached whales.
"The soul of a dancer, then," Ron said with confidence, picking up the conversation again, to be saying something, anything, to fill the silence of the night, and get all thoughts of Carl Rowley out of his head..

A Cold Winter's Deathe

"No," Julianna whispered staring at the snowy ground before them. "No soul." She glanced up at him, her eyes sad. "Of a dancer."

At the slope of the boat launch, the trees opened up and they could see the entire expanse of White Wolf Lake stretching off to the north like a vast arctic plain, a desolate wasteland of ice where nothing grew. Moonlight lay on it like a shimmering blanket. Except for the dark and dangerous center, where the water had yet to freeze over.

"Was that the vehicle of your Goliath?" Julianna asked in a low whisper, and Ron jumped. She cast a quick glance over her shoulder toward downtown, then stood before him and held his eyes.

Ron inhaled deeply and blew out a long, quavering breath.

"Yes. Yes, it was. But I don't want to–"

"Then we shan't," she said. She turned to the lake, and hooked her arm in his. "So. Why a dancer?"

The snow was not deep on the shore. They strolled down the gentle incline of the boat ramp, crunching through the thin crust of ice, until they stood at the edge of the frozen lake.

"Because you're so graceful. So... light." He'd almost said "beautiful," but caught himself at the last instant.

A dozen rustic cottages were scattered along the shore there on the edge of Deathe. A block or so to the east he could glimpse Beth Atkin's solid little cabin between the other houses. There was a light in the window. Ron thought of Alice Louise and Beth, snug and warm in bathrobes and fuzzy slippers, watching *Bull Durham*, while he and Julianna froze on the edge of the lake.

"I think it was right around here," Ron said, glancing around the lake shore. "Yes. There's a spring near that dock," he said, pointing. "About a century ago a young couple snuck away from their homes and had a secret rendezvous here at the lake. They wandered out on the ice and... fell through. It was night. Like this. No one knew they were gone until morning and by then it was too late. The lake had flash frozen overnight. For the next few months the people of Deathe would venture out onto the lake where they could look down through the clear ice and see these two teenagers down there, locked in their final embrace." He shuddered. Julianna regarded him with dark, solemn eyes. Breathless. "I'm sorry," Ron said. "I shouldn't be telling you this."

"Tell me. What happened?"

"Well, it was spring before the ice broke and they could pull the bodies out. They say they were as fresh and beautiful as the day they fell in. Like they were sleeping, just waiting patiently to be rescued."

Julianna blinked languidly.

"You're kind and sensitive," she said. "And intelligent. You would be lovely company for years and years. Interesting. Entertaining."

"Company?" he asked.

She shook her head and turned away from him, a slight smile on her face, her eyes bright with an inner light.

"Remember, I'll always need a personal assistant."

They stood looking out over the glowing lake, side by each, arm in arm. A light wind swept snow across the plain, lifting ice crystals and swirling them in the moonlight. Then Julianna stepped in front of him, alive with secret excitement. She looked up at him, her face intense, her smile mischievous, her eyes devilish.

"Do you trust me?" she demanded.

"What?"

"Do you trust me?" She tugged at his coat sleeves, then took his hands in hers.

"Trust you? I don't know. I... Yah, I suppose." Her eyes blazed with exhilaration and he felt a delightful thrill surge through him.

Of course he trusted her.

She backed out onto the ice, pulling him along with her.

"What are you doing?" he said. He looked around, got his bearings. He glanced toward where the spring fed the lake.

"Come with me." She tugged, and he stumbled along reluctantly.

"No. Julianna, the ice is too thin–"

"Dance with me," she said. "Trust me."

Slowly, cautiously, they ventured out further onto the frozen lake. Ron held back, but Julianna pulled him along persistently, further and further. He shuffled his feet, not daring to lift them off the thin ice. His breath came in rapid, hot clouds.

"Julianna!" His heart pounded in his chest, fear and apprehension constricted his throat. He resisted her, but she was unrelenting, tugging him along with surprising strength. Less than a hundred yards away, between them and the far shore, the middle of the lake lay dark and wet, the ice there so thin as to be almost nonexistent. Julianna began to dance, shuffling her feet slowly, still gripping his hands, pulling at him, beaming at him, her eyes sparkling with excitement.

The ice flexed under his feet.

"Julianna!"

A Cold Winter's Deathe

"Trust me!" she pleaded.

He glanced around, anxious. Somehow they were already a dozen yards from the shore, and still she tugged at him. He planted his feet and a sharp crack reverberated across the lake like a gunshot.

"Whoa!" He felt the ice bounce up and down beneath him as it floated, thin and tenuous, on the surface of the water just below. "Julianna! We have to go back."

"No," she said. "Not yet." She held his fingers in her firm grip. He leaned back, looking longingly at the safety of the shore so far away.

"Dammit, Julianna!" She released his hands and backed away. He grabbed at her, missed. She drifted backwards. Laughing at his distress. The thin ice groaned, popping and cracking around them and beneath them, protesting in a loud voice that carried to the far shore and echoed back sharply. It rocked underneath him like the skin of a water bed, taut, stressed, barely able to support his weight.

Julianna swayed lightly on the thin ice, spinning gracefully, her face always turning back toward him, smiling with delight. He glanced around in a panic, his heart in his throat. *Too far, too far!* They were suspended tenuously over fifteen or twenty feet of frigid water, the ice at their feet not even an inch thick. It complained more vehemently, telling them to be gone, to retreat to safety before it called their bluff and opened up and swallowed them. He could see the surface ice rippling in the moonlight all around Julianna as she spun and swayed in the moonlight.

He stood wringing his hands, panting great white clouds of hot breath. The moon bathed Julianna's pale face in its cold glow as she edged ever closer to the dark heart of the lake. She smiled at Ron with the carefree innocence of a child. His knees were turning to Jell-O, his heart ached for her to return to him. He slid one foot forward, inch by inch, then very gradually shifted his weight onto it. The ice snapped ominously and he retreated, his heart pounding as if to explode.

"*Julie!*" he pleaded in an urgent whisper. "Come back here now!"

She stopped and turned to stare at him for several moments, her expression flat and unreadable. Then she stretched out her hands to him, beckoning him to her with her fingers.

"Trust me!" she said.

"Julianna! Come back!"

She stared at him for a moment longer, then shrugged with resignation and strolled back toward him, pouting at him with disappointment. He could see the ice depressing and flexing under her weight with each step. He edged backward toward the shore, shuffling furiously; the ice groaned and popped. He reached out to her, coaxing her along.

She caught up with him at the shore and threw herself into his arms, giggling with delight. His knees shook uncontrollably and he thought they might fold and he would collapse, but Julianna held him up, her arms locked tight around his waist. Then she kissed him, long and hard, and his breath caught in his chest until he thought he would suffocate, and when she pulled free to smile up into his eyes he gasped for breath.

"You're insane," he said.

"Do you believe in heaven?" she demanded.

He shook his head in disbelief. "What?"

"Do you believe in hell?"

Puck had asked him if he believed in God. "I choose to believe," he had answered.

"Do you believe in eternal life?" Julianna demanded. "In life beyond death? Do you think there are worse things than death, worse fates than hell? Do you believe in love at first sight? In eternal love? Deathless love? Love that spans decades? Centuries? Love unconquered by the grave? Immortal love? Love that can outlast time itself?"

"Good lord, Julianna, what has–"

She kissed him again, desperately, her lips working hungrily at his, and he responded, wrapping his arms around her, pulling her tighter, pulling her into him. The lake beyond them still popped and cracked, muttering its continued annoyance with them.

They stood locked together. She pressed her face into his neck. His chest was heaving in the cold night air for several delicious moments, his breath fogging the cold air.

"I think we'd better go home now," he whispered, "before you take it into your mind to do something even more foolish."

He took her arm to guide them back up Lake Street toward Mrs. Kinderley's.

"Would you like to do something foolish with me?" Julianna whispered.

His heart and body said yes. "I think we've been foolish enough for one night," he said reluctantly. "We could have died, do you realize that?"

A Cold Winter's Deathe

Julianna laughed. "You should have trusted me. No harm will come to you if you trust me."

He studied her face. Her eyes were sincere, aglow in the moonlight.

"You really believe that, don't you?"

"I do. You will too. You'll see. I'll show you."

"You are a curiosity, Julianna. Who are you? Where do you come from?"

"I am here, now, with you. That's enough, isn't it? Tell me it is."

Ron sighed. "It is," he said. And it was.

They reached Ruth's house and stood face to face on the porch, her body pressed against his, her eyes dark, bottomless pools.

"Stay with me tonight," she said.

He fought the overwhelming urge to surrender.

"No. Not tonight. It's too soon. Too late, too.... I don't know. I have to work tomorrow." It sounded as lame as it was.

"What's wrong? Don't you like me?" She pouted prettily.

"Like you? Of course I do! I... I... *like* you... desperately. But this is all happening so fast. We've just met. We don't know each other at all."

And you frighten me, he thought. "Besides, Ruth would definitely *not* approve."

"You will come see me tomorrow night?"

"Yes. Of course I will."

She graced him with a radiant smile, warming his soul with a lingering kiss. Then she turned, opened the door and disappeared into Ruth's parlor, closing the door behind her, leaving him alone on the porch, shivering, wondering what the hell he was letting himself in for. Finally he stepped off the porch and started up the walk toward his stairwell. He could see Julianna in the parlor, standing back from the window, her pale face floating in the darkness, disembodied, watching him. He waved, and she vanished.

17

THE END CREDITS rolled. Alice Louise and Beth looked dewy-eyed at each other and heaved immense sighs.

Alice Louise had no romance in her life. She'd had none in a couple of years, of course, and precious little then. She could not imagine that Beth's boyfriend, Bill Trevarthan, was the romantic type either. Bill had been in her class at the MSP academy. He was a big, funny Yooper with a heart of gold. Stern when he absolutely needed to be, and fearless, but naturally good-natured to the point of being goofy. But romantic?

Alice Louise thought back to her past boyfriends. Especially Alan.

She absently rubbed the third finger of her left hand.

He had shown so much promise early in the relationship. He was a rising star in a stellar law firm, and he dressed the part. Tailored suits, silk ties, and expensive shirts that he really couldn't afford at that point in his career, but essential for playing the role. All button-down and conservative, proper and sober.

The firm didn't do criminal defense, so Alice Louise grudgingly cut them some slack.

He was one of the few suitors (and there had certainly been few enough suitors in her life to begin with) who was tall enough for her.

Alan had always been pleasant and considerate. Interesting. But after a few weeks of dating his true nature began to leak out, as true natures always will.

He'd made reservations at the Atheneum, a great restaurant in a premier hotel on the edge of Greektown. It had been a good day for him. A fantastic day. The firm was offering him a partnership. He was there

A Cold Winter's Deathe

to celebrate. With only two drinks in him, he'd gotten full of himself. Insufferable. He sprawled out, far back from the table, legs spread wide, knees akimbo. Hunched over his dinner. Blathering with his mouth full.

Her memory of the little things was painfully sharp: new Rolex; gold bracelet; manicured nails; razor-edged pant creases with cuffs riding high over new silk socks; polished black wingtips thrust out into the aisle. Cursing the wait staff who struggled to get around or over his feet without tripping or dropping trays of food and drink—calling them clumsy dolts, and stupid cows—when he finally noticed them.

So this was how he celebrated his great successes. She was suddenly not anxious to see how he suffered his losses. But she'd given him another chance. Then another. In the back of her mind, she knew that the day would come. Alarm bells rang. She'd had no other prospects for romance, but didn't care. *Bull Durham* had provided one evening of fantasy and denial.

A tipping point came when she'd introduced Alan to her friends and coworkers and they'd instantly coupled them with the moniker "Alice and Alan Louise." They'd thought it was hysterical. She'd thought it mildly amusing, but she'd found herself cringing in anticipation of Alan's reaction. He had not thought it funny at all.

But then came The Ring, and despite her dark expectations, she'd been too stunned to respond coherently.

After only three days she'd had to yank the ring off her suffocating finger and discovered just how badly Alan reacted to losing. It was beyond ugly. As she'd known it would be.

She remembered her mother's advice and warning: a woman chooses a man for his potential, and expects him to change; a man chooses the woman he wants, as she is, and expects that she will never change. There is rarely a good outcome for either side.

"You ever watch that movie with Bill?" Alice Louise asked.

Beth's eyes sparkled and she flashed Alice Louise a happy grin. "Oh yah. He didn't get any sleep *dat* night, let me tell ya!"

"Did he understand why not?"

"Hell no!" Beth snorted. "But he didn't care much, either! He still thinks I like baseball."

They both hooted with laughter. Then they sighed in unison, draining the last of their Coronas in tandem.

"I don't think I'm ever getting out of this town," Alice Louise said, as Beth turned off the TV and ejected the movie.

"Don't worry. We'll shovel out your car in the morning. I'm sure the Masticator will get the main road opened up tomorrow."

RON CLIMBED the stairs to his apartment, unfolded his hideaway bed, undressed and pulled on his comfortable old flannel pajamas. Then he stretched out in bed and stared wide-eyed into the darkness for what seemed like hours, too tense, too electrified to sleep. It was past midnight before the excitement finally subsided and exhaustion overcame him. He closed his eyes and at once began to dream.

Julianna came to him in the night. She melted through the locked door and stood silently at his bedside, gazing down at him as if he were the body at his own funeral.

He could see her clearly, although the room was pitch dark and his eyes were closed. He tried to open them, without success. He tried to reach out to her, but found he was paralyzed.

Julianna flung the covers off him. She bent over him, her face filling his vision, her turquoise eyes flat, yet curious. Her hand moved over his chest. The top button of his flannel shirt came free and his collar fell open.

18

ALICE LOUISE awoke to the sound of pounding. The racket chased away her nightmares of death and vampires. A light flashed on in the hallway outside her room and she saw Beth go by her door, pulling on a robe. More lights came on and she heard the front door open, then mumbled voices.

"Thelma! It's for you," Beth called from the living room.

Thelma? Then she remembered. She slumped down in the bed, tugged up the covers and pulled her pillow over her head.

"Al?" Beth was in the doorway now, sounding serious. She turned on the overhead light. "I think you need to get out here."

Alice Louise peeled back a corner of the pillow and snuck a peek at the digital clock on the nightstand.

2:12 am.

Chief Woody was again standing just inside Beth's front door, this time looking pale and subdued, working his blue bomber hat in his big hands.

"Chief, I hope we're not going to be making a habit out of this," Alice Louise said, pulling her bathrobe tight as she crossed the living room to him.

"I hope not, too," he said. "We've had another... incident. I kindly need you."

"Now?"

"Yes, ma'am. Right now would be good."

She dressed quickly, pulling on all the warm clothes she had, including the enormous snowmobile suit Bill Trevarthan kept in Beth's closet. Within fifteen minutes she was riding in the back of Chief Woody's ratty old Jeep Cherokee, with Deputy Don driving, the Chief in the passenger seat, and the heater on full, bravely battling back the sub-zero temperatures.

No lights, no siren.

"We had us another accident out by the trestle. It happens. A lot. Ten, fifteen times, some years. Usually when the roads are slick, like tonight. Usually it ain't too bad, just busted up cars and minor injuries. But once in a while... Well, this one's about as bad as they get."

Oh swell, she thought.

They got to the scene in a short time. Deathe's only other police vehicle was there, plus three pickups that the Chief said were fire department volunteers. The road half a mile east of the trestle was still closed from the storm, he reminded her, so Baraga county deputies and EMTs couldn't get through yet.

Flares lined the road. Half a dozen men milled around, now looking relieved to see the Deathe P.D. cruiser return.

The old railroad trestle looked dark and ominous, and solid as granite. She thought it might be smirking.

Headlights and portable floodlights lit the area well, thanks to the glittering white snow and ice. One set of headlights shined on a snow pile next to the trestle. More lights moved behind the snow pile. She saw tire tracks and gouges that started up the pile and disappeared over the top. Beyond, in the light of flashlights, hand held lanterns and the blue-white strobes of camera flashes, she could glimpse something shiny and red.

They climbed out of the car.

Alice Louise followed as the Chief and his deputy scaled the snow pile, struggling up and over, practically on their knees, digging in with their hands and toes, and then stumbling down the other side.

On the far side, a massive red, stretched cab pickup lay on its top, squashed and battered like it had been flung down and stomped on by a giant. All the glass was busted out. The roof was caved in. The driver's side door was hanging open by one hinge, folded forward against the front fender. The other hinge was completely broken away. The inner door panel was ripped, the hard plastic deformed and gouged.

Deputy Don handed Alice Louise a flashlight. She wasn't sure she wanted it all that badly.

She flicked it on and shone it at the door panel.

"How did all that happen? What, a grizzly bear attacked it?"

"You tell me," Don said softly. "We don't have any grizzlies, and if we did, they'd be hibernating now."

A Cold Winter's Deathe

Chief Woody had moved to the far side of the wreck and was pointing his light at something at his feet. Reluctantly, Alice Louise worked her way around the back of the pickup. The tailgate had come off and was stuck in the snow a few feet away like a big red tombstone. She stood at the chief's side. They gazed down.

The body was under a green army blanket. A large body. Fancy alligator skin cowboy boots stuck out from the bottom. Chief Woody squatted down at the edge of the blanket. His hand reached out and paused, and he looked up at Alice Louise and waited. She inhaled deeply, held it for a moment, let it out slowly, and knelt down beside the chief.

He lifted the corner of the blanket and played his light over the corpse.

A large man, with a powerful body, and black, oily hair, wearing a fleece-lined sheepskin coat. The shape of of the body was not right. Twisted somehow. And the face. Cut. Battered. It had gone through the windshield. Strange. It was as if mere seat belts and airbags were not sufficient to hold this giant in his seat.

Something about him was familiar.

"This is... was, Carl Rowley," the Chief said.

"I know him," Alice Louise muttered. "But I don't know how."

The chief peeled his eyes away from the body and studied Alice Louise for a long moment.

"I gotta admit," he said, looking around to be sure they couldn't be overhead. "I kindly got mixed emotions on this one. He was a bad guy, de worst in this town. But now that he's gone... like this? Well, he's got a family and all. I gotta go and break it to 'em tonight."

Alice Louise slumped. "You want me to go with you?"

She hoped he'd say no, and for once she wasn't disappointed.

"I gotta take care of this. It goes with the job. But there's some stuff I want you to have a look at."

"OK. Let's have a look."

"We already are."

She scowled at him in confusion. Then she rose and began to shine her flashlight around, taking in everything around the wrecked truck and broken body. There were first responder footprints everywhere, of course, and... drag marks? She stabbed the light around. It looked like Rowley had been moved somehow. For God's sake, he could not have dragged himself! She followed the gouges in the snow with her flashlight. Around from the other side of the pickup? Not in *this* condition!

"Good lord. You think an animal dragged him here? What? But no bears. So what, then? Wolves?"

"Nope."

She pursed her lips and planted her hands on her hips, staring at the broken body. "So? You got a tyrannosaurus living here now?"

Chief Woody, still holding the blanket aside, glanced up at her. "You heard those stories?"

She shot him a hard look and tried not to roll her eyes.

"Nevermind," he said. "There's no animal prints anywhere to be found. You're missing the obvious." He inhaled deeply and fixed her with a challenging stare. "Where's the blood?"

She felt the breath go out of her lungs, and she began to stab her light around. Desperately. But the chief was right. She could see a few spots of red here and there, but nothing like what would have to have come from the wounds and torn flesh of this big body.

The chief followed in her wake as she stalked around the pickup.

She found a few small smears of blood in the cab of the pickup when she reached the driver's side and bent to look, but even less than she expected, or thought might be typical for a crash of a modern vehicle with airbags and restraints. All of which, she noted, had deployed.

"OK," she said. "I'm stumped. Anything else?"

"Donnie?"

Deputy Don was quickly at the Chief's side.

"Show 'er. I gotta go make a call." Chief Woody lugged his bulk up and over the snowbank.

Don led Alice Louise back to the body. He knelt down a few feet from it and brought his flashlight down close to the snow.

"See that there?"

She looked at the small depression in the snow, and at first it didn't make sense, but then she froze and a chill clutched at her spine. They were footprints. Small. Female-sized. She could see heel prints, like something a woman's dress boot might make.

"Was there a woman in the truck with him?"

"No, ma'am."

"That can't be! You've looked? You've looked everywhere?" She stood erect and stabbed her flashlight all around, into the ditches

A Cold Winter's Deathe

and the woods and up the sides of the old railroad embankment. "I was on a scene once, we were just pulling out to leave when we stumbled onto a purse in the ditch. Then we knew there was more than just the driver, and we found a woman a dozen yards from the wreck. We almost left her there that night, nearly dead, but conscious, freezing in the dark, with all of us milling around just a few feet away for more than an hour." It made her sick to think about it, even now, years later. "You searched? You *really* searched?"

"Ma'am, there was no one else in the pickup. Yah, we searched."

She was reluctant to give it up. But she had to believe him.

"There's more," he said, and led her up and over the snowbank and into the road.

She hadn't noticed before, but there were wooden stick matches poking up out of the snow, red end up. She gave Don a curious scowl.

"We don't have no evidence marker flag things like they have on TV. I just put down matches where I wanted to mark stuff. Like these."

Clever.

He shined his light down. Alice Louise saw another small footprint in the snow in the middle of the road. She looked around and didn't see any other matches close by.

"Where are the others?"

"Well," Don said, "there's one back here." He strode about ten feet up the middle of the road toward Deathe and shined his light on the match and the footprint there. "And another one here." He walked another ten feet up the road and there was another match and footprint. He shined the light up the road and she saw more matches sticking out of the ground, each about ten feet apart.

She wanted to make sense of this, but her mind was blank.

She looked Deputy Don straight in the eye. "Where are the ones in between?"

"There aren't any," he said.

She spun and darted up the road, staying a few feet from the matches, shining her light around, her eyes darting here and there frantically.

No one has a ten foot stride, she thought. *Especially not a woman who wears a freaking size six shoe!*

19

RON FELT a sharp elbow in his ribs. "Huh?"

He hadn't been listening. He had been thinking how miserable and hungover he felt.

He was also daydreaming about Julianna.

Erin Coe gave him an impatient scowl that he interpreted as meaning something like, "what the hell are you waiting for?" As if he was supposed to do something. At that moment, he wasn't sure what.

Erin rolled her dark brown eyes at Spencer Lampi and Abraham Lipschitz.

Erin's eyes were an amazing contrast to the deep turquoise of Julianna's.

He jerked back to the present as she jabbed him in the ribs again.

Spencer and Abraham were explaining the obscure ways of Cavendish Junior College to Erin, while the maintenance crew waited in the conference room for CJC's director of Physical Plant to return and start the staff meeting.

Ed Posen had already stormed in once, carrying about five pounds of folders and papers, and a plastic water bottle. He'd dumped his load on the table with a thud, glared around the room, and barked at Ron something about heat lamps, insubordination, and a forced march to HR. Then he'd drained the water bottle with a tug and bolted out of the room again.

"Where did Mr. Posen go?" Erin had asked with a perplexed frown.

"To take a whiz and fill his water bottle," Ron whispered back. An accurate, if unsettling statement.

"*Eew!*" Erin scowled and tucked her hands in the pouch of her CJC sweatshirt.

Before he could explain, Spencer and Abraham had jumped in and took it upon themselves to offer her a helpful primer on the incomprehensible rules and customs of CJC.

"Ya see," Spencer was saying, "alla da room numbers on da first floor start wit' a one, and alla da room numbers on da second floor start wit' a two."

"Dat's just da way dey do it here," Abe finished with a sigh and a shrug of resignation.

Spencer and Abraham had their routine honed like a vaudeville comedy routine. CJC's version of Groucho and Chico Marx, they were always playing to an audience, and they were—to each other at least—always and forever their own best audience.

"Like there's a better way?" Erin grumbled to Ron under her breath.

"Hey, we don't make da rules!" Spencer said. "Some t'ings ya just gotta live wit'."

"How do you keep all this in your head?" Erin asked, batting her eyelashes.

"I wear earplugs so it won't drain out when I sleep."

"He's got a great memory!" Abe said. "He remembers stuff that never even happened!"

Ron knew they were messing with her.

Ron leaned close to Erin's ear. "Patience, intern," he whispered. But right now he was a bit more concerned about Ed's declaration of insubordination and the threat of duck-walking him to HR.

Sleet peppered the windows. Snow swirled in the eddy currents around the trees and buildings of the campus.

Because of the weather, the maintenance crew was looking a bit skeletal this morning. Janos the carpenter was there, with Jerry, one of his student aides. Janos wore a blue splint on his left wrist. Last Friday it had been on his right. Maybe he'd forgotten, or maybe this was another in his never-ending string of debilitating injuries. Mac the plumber was absent, but that wasn't unusual. Mac set his own schedule, and Ed never objected, because Lucifer defended Mac and covered for him. Lucifer—Lucy Fergusen—the Physical Plant Office Manager and Administrative Assistant, claimed ownership of the department and everyone in it. Including Ed.

Mac was at the top of Lucifer's favorites list.

Ron was definitely not on *that* list. He was on another list entirely.

Of course the college was open despite yesterday's snow and Friday night's blizzard. It almost never closed, whether or not faculty and students could make classes. Most of them lived outside the village limits, and were often unable to get through on the single county road that led into town. They were automatically excused for inclement weather. Lower staff and the Physical Plant crew were not so lucky, and never excused. They were expected to show up regardless, or suffer the consequences. The college (meaning: Ed Posen) did not want to pay them to stay home. So Ron had borrowed Ron Borke's junky Ski-Doo again. The village streets were reasonably clear, thanks to the Masticator, but they got worse farther east.

Erin Coe lived within easy snowmobile distance. She'd wanted to be sure she made it in. Lucifer had warned Erin that if she missed a single day of work she needn't come back for another. No excuses. It would be on her Permanent Record, and Lucifer could promise her a negative job reference that would dog her for the rest of her life. Ron didn't doubt it a bit. Lucifer had wanted Erin for her personal assistant, and for two months she'd fought red tooth and bloody nail against Erin's insistence on working with Ron.

Erin thought she would have an easy day, what with the snow, and virtually no students or staff. At that, Ron had reluctantly pointed out the windows at the piles of snow clogging the doorways and sidewalks, and cited the innocent little clause in their contract that said "and other duties as assigned," to illustrate the depths of her misconception.

Ron closed his eyes to wait for Ed and the pronouncement of his fate. His head felt massive and precariously balanced on his shoulders.

When the alarm had buzzed him awake that morning, Ron found himself naked under the thin sheet, flat on his back with his arms limp at his sides. His pajamas were piled on the bedspread beside him, and he shivered with the cold. Dull pain filled his head, throbbing in his skull and pushing him back into the bed. He was still exhausted, as though he'd not slept at all. Weak, weary, as though every bit of energy had been drained from his body.

He'd managed to pull himself out of bed and stumble to the bathroom to splash icy water in his face. It did little to bring him awake. The image that stared back at him from the mirror was pale and sunken, the eyes rimmed with dull red, the skin blotchy. His head reeled and he leaned heavily on the sink for support. There was a pair of small bruises on his throat. He probed the tender flesh gently with his fingertips. He couldn't remember how they got there.

He'd decided to cover it up with a turtleneck.

Ed finally came back, sat down, and proceeded to sort through his stack of folders and papers, ignoring everyone.

Three minutes later they were startled by a sudden rapping of knuckles on the door frame.

Alice Louise Dubose surveyed the room with a stern expression, an expression which was sadly not reinforced by her puffy, hot pink parka.

"Excuse me, Mr. Posen," she said, "but I need to borrow one of your men for a little while."

She was staring at Ron.

Of course. As if he wasn't feeling lousy enough already today, with a headache and something he could easily mistake for total exhaustion. It had been a rough weekend for him.

"We're right in da middle of an important staff meeting here!" Ed barked.

Alice Louise glared at him, and he cringed. It was indeed a cringeworthy glare.

"On de udder hand, go right ahead. Just be sure to bring him back. Dat snow out dere wants to be shoveled and it ain't gonna shovel itself!"

Alice Louise dismissed Ed Posen with a sniff. She gave Ron a tilt of her chin as she turned and headed for the lobby. Ron offered Erin a quick, tight smile of apology and scurried to follow.

Alice Louise was waiting for him, her fists on her hips, fire in her eyes.

"I want to know what in hell is going on here," she demanded.

Ron shook his head with confusion. "I don't know what you mean–"

"I mean with this town. With you! You look like hell, by the way."

"Well thanks," Ron said. He still felt like hell, too, but wasn't pleased to have it brought to his attention. "I didn't get much sleep last–"

"I want to know what you were doing at that camp yesterday, and what all these rumors and reports are that are circulating around town. That you were having some kind of running feud with Carl Rowley, and that he threatened you with a shotgun." She stared hard at him, watching his reaction.

"We already talked about this. I told you all this last night," Ron said, his heart in his throat.

"Yes. You had a confrontation on the main street with Rowley Saturday. There were reports that a big red pickup was seen following someone on a snowmobile yesterday—someone who just might have been you—just a short time before–"

"I told you about that."

"–you showed up *unexpectedly* at Sid Francis's camp. There were also two reports of gunfire out on the road near that old trestle. And..."She hesitated, and Ron could see the uncertainty clouding her blue eyes. She glanced away, took a breath, then turned back to face him. "I've been having nightmares. And some of them involve you." She glared at him, daring him to make some dumb remark. "And this Carl Rowley person. Something happened in the bar between you two Friday night. I know you told me about it, but I... I still can't quite remember it. And since that night, strange things have been going on here. Your chief of police has his hands full and he just won't leave me alone. And somehow, you're in the middle of all of it. Don't lie to me!"

She put on her cop face and held his eyes, unblinking, with an ice cold stare, while Ron weighed his response. But she blinked first.

"Carl Rowley," she added softly, "is dead."

The room spun. There was a bench bolted to the lobby wall. Ron stumbled backward until his legs touched it, then he sat down hard.

Relief. Horror. Confusion. Sorrow. A collage of emotions flooded over him and through him in an instant, and looped again and again like a stuck record.

Somewhere in the building a phone rang three times, then went quiet.

"Are you sure?" Ron said. "How?"

"Oh, yes. Very dead. He went off the road just east of town. Over an embankment. Probably bounced off the old trestle, and rolled it."

Ron stared at her, hearing but not fully comprehending.

"He's dead?" His thoughts turned from personal relief to Carl's family. Not just his minions, like Shelby and Dennis. He knew there were others; people intensely loyal to Carl. But there was also his wife, Viola, whom Ron had sometimes seen riding in Carl's truck in the summer—a small, mousy woman, with stringy dishwater blond hair, and a slack expression that looked perpetually defeated and vacant; Greg, Carl's oldest son, who had been subdued at the Buck Snort, but with his father on the street Saturday afternoon, that time angry and dangerous; Carl Junior, the youngest; Carl's daughters, Carla and Carlotta. There might have been more, Ron couldn't recall. He only knew them through Beth, who knew them or had had them in her classes at Deathe Consolidated.

There was a commotion in the hallway, and Spencer and Abraham burst into the lobby, followed by the rest of the crew. Ron looked up at them, almost without recognition.

"De college is closed!" Spencer exclaimed. "Dere's anudder big snowstorm on de way, and we get to go home before it hits!"

They rushed through the lobby, a jubilant parade dancing in double-time, and disappeared into the stairwell with Janos bringing up the rear, limping along in a big blue plastic bootie. Erin followed. She looked expectantly at Ron, but then her eyes fell on Alice and they darkened.

Michigan State Police Trooper Alice Louise Dubose had had Erin fingerprinted by her Crime Scene guys in the fall, when Erin had first fallen in with Ron and then gotten caught up in the Bedderhoff murder investigation. She'd felt violated then. It didn't help when Ron joked that having her fingerprints on permanent file with the State Police meant she would have to be a law-abiding citizen forever.

Erin passed through and out the door, casting a quick, accusing glance over her shoulder at Ron. Or Alice. He couldn't tell which, and it didn't matter. She would either hold a grudge, or forgive, or at least get over it. Or not. He had apologized, but he had no control over her feelings.

"Is that your girlfriend?" Alice asked, and Ron's eyes darted around the lobby for an instant before he realized she was talking about Erin, and not Julianna.

"Of course not! She's a student here. Erin Coe. My intern."

Alice made a "whatever" noise and trudged over to the bench to slump down beside Ron. She muttered an angry oath.

"I should get back to town."

"I can give you a lift to Beth's on my neighbor's snowmobile," Ron said. It would be a long, cold slog of several blocks, into the wind, through drifts and snow piles pushed up by plows, and blown into mountains by the Masticator.

Mark Wolfgang

"No need," she said. "Chief Wood loaned me his old Ford Bronco." She shook her head with despair. "Worthless piece of tin crap. Hardly bigger than a damned golf cart, and half its weight is tires."

"You gotta have good tires up here–"

"And the other half is rust. Wind blowing through all the holes in the body."

"Well, I guess holes don't weigh much."

Ron knew the vehicle. A 1984 Bronco II, built at the nadir of Detroit downsizing, now more holes than metal. He was surprised Trooper Dubose would allow it on the roads, let alone drive it herself. He assumed she hadn't noticed that the license plate had expired at least ten years ago.

"*I'm doomed.* I'll never get out of this place," she said. "Hundreds of miles from home, my car's entombed in a snowdrift, and the county road is still impassable. Pretty soon we'll *all* be stranded here. Eating each other."

Of course *his* car was entombed in a snowdrift, too, with all the windows busted out.

She put her face in her hands and heaved a weary sigh, and without sufficient forethought, Ron slipped his arm around her shoulders. Tall as she was, even sitting down, he had to stretch up to do it. Alice Louise relented and actually leaned into him for about half a second before she stiffened and drew back, bolting to her feet and stepping away from him.

"I will see you later," she said, her eyes stormy. "Don't leave town," she added, then looked appropriately sheepish. She bolted for the door and was through it and gone before Ron could say goodbye.

"Well," Ron said to himself, "I guess I'll ride home alone."

20

IT WAS ALREADY starting to snow in earnest. Again. Black clouds gathered their forces beyond the ridge of hills that ringed the Iron Bowl on the northwestern shore of White Wolf Lake, preparing a fresh new assault on Deathe.

Alice Louise eased the Bronco through Deathe, bouncing and thudding over the brutal ice-covered streets. At the four corners she saw Chief Wood's SUV parked in front of Hoolie's Café. She angled the Ford into a cut in the snowbanks behind the Jeep, managing to leave just enough room on the street for a vehicle to get through. She killed the engine and headed inside.

Chief Wood sat at the window table with a cup of coffee and three slices of pie.

"I couldn't decide," he said.

Alice Louise dropped into the chair opposite. She looked at the chief's pies, saw something that might be coconut cream. Unwrapping a fork, she took a taste. It was amazing. She snatched the plate and pulled it in close, then flagged the waitress and motioned for coffee.

"What's in the file?" she asked, pointing her fork at a brown folder on the table between them.

"Carl Rowley's records. I was just going over them again."

She picked it up. Felt the heft of it in her hand. Probably no more than a hundred pages.

"Thinner than I'd expect, based on his reputation." The coffee came and she nodded her thanks to the waitress. She took another bite of her pie and nearly swooned.

"Yeah. Forty years worth of records there. He really tore up the place in his youth. A whole lot of complaints against him, especially early on. A goodly bunch of investigations. But no arrests. No prosecutions. No convictions. Witnesses recanted. Complaints and charges got dropped. Evidence disappeared. Everybody knew what kinds of things he did. That never stopped. He just got better and folks got wiser. And more scared. With good reason."

Alice Louise shuffled through the files between bites.

"Never had a job in his life," Chief Wood said, "but he'd go downstate and buy a $50,000 pickup with a stack of hundred dollar bills. Go figure."

There were no mug shots of Carl Rowley, but several photos. Many were black and white, others color but faded with age as if they were taken decades ago. She saw the steady progression of a rangy, tough-looking kid growing into a beefy, dangerous thug. A man who obviously knew nothing of moderation—who didn't work out, but had the bulk and strength of a bull through the magic of genetics.

Several played out like a set in a photo shoot: Here's Carl, slouching with a cigarette dangling from his lips, smirking, or glaring, at the camera. Hair slicked back in a bad imitation of Brando in *The Wild One*. A beer or whiskey bottle in one hand, and more often than not a firearm of one type or another—a fully automatic assault rifle or machine pistol with an illegal magazine—in other. And another. And another. In three pictures, his beefy arms wrapped around the necks and shoulders of obviously underage girls. They sagged under the weight, with fear glazing their eyes.

"He liked 'em young," Chief Wood said, his voice a low rumble, and she realized she was staring at them in disgust.

She thumbed through some of the complaints. Accusations of vandalism. B & Es. Assaults. Fights. Reckless endangerment. Firearm violations. Grand theft auto. Even animal cruelty.

"We had a couple of your state boys give him a 'come to Jesus' talk when he was younger. He didn't come, though. Like tryin' to teach a pig to sing." Chief Wood finished his last piece of pie with an expression of profound remorse. He raised his weary eyes to meet Alice Louise's. "The worst one was when he got goin' in some kind of blood feud with his brother-in-law. Ugly. Violent. Then after we thought things had settled down, the guy was found killed in the woods. Huntin' accident. Or so the report says. No leads, no arrests. The case is still open."

Alice Louise closed up the report and pushed it across the table.

A Cold Winter's Deathe

Chief Wood said, "At least Carl didn't dress him out and hang him in the barn." He had the good graces to offer a guilty wince.

She took a deep breath.

"I hate to even ask this, but what else have you got going on today?"

Chief Wood wiped his hand over his weary face.

"Long night last night," he said, his eyes hollow and rimmed with red. "I hadda buck through a couple miles of drifts and get all the Rowleys outta bed to tell 'em about Carl. It was not good." He cast a guilty glance at Alice Louise. "I gotta say, I got mixed emotions about Carl bein' gone. In some ways... well, it's a relief for de town. But de way his family carried on." He shook his head at the memory. "Quite frankly...." He glanced around the café and lowered his head and his voice. "Dey scare de hell outta me. All of 'em. And dere's a whole buncha Rowleys out dere in de bush. Greg, de oldest boy, he carried on and said he'd do anything to get his father back. Anything. He was ready to kill me and anyone who ever crossed de old man. And Carl'd whipped dis kid's ass so many times I can't keep count. Dey're all crazy,"he said, shaking his head. "Crazy as loons."

"I'm sorry," Alice Louise said. It sounded lame, but it was all she had.

"We put Carl's body in de mausoleum out at Fairview Cemetery."

Alice Louise jumped. She felt her heart falter, skip a beat, then stutter back into an unsteady rhythm. Her eyes lost focus, her vision went gray.

The mausoleum. Where Ron said he and his vampire hunter buddy had supposedly gone to check out Sid Francis's body for signs of impending vampirism.

She realized Chief Wood was still talking.

"No way to get him outta town for prob'ly a few days now." He glanced out the window. It was growing darker by the minute, and the snow was falling with grim determination. "We were gonna stick him in the shed behind the station, but we got worried about freezer burn. *Haw haw!*" Wood, recovered now from his memory of last night, looked pleased with his dark humor. Alice Louise cringed. "The temperature in the mausoleum dere is just about right. Not too cold. Not very dignified, but dere ya go." He downed a final slug of coffee.

"Was there anything..." Alice Louise started, then considered carefully what she was going to ask. She couldn't think of a good way.

"The mausoleum. What's it like?" she asked, and took a quick and innocent bite of pie.

Wood watched it go into her mouth.

"Buncha old stone and concrete crypts line the walls. Most of 'em a century old an' more. Except for Sid Francis's vault. We wrapped Carl up pretty good and laid him out on toppa Sid. Guess we'll be buryin' both of 'em when the weather breaks in the spring."

Alice Louise breathed an inner sigh of relief. If there had been anything disturbed–

"There was one other thing," Wood said, sipping his coffee and calling for more. "We suspect some kids musta broke in there recently."

Alice Louise held her breath.

"Dere wuz handprints in the dust on a couple of the old vaults. Looked like someone had maybe even pulled one o' the lids off, had a peek, and then stuck it back on."

Stay casual, Alice Louise thought. She took a sip of coffee to steady her nerves.

"Anybody you knew?" she asked, trying to sound light and natural.

"Nah. One of the Reindhart women. Died about a hunnert year ago."

Her heart stopped again. Was Ron's insane story true? He had his facts straight.

He had been there!

She knew what was the right thing to do. Tell Wood. Bring Ron in for questioning. Get to the bottom of it. Find the Yooper vampire hunter and get him off the streets. Do an assessment. On both of them.

Instead, she changed the subject.

"When did you say you can get Carl's body out of town?"

"Don't know. Not for a couple days, we're guessing. More snow on the way."

Trapped here, she thought. *For days.*

"I trust you locked the door." She thought of vermin—rats, squirrels, raccoons. Not just her friendly neighborhood vampire hunters and crypt robbers.

Woody nodded. "Big padlock."

"So...." She had to ease into another mystery. "What did you make of those footprints in the snow at Carl's wreck?"

"Footprints?" Wood said, his bushy eyebrows squirreled up on his forehead.

A Cold Winter's Deathe

"Yeah. Those little size six boot prints that were about ten feet apart."

Staring hard at nothing on the table, the chief scowled and pouted out his lower lip.

"Chief Wood! You remember them. The same as the footprints at Sid Francis's camp! Right? *Right?*" She stopped and clamped her mouth shut.

"I guess I'll have to go back over mah notes," he said, scratching at the stubble on his chin and shifting his gaze off into the distance. "I don't rightly recall anything like that."

Amnesia? Wasn't this exactly what she was experiencing with the brawl she vaguely remembered Friday night at the Buck Snort? And their expedition to Sid Francis's camp yesterday. Everything about that was still fuzzy in her mind. She had to struggle, to focus hard to bring back the images, the... the tiny footprints in the snow, which she'd almost forgotten again until just this minute.

And the stench of the coffin in the cellar.

She realized that Chief Wood was talking.

"Well, now... there is this one other thing you should maybe know about."

She pushed the pie plate away, sat back, and took a deep breath. "Hit me."

"We might also have an intruder in town," he said, and that piqued her interest. "Tino thinks there's somethin' or someone living over the Buck Snort. He found a pile of rags an' a stash of stuff up there in the old ballroom. But no bodies yet. Excuse the image. Plus there's been a rash of peeping Tom calls lately."

"Have you checked into any of this?"

"Not yet. I been short-handed today. I'll put someone on it tomorrow."

She suspected a connection here. To everything.

Yet she still hoped it was some kind of elaborate joke, for which there would be hell to pay.

She felt a sudden urge to start poking around and see what developed. She knocked back the dregs of her coffee and slammed the cup down on the table.

"Let's go have a look," she said.

131

21

NATURALLY, ED did not let Ron off so easily as the others. At least he didn't have to shovel snow. Ed made him stay to change the light bulbs in the Liberal Studies Building elevator. A week earlier, Ed had directed him to put in the tiny, incredibly bright, blue-white quartz bulbs. Ron knew there would be trouble. The little car was lit up like a tanning booth, only brighter. And hotter. The very next day, one of the teachers had suffered a panic attack and collapsed, claiming the new lights sucked all the oxygen out of the elevator, and he couldn't breathe. He'd had to be rescued by Public Safety officers, and tended to by Deathe's volunteer EMTs.

Of course this had somehow been Ron's fault.

Erin helped Ron put the old bulbs back in, then after a while she jumped on her snowmobile and raced away home ahead of the storm.

Ron didn't manage to escape the campus until past noon. By then the wind was howling in the bare trees, driving the snow directly into his face, stinging like needles as he rode the Borke's Ski Doo toward home. Despite thoughts of Julianna, perhaps sitting alone and bored at Mrs. Kinderly's, he had made time to stop at the Buck Snort for one of Tino's trademark "Heart-Attack-Inna-Sack" lunch specials. He ate it in the booth under the stairs.

After a couple games of pool, it was suddenly happy hour. Then Ron was recruited to join a round of fifteen-two—what Lopers and the rest of the world might call cribbage.

Only a handful of regulars were there, seeking shelter from the latest storm, settled in for the duration. No better place to be.

A Cold Winter's Deathe

Ron settled in, too. He wanted to rush back to his tiny apartment at Ruth's, but he was afraid that Julianna might not be there, and afraid of what it might mean if she was. Or if she wasn't. It was all too confusing.

He'd spent five years in the U.P. without the company of a friendly, unattached woman. He recognized that he was losing his social skills, especially during those times when he would hole up at Cavendish House in total solitude, not seeing or speaking to anyone, occasionally for days at a time. Coming into town after those spells was unsettling. He sometimes found he could hardly put a coherent sentence together.

Besides, he was sure he was coming down with something. Flu, maybe. Every time he stood up he got a head rush.

Ron watched the flashing colors on the TV screen that hung in the corner, absently reading the repetitious news banners crawling across the bottom. He allowed his mind to empty out. And all in all, things were not bad.

Staying here delayed the need to commit himself. To go, or not to go. That was the conundrum.

He blocked all thoughts of Carl Rowley out of his mind, instead welcoming thoughts of Julianna in.

Tino entertained the crowd with jokes and tall tales of Deathe, and his latest story.... Ron listened as he told Harv Harkonen and Bob Lipinski how he suspected there might be a bum living in the empty second floor space above the bar.

Ron's ears perked up.

Tino had found what he called "a nest" up there. Old blankets, rags, cardboard and newspapers, all gathered up into what Tino said reminded him of a "fort" a kid might build in the corner of his bedroom. Apparently he had even called Chief Wood to check it out.

Puck.

He'd heard enough. When no one was looking, Ron slipped out of his booth and snuck around to the stairs that led up to the second floor. The thick oak door was secured with a heavy padlock and hasp. He tugged on it, hard, but it was solid, no give to it.

Did that mean Puck couldn't get up there? Or did it just mean that Ron couldn't?

He'd slipped back into his booth just before Tino came to check on him. The sullen bartender tipped his chin toward Ron's empty bottle as he wiped his paws on a dish towel.

"Um, no thanks," Ron said. Tino scrunched up his face in confusion. "I got this monkey on my back," Ron added.

Tino stretched his neck to peer around behind Ron's shoulders.

"Yup," he said, expressionless, nodding with solemn understanding. "It's still there."

"Hey," Tino said, "Dat little filly find you yet?"

"Little filly?"

"Yah. Fine lookin' little wench with long hair and funny eyes. Came in Saturday evening smellin' of wood smoke, asking a lot of questions. She seemed mighty interested in you. Or maybe it was your neighbor, dere, Ron Borke," Tino said, scratching his head. "Whatever. Wanted to know where you lived, and you both live out on the west end, so I pointed her your way."

Julianna. Ron felt warm for the first time that day, just thinking about her. She had known about him before she even came to Ruth Kinderly's house. Interesting.

"Wood smoke?" Ron asked.

"Yeah. Pretty t'ick at first, I thought. But den I hardly noticed it later."

"She give you her name?" Ron said. Not that it mattered. He knew it was Julianna.

"Nope. And next t'ing I knew, she was gone."

Tino turned and ambled back to the counter.

Unwilling to grill Tino, Ron stalled for a while and listened for more clues, but by then Tino had moved on to other topics.

ALICE LOUISE dropped her shovel and bent over, panting, sweating under her ski jacket. Her jeans were crusted with snow and ice, her feet frozen blocks. Her lungs burned with the exertion of shoveling for the past half hour..

Her car was barely half exposed. And it was still snowing.

Beth continued to fling great shovels full of snow high and long, until she saw Alice Louise bent over with her hands on her knees.

"Malingerer!" Beth crowed. "I thought you wanted to go home!"

"*Home?* No such luck. Home is a long way away, and I think Gray Mackie at the Ironwood post would miss me after a few days. But get out of *here?* Oh yeah. That's my life's goal right now."

Dusk was gathering again. The Masticator had broken down Sunday, or run out of coal or plutonium fuel rods, or whatever it burned,

A Cold Winter's Deathe

but now it was reported to be back out on the roads, trying to break through the big drifts east of town. Rumors were circulating that the road might be passable all the way through to L'Anse by nightfall. Or by morning at the latest. Alice Louise wanted to be ready.

Beth jammed her shovel into the hard snow mere inches from Alice Louise's Monte Carlo.

"Hey! Mind the paint!" Alice Louise barked.

"This ain't my first rodeo," Beth drawled. "Why don't you get started on the driveway up at the road and leave me to the fine detail work."

Alice Louise took in a few more deep, frigid breaths before shouldering her shovel and wading out to the end of the driveway. The street was still thick with snow. Half a foot at least, with drifts and ridges a foot deep and more. She fretted that the Monte Carlo would never even make it downtown, let alone to L'Anse. Assuming they could even get it up and out of Beth's driveway. She pulled her chuke down tight over her ears, hiked up her gloves, and dug in her shovel, intending to work her way down from the street to the rear bumper.

The snow was packed hard. She beat at it and stabbed at it, repeatedly, breaking it up into smaller chunks that were still as big as her head and twice as heavy. She grumbled to herself, cursing and swearing at the snow, the ice, the cold, the U.P., Lake Superior, and the damned Canadians, who kept sending down those frigid arctic blasts to make her life–

She was aware of Beth shouting at her, but she couldn't hear over the clamoring din that filled her ears.

"What?"

Beth was waving frantically. "*Run!*" she screamed.

Alice Louise glanced over her shoulder to see a massive wall of spinning blades that towered over her head—bearing down on her fast.

She dropped her shovel and dove toward Beth as the Masticator thundered past, shaking the earth and darkening the sky, spewing out a blizzard of snow and ice like a volcanic eruption. She ducked and rolled, curled up on her knees, and flung her arms over her head as a hailstorm of ice chunks pummeled her back. A boulder the size of a bowling ball thudded to the ground a foot from her head.

The beating slowly subsided. Smaller pebbles of ice still clattered to the ground all around her. She waited them out, then she cautiously lifted her head up to peer out from under her gloved hands. Something whistled down from the sky, and the mangled snow shovel clanged off the roof of her car and spun down the snow toward the lake to its death.

Beth peeked up from the far side of a fresh new snow pile.

"*What in the hell was that?*" Alice Louise bellowed.

Beth came out slowly, shedding chunks of ice and brushing snow off her old barn coat.

"*That*, I'm sorry to report, is your only hope of getting out of here any time soon. Probably going back to the maintenance garage to feed on its fresh kill." She shrugged, but her eyes were immense with the reality of the close call.

Alice Louise pushed to her feet and glared off to the west, where clouds of snow billowing up through the trees marked the passing of the beast. She turned to Beth, who was standing behind a huge pile of snow, and realized that under it was her car, buried again. Deeper than ever.

"Who the hell is driving that thing?" Alice Louise demanded.

Beth looked appropriately sheepish. "We have no idea. That's the stuff of myth and legend. No one's ever claimed the job. And no one really wants to know."

Alice Louise sucked in a deep, intensely cold breath and blew it out in a cloud.

"No offense, but if I get out of this town alive, I'm not coming back. Ever. I love you like a sister, but from now on you'll just have to come to me."

RON CAME home to a cold, empty apartment.

He knelt at the register. A scratchy old record played softly downstairs, some wistful big band number from decades ago. Probably lamenting a lover gone off to war. He heard Ruth puttering in the dining room, humming along with the music. He called her name, and she answered.

"Is Julianna home?" he asked.

"No, Mr. Blank. I... I was hoping you might have seen her. She's been gone all day, you see, I haven't seen her at all. And... well..." She lowered her voice, as if she hesitated to imply anything unsavory. "It doesn't look as though her bed was slept in."

"Oh." Ron's heart sank. "I'm sorry. I just got home. I haven't seen her at all today, either." He hoped she believed him. It wasn't as if he had a reputation to protect or defend, but probably Julianna did. Plus

A Cold Winter's Deathe

he liked Ruth and valued her respect, but she wasn't very good at keeping secrets.

He heard a horn honk. Even though he knew (*knew!*) Carl Rowley was dead (*dead!*) he sidled up to the window and carefully eased back a corner of the curtain. He peeked out to see Beth's Jeep idling at the curb in front of the house. Curious. She blew the horn again and Ron suddenly realized this was Monday night, and they had rehearsals for the Deathe Founder's Day play at the Consolidated School. Beth had reminded him yesterday, he'd immediately forgotten. Considering the recent weather, he figured he could plead out, and say he assumed rehearsals had been canceled.

Beth honked again. Ron sighed. He was committed. He pulled on some boots and his winter gear, and, with a last lingering thought about Julianna, he headed out before Beth had to come in and get him.

22

Ron helped guide the little kids off into their parents' cars, while Beth turned off lights and locked up the school building. Alice Louise sat in Beth's Jeep. Not happy to be out at night in this weather.

Snow swirled in the the yellow cones of light beneath the parking lot utility poles. Pitch darkness loomed above and beyond, in all directions. The temperature had been dropping steadily since sunset. Winter was settling in for a long visit.

Only Deathe would hold a Founder's Day Celebration in January in the Upper Peninsula. Rehearsals had begun two weeks earlier and were held every Monday night. Fortunately, Beth was a harsh task mistress, and she made sure everyone was out of the building by 8:00. Ron had hoped evening events at the Consolidated School would be canceled, but the Masticator had gotten the road opened up enough that thicker heads had prevailed. Yooper *sisu* resisted surrender to mere winter blizzards.

So rehearsal had gone on. Beth had not let him out of his commitment.

Again, as the week before, and the week before that, the play rehearsal was barely controlled hysteria. Chaos reigned. Alice Louise, once she'd finished grousing about being trapped in Deathe, sat in the bleachers of the multi-purpose room and laughed at Ron and Beth.

Beth had taken what Ron considered to be unfair advantage of their friendship, and pressured him into volunteering to help corral the elementary school kids into some semblance of an amateur theater troupe. The script had been written a century ago by a member of the Cavendish family—perhaps even Miss Catherine herself, the Cathy Cadaver of Deathe legend—and was strictly adhered to. The challenge

A Cold Winter's Deathe

now was in getting new generations of kids motivated, and holding their interest for a few short weeks, especially with all the obligations and distractions of the new age.

He'd envisioned the job as mere babysitting for a couple hours a week. As it turned out, General Eisenhower couldn't have had a tougher job organizing D-Day. At least now Ron got free transportation from Beth, since his car was still windowless and buried under a snowdrift.

They'd held try-outs in December, but in a school with fewer than a hundred students, it was a given that anyone who tried out would land a part. Ron rode loose herd on seventeen kids, aged six to thirteen, and somehow found the strength to guide them through the first act. It pretended to reenact the founding of Deathe, in 1849, when there was a copper rush in the Upper Peninsula that rivaled California's gold rush of the same year. The area around Copper Harbor had grown by leaps and bounds then. Calumet, a dozen or two miles north of Houghton-Hancock, was the first city in Michigan with gas streetlights, boardwalks and an opera house. Deathe had been loosely settled then.

The play was an annual ritual, sacrosanct and unbreakable.

Three cars sat idling softly, enshrouded in white vapors, while the little monsters piled into the back seats and strapped in for the ride home. A group of kids babbled excitedly around a big Chevy Suburban, then one of them saw Beth and came to her at a dead run.

"Did you see it? Did you see it?" Maria Lopez cried. She slid to a stop before Beth and Ron, puffing clouds of steam, excitement dancing in her black eyes.

"See what?" Beth asked.

"The ghost! It was right over there!" Her hand shot out and she pointed to a line of bushes at the far side of the parking lot, just at the edge of the circle of light cast down from the utility pole. They peered into the darkness. There was nothing there now.

"No," Beth said. "Sorry."

"It was right over *there*," Maria insisted.

"I'm sure it was." Beth put her hand on Maria's shoulder and turned her around and guided her back toward the car. Ron stood and watched them walk away. The other kids surrounded Beth, clamoring for her attention. She divided it evenly. She was good at that.

Ron struck out alone across the parking lot and soon passed under the buzzing mercury light near where the ghost had been spotted. He wandered around for a minute in the icy cold, under the obsidian sky, staring at the snowy ground. At last he saw them. Small footprints. Shallow; very faint. Not many, but a few. Footprints made by small boots. He turned and headed back to where Beth's Jeep was warming.

"See anything?"

"Nothing at all," he said.

23

THE PHONE was ringing when Beth and Alice Louise hit the door.

"That had better *not* be Chief Wood!" Alice Louise barked.

"Don't worry. It's probably Naomi Borke. While you were out earlier visiting your boyfriend–"

"My *what?*"

"–I talked to Naomi. She was hoping they'd canceled everything for the next few days. Her husband Ron is really sick, she needs the day off. I forgot to call her back with the sad news."

Beth answered the phone with a cheery, "Hi, Naomi." Then she turned a dark eye on Alice Louise. "Yah, sure, she's here."

Alice Louise's eyes popped wide and she made a quick throat-cutting motion with her hand, silently mouthing *"No no no! Hang up! Hang up now!"*

Beth cupped her hand over the mouthpiece. "Sorry." She held out the phone.

Alice Louise took it reluctantly. "Hi, Chief. What's up?" She cut a lethal glare at her friend, and mouthed "traitor!" as she sat down to pull off her boots.

"Trooper Dubose," Chief Woody said, "I am dreadfully sorry to be bothering you at this time of night again."

She could hardly hear him over the static of the Deathe telephone system's notoriously bad connections.

"Chief, you'd better be calling to tell me the road east out of town is clear, and I can get out of here in the morning."

"Oh, no. Dis storm today skipped right over town and dumped its load all over the place east of us for a couple miles. Just beyond the school. Drifts ten feet deep in places. All the county plows are either overworked or broke down. Mostly, I just wanted to make sure you're still in town," Chief Wood said, "and available if we need you. Also to give you a little heads up."

"I am still in town." Alice Louise sighed. "What heads up?"

"Well, I don't really know perzactly how to say this..." He took a deep breath and Alice Louise waited impatiently. He lowered his voice as if afraid of being overheard. "Carl Rowley's body has gone missing."

"*It what?*"

Alice Louise realized she was on her feet.

The static came and went. She hoped she misunderstood. "I thought you said you'd secured Carl's body! You said you'd padlocked the doors!"

"That we did." The Chief sounded appropriately humble. And humbled.

"Then how?"

"Someone snapped the lock off. Donnie saw it when he was on patrol this evening. The doors was busted open. He stuck his nose in there, and Carl was gone."

She heard another phone ringing on the Chief's end of the line.

"What the hell?" she snapped.

"We don't rightly know what the hell just yet. We're suspecting some of his family came and stole the body, but right now we don't know anything. Maybe his brother-in-law, one or more of the kids. Maybe even his wife, we don't know. They're all just about crazy enough. But, well, you being a state cop and all, I felt duty-bound to report in with you first."

Oh goody, she thought. *And you wanted to share the horror of this with me.*

The other phone at the Chief's end went silent after the third ring.

She heard a commotion in the background. Chief Wood excused himself. She could hear voices, muffled by the Chief's paw over the phone. It sounded like Wood saying, "Donnie, call up the fire chief and tell him to round up some men."

The phone line hummed and crackled.

"Chief?" Alice Louise said.

"We just got another call in."

What else could go wrong in this town while she was still stuck here?

A Cold Winter's Deathe

"OK, there's something else you should know," Wood said, and she wondered why he was still on the line, talking to her with another caller on the line—and she awaited his next, inevitable request, which would mean a long, cold night, tracking down *body snatchers*.

"I been gettin' some pretty strange reports from around town," Chief Wood said. "Not just from a couple of guys steppin' out of the Buck Snort a while ago, but just now from a couple of upright, sober citizens."

"Go on."

"OK, this is a little bit hard to believe..."

Alice Louise somehow knew she was not going to enjoy hearing this.

"But we been getting reports that... well, for starters, old Mr. and Mrs. Farnsworth on Mill Road near the cemetery just now called, and they swear to God they just saw Carl Rowley walking past their house. Headin' downtown."

Alice Louise jerked the phone away from her face and stared at it as if it might bite her.

Beth was on her feet. "What?"

"I gotta go," Chief Wood said.

"Wait! Chief! You said the mausoleum door was busted open." She formed a new question in her mind. It was crazy. But how could anything get crazier than it was already? "Did Donnie happen to say... was it busted *in*, or *out*?"

After a moment of silence, Wood said, "Hang on a sec." She heard his muffled voice as he talked to someone else in the room. She waited, listening to the crackle and hum of the phone lines, her breath still in her chest. "Um, Donnie hadn't rightly thought about it, but now that you mentioned it..."

"*Do not tell me this.*"

He told her anyway. "He says it looked like de door was busted out from the inside."

Alice Louise saw stars. Her head swam.

"*What the hell is going on here?*"

The line went dead.

Alice Louise sat down hard, numb, clutching the phone in her hand. Beth rushed to her side and gripped her arm, her eyes wide with alarm.

143

"I have to go see Ron Blank," Alice Louise said. "The instant I'm gone, turn off all the lights and lock all the doors. The *instant* I'm gone. And if the phone rings again, *don't answer it!*"

24

R‍ON SAT bolt upright, startled awake by someone pounding on his door, inches from his head. He lurched up off the couch feeling like death warmed over, and made a grab at the baseball bat he'd taken to standing in the corner, within easy reach, whether he was watching TV or sleeping in his bed. His head swirled and he thought he would collapse on the floor.

But Carl was dead, and he hadn't seen the Yooper kid since yesterday. And besides, whose head did he really think he could bash in? The bat was an empty threat. Right now he could barely see straight, with all the stars swirling before his eyes.

But the bat still felt good in his hands. He pulled up his collar snug around his throat as he eased the door open a crack and looked out to see...

Alice Louise Dubose. Again. She pushed the door open as if he wasn't even there, wasn't trying to hold it closed against her, and she barged right in.

"Where *the hell* is this Yooper vampire hunter idiot you claim to know?" she demanded, her hand on Ron's chest, pushing him back into his apartment.

"I told you, I don't really know–"

"Don't know, or won't tell me? You had some kind of an idea about it last night. Spill it. Better yet, take me there. *Now!*" she added when he didn't answer instantly.

He told her his suspicions.

Alice charged Chief Woody's old Bronco down the deserted streets of Deathe. Bitter blasts of arctic air and ice gushed up through the holes in the floorboards. No heater could compete, and the Bronco's probably didn't work at all anyway. She slammed it into a vacant space in the no parking zone in front of the bar, hustled Ron out, and practically pulled him through the door and into the Buck Snort. She led him stumbling through the crowded saloon, straight up to Tino, who was polishing glasses behind the bar, and jammed her badge in his face.

"Take us upstairs. Now!" she demanded, when he stood frozen and wide-eyed before her.

They followed Tino as he led them back to the front door, but they didn't go outside. Instead, he rummaged through the keys in his pocket and selected one, and slid it into the padlock on the door that led up the enclosed stairway to the upper floor. The lock snapped open. He folded back the hasp and pulled open the door. The hinges were rusty and it took some effort. He began to climb the creaking old steps into the murky darkness.

Ron and Alice Louise followed closely behind.

The upstairs had been officially, legally condemned a couple years before. The floor was no longer able to support much weight, but it was still strong enough that it hadn't been deemed necessary to condemn the entire building. The stairs ended at a small foyer. Ron and Alice bumped against Tino as he paused at the top. In decades past this had been a ballroom, wide open for the full width and depth of the building. Two large windows pierced the front wall, overlooking Main Street and the Close Finnish. The mercury light over the intersection struggled without much success to penetrate glass so grimy as to be nearly opaque. They strained their eyes to see into the gloom. Slowly, they adjusted.

The other walls were blank, peeling wallpaper and colorless paint. The oak planks of the floor were heaved and buckling, and thick with the dust of the ages. Three ancient, dark brass chandeliers dangled loosely from the high ceiling, enshrouded in cobwebs.

"You know what we're here for," Alice said.

"Yup," Tino replied. "I know."

He edged away, cautious with his footing on the uneven planks.

Ron nudged Alice.

"He knows? He knows what?"

"I've already been up here before. This afternoon. With your Chief."

Ron's head swirled. Of course he'd heard Tino say he'd called Chief Woody about someone maybe living in the old ballroom upstairs,

A Cold Winter's Deathe

but he'd missed that the Chief—and Alice—had checked it out already. What did she expect to find now that she hadn't found earlier?

"What did you find then?" He had to ask.

"A nest," Alice whispered.

Ron found a light switch—the old push button style, the same as in Cavendish House. He punched it on and off a few times, but of course nothing happened.

Tino led them, stumbling in the darkness to the far corner. They saw only the shadows of unfathomable black shapes huddled low in the corner.

Alice dug into her pocket and pulled out a small flashlight. She flicked the switch, and nothing happened. Of course. She slapped it in her palm until it flickered and cast out a half-hearted beam of pale light.

Tino crouched down and reached into the shadows. Ron and Alice squatted beside him. Ron reached out hesitantly. He felt thick old cloth in his fingers. And cardboard, and newspapers. Alice's light went out and she thumped it again.

"I clean it up," Tino said. "It comes back."

The blood was pounding in Ron's ears, drowning out the silence. He has suspected. Now he knew. He stood and looked around the room, hard, concentrating like hell, straining his eyes to see every shadow in every corner of the room, forcing himself to pay attention, miss nothing.

Finally Ron saw him. A wraith standing just beyond their reach, slightly darker than the surrounding gloom. Ron stood and stretched out his hand to him, pointing at him, focusing on him, until he finally became clearer, as though materializing out the mist.

Alice Louise gasped.

Tino jumped to his feet.

They could see him, too. Ron grinned with triumph. Alice pinned him with the anemic glow of her flashlight.

"Folks, I'd like you to meet Puck!" Ron said. "He's really *not* a figment of my imagination."

"Dese ain't de droids yer lookin' for," Puck muttered with downcast eyes and a feeble wave of his hand. "Move along."

But it was too late. He looked like a little kid who'd been caught in a big lie. Whether disappointed in himself, or merely mortified at getting caught, Ron couldn't be sure.

Mark Wolfgang

"OK, now I'm pissed," Alice Louise snorted. "I'm not some simple-minded drone, you know! If you think that kind of crap is going to work on me, you got another think coming! *I can see you now!*"

"Dese ain't de droids we're lookin' for," Tino muttered, his voice flat. Ron and Alice stared at him in disbelief. "Let's move along," he said. He was gazing around the room, a blind buzzard smelling an unseen carcass.

Alice Louise jiggled the beam of the flashlight and shadows jittered across the kid's face. She started to point. "He's right–" But, glancing at Tino, she realized that only she and Ron could see the kid. "Tino, go back down and put on some coffee. I think we're going to need it." She turned to Ron. "Well, now maybe we'll get to the bottom of all this."

Ron sincerely doubted it.

A Cold Winter's Deathe

25

ALICE LOUISE stared across the table at Puck with an uneasy fascination. He regarded her with equal suspicion. But she had the presence and demeanor of a cop. He was just a sullen, gawky kid in an over-sized bomber hat.

Or so Ron wanted desperately to believe. But he had seen the instruments of horror in Puck's tackle box. He knew the kid must be capable of much more than his age and appearance let on.

But Puck was stubborn.

Ron teased Puck back down into the light. begging for his help, hinting at the situation building within the town of Deathe, just beyond the safe walls of the old saloon. Whenever Puck balked, Alice gave him a push.

They took up their place in the booth under the stairs, Alice and Ron on one side, Puck, the alleged perp, on the other.

The interview didn't go well. Puck remained cagey, offering nothing for free.

He hadn't offered any good answers yet, despite Alice's best efforts. Ron was sensing her growing desperation. She was probably wishing for bright lights and a rubber hose. They were getting nowhere.

"Carl Rowley is dead," Alice said. "You know who he is, right?"

Puck nodded. "Yah. I know. I heard."

"They stuck him in the mausoleum for safe-keeping," Alice said. Puck was nodding. "The mausoleum where you and Ron went Friday night to visit Sid Francis's body. Right?" She sounded accusing, but she was just saying what they all knew she knew. Puck and Ron nodded. She drew a deep breath. "Now Chief Wood tells me that people are reporting seeing him walking the streets tonight."

Ron reeled back in his seat. *"What?"*

He stared at the side of Alice's head as she stared hard at Puck. Unflinching. Dead serious. *But how could she be?* he wondered. This was insane!

But Puck remained passive. He gazed at the scarred tabletop, nodding thoughtfully.

"Dis is what I expected," he said. "What I been waiting for. It's gathering its forces against us."

"Why?"

Ron continued to stare at Alice, expecting her to break, to give herself away that she wasn't serious, that she didn't believe any of this for a moment, that she was just toying with Puck to get a reaction.

"To protect itself. It knows I'm here. It knows I won't stop at nothin' to destroy it, and it can't permit that."

"Why did he come here in the first place?"

"Alice," Ron said, "you can't be–"

She shushed him without taking her eyes off Puck.

"To escape me," he said. "I've chased it all across Nort' America for years, always doggin' it, never givin' it time to rest for long before I find its lair and track it down, and close in on it once again. It came here to prey on the unsuspecting, de ignorant and naive." He turned to Ron with an apologetic shrug. "Sorry, dude. You're OK. But you know what I mean. And to hide from me," he added to Alice.

"How will he go about gathering his forces?" Ron asked.

"It's begun already, dude. Starting wit' your friend Carl."

"*Carl?*" Beth exclaimed.

"Now he'll be a servant to it, a slave. And dis Carl, he can influence others. Family. Friends. T'rough their loyalty to him in life, or t'rough fear and intimidation. Whatever's necessary. His powers will develop over time, if we allow it. He'll get stronger. But for now, he'll kill anyone who threatens his maker. Dat's why he was created." Puck shook his head slowly, and Ron detected a note of helplessness in his voice. "He's gonna be a problem."

"He was just a bully," Alice protested. "A coward. A spineless jerk. Besides," she added angrily, "he's dead!"

"He's more dangerous now den he ever coulda been when he was alive."

A Cold Winter's Deathe

"I can't imagine that," Ron said, more to himself than to Alice or Puck.

"You might not have to imagine it," Puck replied evenly. He looked hard at Ron. "Dis is a problem we gotta take care of. Tonight. *Right now.*"

Understanding passed between Ron and Puck, and Ron felt a chill shiver down his spine.

"What?" Alice huffed, glancing angrily back and forth between Puck and Ron.

"He wants to break into the mausoleum again," Ron said with a groan.

"No," Puck said with a shake of his head. "We should stake out the cemetery. Observe. We must keep a safe distance this time."

"Damned right I'm going to keep a safe distance! Carl had it in for me after what happened here last Friday night. I'm not going anywhere near that cemetery."

"Ron!" Alice barked. "You're damned right you're not going anywhere near that cemetery. None of us are. We're going to wait until morning, then go do a thorough investigation. With Chief Wood and his deputy. Listen to yourself! Listen to *us!* We're talking about vampires like they're real, for cripe's sakes!"

Ron slumped in his seat, suddenly realizing how ridiculous this conversation really was. But the fear still clutched his heart in an icy death grip.

"We gotta go watch. To prove it to yourself," said Puck.

"Oh right!" Alice spat. "You went *into* the mausoleum last Friday night. Why not now? Huh?"

"Too dangerous, man," Puck said with a shake of his head. "Too dangerous. We can't go back dere wit' Carl on de loose! We need to stay safe somehow."

Ron let this percolate in his head while Alice continued to grill Puck on what she called his "beliefs." Puck was adamant, unwavering. She was talking about footprints now, and their interrupted visit to Sid Francis's camp, and something in the root cellar.

Of course Puck was insane. But. There was only one way to know for sure.

"I have an idea," Ron said. "We'll need your old Bronco."

Alice turned to him as if she hadn't realized he was still there. "Why?"

"We'll use it to stake out the cemetery tonight. Keep an eye on the mausoleum, see if anyone comes out or goes in."

"You're insane," Alice said.

"Puck, it's your call." The kid nodded his head. "Then it's settled."

They both stared at Alice, awaiting her answer.

"No way, bucko!" she said.

"We have to do it, and we can't stand around out in the cold, unprotected. C'mon, Alice. Please."

"No. I'm not going to let you make a fool out of yourself. And me."

"Trooper Dubose." Ron heard Puck's voice, so soft that it almost seemed to speak directly into his mind. Alice was still glaring at Ron as though she hadn't heard. Ron glanced at him. He was staring at Alice. Hard. "Give him the keys," he said softly.

Alice hesitated, her resolve failing.

"No," Ron said to Puck. "Not this way."

"Trust me," he said, and to Ron the phrase sounded uncomfortably familiar.

Alice seemed frozen at Ron's side, her eyes glazed. But then she blinked, as though coming out of a trance, as Ron was sure she was. She glanced at Puck accusingly.

"I don't think she's susceptible," Ron said. Too strong of will, he thought. She could see ghosts. She could see Puck. She was, at once, both open to the supernatural, and defiant against it.

"No one is going anywhere tonight, except you," she said to Puck. "I think we're going to put you in protective custody for the night. For an absolute fact, no one is going to the cemetery."

A Cold Winter's Deathe

26

THEY BACKED the drafty old Bronco II into a grove of pines that faced the cemetery across Deathe's main road. A cinnamon moon hung low on the western horizon, just past full, and gradually faded to ginger and peach as time passed and it disappeared over the western ridge. The sky faded to black with the retreat of the moon. Stars poked through with renewed intensity.

It had been near last call when Alice had directed Tino to fill two Thermos bottles with hot black coffee. Ron wondered if Puck had influenced her. But he couldn't believe Alice was susceptible. So she had changed her mind.

They'd dashed to Beth's house for blankets and provisions, then to Ron's for warmer clothes, although he hardly felt the need for them now. The bitter cold wasn't as bad as he'd thought it would be. He felt fine now. He felt great. His nerve endings seemed to tingle with energy.

Ruth's house had been dark. No lone figures haunted the windows. Ron had hoped that Julianna, and Ruth, were safe in their beds with the doors locked.

Puck broke into the donut bag within the first few minutes of the stakeout. Alice slapped at his hand, but he was too quick.

"I gotta keep up my strength," he said. "I'm de Super Vampire Hunter. Donuts to me are like spinach to Popeye."

They sat in silence, bundled against the cold, the windows open a crack to let their breath out and prevent the glass from icing up. Alice sat behind the wheel, Ron took the front passenger seat. Puck sat alone in the back with his little tackle box for company. The mausoleum was barely visible in the deep shadows, perhaps fifty yards away.

"I seem to remember your BFF Pud is *supposedly* buried right over that ridge," Alice said to Ron. Sarcasm iced her voice. She didn't believe for a moment that Pud, her nemesis from the college when she was investigating the Bedderhoff murder in October, was buried anywhere. She was still convinced he was pulling a scam, pretending to be dead, while hiding out in plain site on the campus, for reasons she couldn't fathom. She was sensitive to ghosts and other supernatural stuff. Ron guessed that was how she managed to see Puck when no one else could. But she still had to concentrate to do it.

"He's not my BFF," Ron protested. In fact, he had been a thorn in Ron's side for nearly five years before Alice showed up. Now, he was mercifully gone. To where, Ron had no idea.

They could see the shattered door of the mausoleum hanging outward on its iron hinges. They had not gone to look inside. In a quiet voice, Puck had recommended against it. Ron had conceded without protest. Alice had put up a brave front, suggesting that they should at least peek through the gap, but in the end she hadn't insisted.

"But, Puck," Ron said, "can we really expect him to come back here? What if he's gone home? Bitten someone in the family? Greg, or Dennis, or his wife Viola. What if they're vampires now–"

"It don't always work dat way," Puck said. "Odds are, he's killed already." He shrugged a helpless shrug. "We just haven't heard about it yet. He's new to dis, you understand. Right now he's driven by a lust for blood. He was drained, you said–"

"I didn't say that," Alice protested.

"Well, you said dere wasn't no blood at de scene. So we gotta assume he's just got a blind, mindless craving. Raw nerves. He's little more den a zombie, a wild animal, widdout even self-awareness. He has to adjust to his condition. After several kills he'll gradually become aware of his condition and gain control over his blood-lust. Den he has to be taught by his creator. It takes time."

"Several kills?" Ron said.

"Yah. Unfortunately. But it don't need to be humans! Animal blood is almost as good. At this stage dey can't be choosy, and dey don't have the intelligence for it. Dey need fresh blood more often in dis climate. Dey generate little or no internal body heat, so if dey don't drink warm blood dey get lethargic. That would be dangerous for them. But under de right conditions dey can take advantage of the situation and slip into something like hibernation. Or, dey can freeze solid."

"And then they're really dead, right?"

A Cold Winter's Deathe

"Nah. When dey thaw out, dey pick right up where dey left off."

Alice murmured, "Bull."

Puck pretended not to hear.

Ron wasn't sure why she even agreed to this madness. She kept her own counsel. He was sure Puck now held no sway over her, if he ever did. She just seemed grimly determined to see this through, to prove them all wrong, so they would look and feel foolish, and she'd get back to her life outside of Deathe.

"And den dey need blood more den ever to recuperate their strength," Puck continued. "De bite of a vampire don't always cause vampirism. Dey don't procreate by accident. It's a process, and sometimes it's prolonged intentionally by the vampire. It can be like... *courtin' a lover!* A long, slow seduction—pardon my French," he said with a wary glance at Alice. "Dat eventually ends in the death of the chosen victim, anna unholy resurrection about t'ree days later."

"Three days?" Alice said sarcastically. "Do you hear yourself? That sounds almost Biblical. Carl was just killed Saturday night, now he's... well, *reported to be*... walking around tonight."

"T'ree days, more or less. It ain't no accident, you can be sure. You tell me he died in an auto accident. OK, so dere was an accident, probably caused by de vampire. Then it jumped him as he lay dyin', and fed on him. And then *it* fed *him*. And he died with de vampire's blood in his veins, and dat created him. It was done quick, yah, but it was done intentionally. I seen it before, in Savannah several years ago."

"Georgia?" Ron prompted.

"Gimme a break," Alice said under her breath.

Ron poured them each a cup of coffee from the Thermos. It billowed steam. He lifted his to his lips, but the smell of it, which he loved more than drinking it, made his stomach do a quick roll. He set the cup on the dashboard.

"Don't set that up there," Alice warned. "You'll steam up the windshield and we won't see anything."

"You really expect to see something?" Ron said.

She leveled a warning glare at him.

"Why procreate in the first place?" Ron said to Puck. "Except for protection? For slave labor? Is that it?"

"Not at all. Sometimes they do it for company."

"What? You told me they have no human emotions. They're not capable. Now you tell me vampires get *lonely?*"

"Vampires ain't no more capable of human emotion den a shark is. But dey have needs. Biological needs. Spiritual needs, so to speak. Dey're driven to procreate, like any lower animal. And dey can live for a *long* time."

"Go forth and multiply," Alice said sharply. "Are they doing God's bidding then?"

"Oh, Alice–" Ron said.

"No," Puck interrupted. "Let her have her opinion. Dere was a time I didn't believe either, ya know."

"What changed your mind?"

Puck looked away over the moonlit snow, frowning. He swallowed hard, the noise embarrassingly loud in the tight confines of the Bronco. Then his head began to shake in tiny, quick motions.

"I can't talk about dat right now."

"When?" Alice asked, with more benevolence than Ron would have expected.

"I don't know. When all dis is over, maybe."

He sighed, and a door seemed to close. Alice opened her mouth to speak, then thought better of it.

They sat in silence, drinking coffee and eating donuts, shivering in the cold and taking turns dozing fitfully. Except for Ron. He had no appetite for donuts. He was already as wide awake as if he'd been slamming down the energy drinks the kids at the college were always buying, and eating chocolate Zingers by the case—so full of sugar they crunched with every bite.

Occasionally, despite Puck's vehement protests, Alice would start the engine and let it run long enough to coax some warmth out of the heater and defrost the windows. Then she'd turn it off and they'd sit in silence some more.

The world was quiet. There was not a breath of wind. Ron thought he could detect the faintest hint of dawn in the east.

Alice rested with her head against the side glass, eyes closed and lips parted slightly, breathing evenly, lost in sleep. Puck slept in the back, clutching his tackle box to his chest.

Ron rolled his neck to work out the kinks and glanced around. A sudden dark movement across the road riveted his attention and he sat bolt upright, peering into the gloom. Alice had brought binoculars, but now he had no idea where they were. His frantic searching roused Puck. He came awake quickly.

"What's happening?"

A Cold Winter's Deathe

"I don't know," Ron whispered. "I thought I saw something."

Alice stirred and shook herself awake. "Saw what?"

"Something moved over there." Ron pointed toward the east edge of the cemetery. "Where are the binocs?"

"Probably a dog or something," Alice said, then she gave herself over to a huge yawn. "What time is it?"

Ron shushed her. "Too tall to be a dog."

"Did you just shush me? You don't shush me!"

Puck found the binoculars and was training them intently on the hedge row along the east fence. Alice was twisting awkwardly, trying to read her Shopko watch in the darkness, swearing under her breath. Ron strained to see into the shadows surrounding the mausoleum.

Carl Rowley stepped out into the light.

"Holy man," Ron breathed.

Puck jerked the binoculars toward the mausoleum and let out a small groan.

"What?" Alice said, too loudly. She glanced between Ron and Puck in confusion. "What?"

"There," Ron said, pointing at Carl.

From this distance it was hard to tell. In truth, it could have been anyone. But the figure that stood at the old iron door of the mausoleum was big—bigger than an average man. Even in the meager light, Ron could see that he wore only a dark, ill-fitting plaid flannel shirt, rumpled and unbuttoned over a dark-stained T-shirt, and torn trousers. No coat, no hat, and the temperature barely above single digits.

"I believe it's your friend," Puck whispered. Ron shuddered at the word "friend."

Carl glanced furtively around as he stood at the door. There was a quick, animal quality to his movements. A nervousness. Wary, fearful, he seemed to be sniffing the air.

Alice squinted into the darkness, shaking her head with disdain.

"You can't tell me that that's—"

"Shh."

"Dammit, Ron—"

"Alice," Ron hissed, "will you *please* be quiet."

Carl's head snapped toward the Bronco and Ron's heart seized. The bear was out of the cage. The dead bear. Bigger and meaner than ever.

Carl froze in place, staring directly at them like an animal that had just heard potential prey and was trying to locate the source.

Puck pawed through his tackle box.

Alice thrust out her hand to Puck. "Give me my binoculars."

He reluctantly handed the binoculars to her, then concentrated his efforts on finding something in his box.

"I think he sees us," Ron managed to squeak.

"I know," Puck said.

Alice pressed the binoculars to her eyes and worked the focusing wheel.

"What do we do?" Ron asked.

"Wait and see."

Alice suddenly cried, "*Holycrap!*" She jerked the binoculars away from her face and looked Ron, eyes wide with terror. "That looks like Carl Rowley!"

Ron could have laughed, but it would have sounded hysterical, and there was no time. Carl was suddenly in motion, running toward them, lumbering across the snow like a charging bull, gathering speed and force with every step. His open flannel shirt flapped out behind him like a flag. His undershirt was tattered and blotched with dark patterns.

Alice shrieked and dropped the binoculars.

"Lock de doors!" Puck huffed quietly, his voice strained, but it was almost too late already.

The Bronco shuddered as Carl flung himself onto the hood. Carl's swollen face pressed against the glass, incredibly close, ashen with death, distorted with rage, mangled from the impact of his fatal accident. His eyes and mouth were pure black. Horrible teeth flashed and clacked against the windshield as he tried to bite his way through the glass to get to his prey inside. Ron jolted backward in his seat and Alice screamed.

"Lock de freakin' doors, *now*, please!" Puck shouted. "*An' start de car!*"

The Bronco rocked as Carl flailed on the hood, battering the hood and windshield with his fists. The sharp sound of the impacts turned dull as the windshield succumbed to his blows and cracks spread like spider webs. He was screaming wordlessly, howling with bloodlust, trying to crawl through the glass.

"*Start de damned car!*" Puck pleaded, shouting to be heard over the bellowing demon just outside. He jerked around the back seat, fumbling in his tackle box.

Alice seemed to hear this time. She fumbled frantically for the key, fighting without success to find it and twist it. Carl flailed on the

A Cold Winter's Deathe

hood, insane and out of control, then he jerked toward Alice's side and tumbled off onto the ground. Ron reached across behind her and punched down her door lock button an instant before Carl found the handle and yanked. The Bronco jumped sideways with the force.

Carl slammed his arm into the side glass as Alice turned the key and the starter ground. The glass crazed and depressed. Ron knew it wouldn't withstand the next blow.

Alice was huffing from deep in her gut. The engine caught. Carl thrust his elbow through the window. He reached in as Alice yanked the gearshift into Drive and stomped on the gas.

The Bronco lurched forward, and Ron thought they were going to be safe, but Carl's immense hand gripped the door and the truck jerked sideways. Then they were suddenly in freefall, tumbling around in the cabin. The world spun outside the windows. Everything in the Bronco came loose and Alice fell on top of Ron as the car rolled over on its side.

The engine screamed and died.

Ron lay pressed against the passenger door with Alice's weight crushing down on him. She yelped with pain. The passenger side window beneath his head had shattered and snow and broken glass pressed into his face. He heard Puck babbling wordlessly in the back seat and Alice was still lying on Ron, sobbing with panic and gasping for breath, flailing her arms. He tried to push her away.

The windows exploded all around them under the impact of Carl's blows. He beat on the roof and it dented in. The headliner popped loose. Alice shrieked, and then an enormous arm reached through the gaping hole where the windshield used to be and gathered up a huge handful of Alice's coat.

Then she was gone.

Ron saw her feet vanishing out into the night.

He screamed "*Alice!*" and scrambled to follow.

"Help me," Puck demanded from the back seat of the car.

Ron saw Carl dragging Alice, kicking and screaming, across the road, toward the cemetery and the mausoleum. Alice Louise. Over six feet tall, an Amazon in a puffy pink parka, but she looked like a little rag doll tucked under Carl's arm.

"*No!*" Ron bellowed.

Carl paid no attention. Alice flailed in his arms and cried out for help as he lumbered forward.

Puck clambered over the top of Ron and crawled out of the vehicle, limping to follow. He had something in his hand, Ron couldn't see what. Ron scrabbled to pull himself out through the windshield hole, and he ran too. Sharp pains shot through his body like fireworks, but he passed Puck and launched himself onto Carl's back. Carl staggered under the extra weight, and Alice almost slipped away.

"Stand back!" Puck yelled, but there was no need. Ron was airborne as Carl flung him away.

Ron hit the ground, tucked and rolled up on his feet, unharmed. He looked back to see Puck press his hand into Carl's back. There came a sharp snap like a gunshot and Carl convulsed violently, popping up off the ground. Alice exploded from his grasp and hit the snow hard with a *woof.*

Carl went rigid, then collapsed and spasmed on the ground, incapacitated, back arched, hands turned to stiff claws, face contorted even more horribly.

Puck stood over him, panting.

"Get my box!" he shouted to Ron.

Alice stirred listlessly just beyond Carl and Puck. Puck turned on Ron.

"*Get my box! Now!*"

Ron stumbled back to the Bronco. He threw himself through the shattered windshield. Everything that wasn't bolted down had fallen to the low side, the passenger side. On his hands and knees, he pawed through clothes and blankets and donut bags and cups and broken Thermos bottles until he found the tackle box, then backed out and pulled himself to his feet again.

Puck had moved a respectful distance from Carl. He glared down at the monster with wary anger, still holding some kind of weapon at the ready in his right hand. Alice was scrabbling away from them as fast as she could crawl, making hoarse whimpering noises in her throat.

Ron made his way back to Puck and tossed him the box. Carl was writhing in the snow, like a turtle stuck on its back, kicking and lashing out, and Ron feared that at any instant he might turn over, get up, and come after them again.

Puck handed Ron his weapon. Ron saw that it was a plastic gun-like device, with two steel probes. An electric shock gun, probably capable of delivering several thousand volts for a few seconds.

A Cold Winter's Deathe

"Dammit!" Puck was pawing frantically through his box. He looked up at Ron. "De stake. De hammer. Dey musta fallen out in de car. Go back and get 'em."

Before Ron could turn and go back, Carl rolled onto his knees and labored unsteadily to his feet. Puck grabbed the stun gun out of Ron's hand.

Carl moved away, unaware of the three of them, staggering blindly toward the mausoleum. Ron saw that the sky was brightening toward the east, coming alive with the rosy glow of morning. Carl stumbled and fell heavily, crawled a ways, then regained his feet and lurched on. Puck followed behind, the weapon in his hand trained on his prey.

"Kill him!" Ron yelled frantically. "Kill him!"

Puck seemed not to hear. He stalked the lumbering vampire at a safe distance.

Alice moaned and Ron forgot about the stake and hammer. He went to her. She clutched at him weakly, and he pulled her to her feet and helped her, limping, back to the Bronco.

Puck followed Carl to the mausoleum, still maintaining a respectful distance. Carl slumped against the door and looked around with eyes black, glazed, and unfocused, his expression filled with pain and weariness. In an instant he was gone, though Ron never saw the heavy door open or close.

The sky grew brighter with each passing second. Alice and Ron leaned heavily against the Bronco's roof, gasping for breath, their hearts pounding with panic.

After standing guard at the mausoleum door for several minutes, Puck turned and staggered back to the vehicle. Alice stared at him in horror.

"Th—they—they're real!" she stammered. "I can't freaking believe it. You gotta kill them. Kill them all!"

"We can get him now," Puck said, bent over at the waist with his hands on his knees, panting as though he might throw up. "We got all day," he managed to say between deep breaths.

"No!" she shouted. "Now!"

Puck looked as if he'd been slapped. His eyes were wide, with.... fear? Ron wondered.

Alice clung to Ron, shivering with cold and panic. Her breath came in short, ragged gasps.

They took a quick inventory. All had cuts and sprains and abrasions—Alice worst of all. Ron worried that her left wrist might be broken. It was badly swollen already and she jumped and whimpered when he touched it. He ached from head to toe. His head throbbed, and the gathering sunlight, soft and diffuse as it was, burned his eyes.

He wanted to get Alice to a hospital, but of course that was impossible with the closed roads.

He looked the Bronco over. Most of the glass was broken or caved in; the roof and hood were badly dented; dark fluids leaked out of the engine compartment and stained the snow. It was resting on the passenger side, on a slight incline. That was good. At Ron's urging, he and Puck gripped the luggage rack on the roof and heaved. Alice helped with her good hand, and on the third try it pivoted upright and bounced on its tires.

And to think Alice had earlier *complained* about how light it was.

The engine groaned to life after a few long seconds of cranking, and chugged erratically. But it ran. Ron eased the truck out of the ditch and aimed it toward Beth's cabin. One headlight worked. There was still some windshield glass on the driver's side, but none on the passenger's, so he drove slowly. Alice huddled against him, wrapped in a blanket, trembling violently in the icy blast of wind that whipped through the interior, even at twenty miles an hour.

They only had to go a few blocks, so there wasn't a lot of time for coherent thought.

"We have to stop this," Ron said to Puck.

The Yooper vampire hunter sat in the back seat, rubbing his leg. Ron glanced at him in the mirror. He seemed to have aged a hundred years over night. His eyes were still enormous.

"Yah. We will," Puck said softly, and without, Ron thought, much conviction. "Dis time for sure, we will."

Ron wondered if any of them were up to it. And if they ever would be.

27

RON DROVE them to Beth's cabin and woke her up by pounding on the door.

Alice Louise was dimly aware of how he sagged under the weight of her leaning heavily on his shoulder, but she was in no condition to care, or do much to help him.

Beth stood in the doorway, in her bathrobe, staring at them in shock until Ron had to push her out of the way to pull Alice Louise in.

Her head swam. Her left wrist burned as if it were on fire.

"What the hell happened to you two?" Beth demanded

Two? Alice Louise glanced past Beth toward the door, looked around the room, realized that the Yooper kid was not with them. She shot a look at Ron, but he shook his head and mouthed "later." She seemed to see him as if from a distance.

"Small accident with the Chief's car," Ron said to Beth as he muscled Alice Louise into the house. "I think we'll be OK."

Beth peered outside. *"You rolled it?"*

"Icy out there, ya know."

The sun was just breaking over the horizon, orange sunlight leaking in through the east windows. Alice Louise leaned against the table. Ron had melted into the shadows.

Beth helped Alice Louise out of her boots and coat and snowmobile suit and about three layers of heavy winter clothes, and made her comfortable on the couch. Then she bustled into the kitchen and raided the freezer. She wrapped a bag of frozen peas in a dish towel for Alice Louise's wrist, all the time shooting angry glances at Ron. Alice Louise winced at the pain that shot through her arm when Beth gently poked and prodded.

"I don't think it's broken," she pronounced, her eyes searching Alice Louise's.

"It's OK," Alice Louise whispered, thoroughly humiliated by now. In pain, an invalid, she wanted to be strong, invincible, but her arm hurt like hell and her head felt as though it had been split open with an ax. The morning sunlight reflecting off the white lake stabbed her eyes like ice picks. "We could really use something to eat."

With a gentle pat on Alice Louise's knee, Beth retreated to the kitchen and rifled through the refrigerator, working to throw together a simple breakfast, and brew some fresh coffee. The cabin was warm and comfortable after the bitter cold night, and Alice Louise's eyes were heavy.

With Beth out of earshot, Alice Louise asked Ron, "What's next?"

Ron, from the shadows, shook his head with resignation.

"I can only imagine," he said. "We have to go back, find Carl, and..."

She didn't want to hear it. He didn't want to say it.

"Can't we catch some sleep first?" she said. "I'm practically dead."

Poor choice of words, she thought.

Beth came back with coffee. Alice Louise took the mug in both hands and held it to her face, luxuriating in the warmth and aroma. It seemed to weigh a ton at least. Her adrenaline was spent and she wanted only to collapse into her bed.

When Beth returned to the kitchen, Alice Louise asked Ron, "Where's your... friend?"

She peered around the cabin. Her fear was that he was in the room somewhere and she just couldn't see him.

"He didn't come in," Ron whispered with a glance at Beth. "Said he had to go back to regroup and strategize, whatever that means."

"If it means killing Carl Rowley—*again!*—I'm all in favor of it." She heard her voice saying it, but she couldn't believe that those were the words coming out her mouth. Her brain was still trying to struggle up out of a fog. "What day is this? Tuesday? Don't you have to go to work or something?"

Ron looked stricken. "I guess I'll just have to blow it off. You need to get some sleep. *We* need to get some sleep. Ed will be furious. But then again, when isn't he?"

"Don't you think we should go now and get it done?"

A Cold Winter's Deathe

"No. We need sleep first. Just a couple hours." Ron looked wretched. Pale, with droopy, red-rimmed eyes. He shook his head wearily when she protested. "An hour," he said. "One hour. We've been up all night, and now we have all day. Puck said so."

She slumped back on the couch, almost nauseous with fatigue.

"What the hell did the little imp use on Carl?" Alice Louise glanced at Beth in the kitchen. Breakfast was almost ready. "I think I heard you talking about it on the way here." Her memory was vague, mostly just images and wordless voices, bitter cold and pain.

"Some kind of electric stun gun." Ron hesitated, then relented. "Something highly illegal. Capable of delivering 180,000 volts, he said. Normally used, I imagine, by sadistic police interrogators in small Central American countries. I didn't ask how he got it" he added before she could grill him on it.

"He told me that although vampires aren't technically 'alive' by our understanding, they're animated by electrical impulses along their nervous system, just like in life. The stun gun can jangle those impulses and disable them. He'd used it before. But the only sure way to kill them," Ron added, "is to drive a stake through their heart, then cut off their head."

There. He said it. The thing she was expecting. Her stomach turned a lazy somersault. Alice Louise heard the words, but already the reality of the night was fading, and it sounded insane. It *was* insane. She realized she was cradling her arm.

She had to man up.

Beth was setting out breakfast. Alice Louise sat up straight, got up and went to the table. She rebuffed Beth's attempts to help her. Ron followed. They sat down and ate while Beth peppered them with questions. Alice Louise cringed inwardly as she lied to her best friend, over and over, until Beth had to rush around and get ready for school.

"Out chasing bad guys," Alice Louise heard herself saying. "Assisting Chief Wood. Investigating some petty crimes."

Stupid lies that anyone could uncover with a phone call.

RON SAT huddled in on himself, his back to the windows, eating sullenly. He felt like he had the worst hangover of his life, which made it easy enough to convince Beth to call the maintenance department at Cavendish College and tell them he was sick. She did.

"I talked to Lucifer," Beth told Ron.

"She was in her office?" Ron exclaimed. "She's *never* in her office." He glanced at his watch. "Especially at this hour."

"No. I think she has her office phone forwarded to her *lair*. She said you have to have a doctor's excuse to have today off, have it witnessed and notarized, and you have to bring it in and hand it to her personally before noon today or she'll haul you to HR. Of course, if she took just one look at you..."

"Thanks," Ron muttered. Swell, he thought. No doctor in town, no way to get to L'Anse to see one, and what the heck's the point of taking a sick day if you have to drag yourself in to work to prove you can't come to work because you're sick and you need a sick day? Typical Lucifer Rule: arbitrary and punitive. Fortunately, she didn't actually have any direct control over HR. Or Payroll. Just her usual undue influences. Ron would deal with it later.

As energized as he'd been last night, he felt like hell this morning, and obviously looked equally bad.

When Beth was finally gone—("*To school?*" Alice had barked; "is this some of that *sisal* crap you keep talking about?" "*Sisu*," Beth had corrected, and confirmed that, yes, school was open, but just starting a little later than usual in recognition of the brutal weekend weather and six-foot drifts)—they were both on the verge of collapse.

ALICE LOUISE'S head drooped. Her eyes kept falling closed.

"We need to sleep," she said.

"We should find Puck... and get back to business," Ron said. He was slumped on the couch.

"We have all day." She was cradling her wrist again. It ached, dull and deep. "I'll set my alarm clock."

She realized she was talking, but Ron wasn't hearing. He was passed out already. She did what she could to get his feet up and stretch him out on the couch. He winced when sunlight fell across his cheek, so she closed the blinds and covered him with a quilt (another piece of work created by Beth's color blind grandmother). Then she stumbled into her bedroom, fell on the bed, and was instantly asleep.

THE NIGHTMARES were worse than ever. Puck was a vampire now. He killed Alice. He killed Beth. Then Julianna came and covered his eyes and took him away, whispering gentle reassurances to him, kissing away his fears, telling him that if he only trusted her, everything would be all right. Forever.

A Cold Winter's Deathe

Ron awoke to Puck shaking him violently. His face was close to Ron's. He was shouting. Ron hated him and struck out and caught him on the chin with his fist and Puck fell away. Ron sat up on the couch, blinking and squinting in the bright sunlight.

Puck stared at him in surprise from across the room, touching his fingers to his chin. Ron saw a bright glint of blood.

After he'd settled down, Ron stalked to the bathroom and splashed cold water in his face and tried to wash the nightmares and the hatred from his mind.

"We have to go now," Puck said. He didn't mention Ron's attack.

"What time is it?"

"Past noon."

"Damn!" They'd overslept somehow. No matter. They still had a few hours of sunlight. "I suppose we're going back to the cemetery."

They snagged the keys to the Bronco and snuck out, leaving Alice sleeping in her room.

It should have been quick and easy. So naturally, it wasn't.

Ron herded the broken Bronco II to the cemetery. He parked, and they tried to creep in unseen. A tough trick in broad daylight on a Tuesday afternoon, but he thought they made it. Like so many Michigan days, this one had started out crystal clear and sunny, but the clouds had formed by mid-morning and now the sky was evenly overcast, blanketed with leaden clouds from horizon to horizon. But the glare of the sun on the snow stabbed his eyes.

Ron had bundled up like an Eskimo, with a stocking cap pulled low over his eyes and a scarf wrapped around his neck, covering his face up to his nose. He'd found sunglasses in the glove box, bent and crooked, and wore them snug over his eyes to shade them against the glare.

They reached the door of the mausoleum. He could see now that it was thick wooden planks, clad in steel or iron, peppered with massive rivets. The hasp and hinges were still broken, the doors hanging partly open, not even wide enough for Ron to slip through.

"Did Carl really do this?" Ron asked.

Puck nodded his head. It bobbed under the bucket of the ratty bomber hat. Ron saw new fear in his eyes.

They pried the doors open enough to squeeze through into the mausoleum. Ron saw Puck's hand shaking.

Carl was nowhere to be found. The tarp he'd been wrapped in lay in crumpled on the stone floor.

Puck heaved a ragged sigh.

"He's not here," Puck said. "We're too late."

Ron didn't want to believe it. He examined every inch of the crypt.

"Where the hell is he?" Ron demanded. "He couldn't have dragged himself out of here in broad daylight. Could he?"

Puck had to think about that for a minute.

"Not in de daylight, of course. He wouldn't get far. We can look around. Remember, his mind is scrambled, from trauma, death, resurrection... vampirism. He woulda needed help. Guidance. Dat's what worries me. Someone else coulda come and taken him."

Ron's mind went blank and black for an instant. Then he remembered Puck telling them how vampires could have influence over weak minds.

Like Carl's relatives.

"Greg," Ron said.

"Who?"

"Carl's son. Alice was telling me about him last night, when we were going to find you at the saloon. She said Chief Wood told her Greg went crazy when he learned his father was dead. He said he'd do anything to get his dad back. Anything."

They squeezed out of the mausoleum and looked around, and soon found deep footprints in the snow that they'd overlooked when they'd first arrived. Something had been dragged away. Carl's body, they guessed. They lost the trail within a few dozen yards.

"It had to be Greg," Ron said. "Him and his family."

The Rowley house was a mile southeast of town. They drove slowly in the battered, wobbly, rattling Ford, shivering and squinting in the cold wind that blew through the gaping side windows and the remains of the shattered windshield, their eyes watering, faces freezing.

They reached the end of the road, where the Masticator had had to give up and turn back in the face of a twenty-foot snowdrift. There was no road visible to the east, only miles of virgin, trackless snow.

But the long driveway to their right was plowed just enough for the Bronco. They turned south and bucked their way through to the end.

The Rowley homestead was a big, ramshackle old farmhouse that hadn't seen a fresh coat of paint in twenty years with a detached garage and a large pole barn—the better for stashing lots of stolen

A Cold Winter's Deathe

goods. After their insistent pounding on the back door, Viola answered looking like a wrung out dishrag. She was small and haggard, although Ron knew she was not even thirty yet. Second wife. Carl had divorced the first and married Viola when she was only seventeen and he was facing a statutory rape charge. A quickie marriage, and the charges went away. A few months later Viola had borne Carl Junior.

She opened the door a crack and blocked it with her body.

Ron introduced himself and told her they'd come to talk to Greg.

"Greg ain't here," she stated bluntly.

Ron's heart sank. He managed to ask, "Do you know where he is?"

"It's a school day!" she snarled, and added an appropriate title for Ron.

He looked at Puck and Puck looked at him.

"Allow me," the Yooper said.

He brushed past Ron and grabbed Viola's small head with both hands. She tried to jump back, her arms jerked up to ward off the kid, but then she went suddenly rigid in Puck's grip. They stood motionless, face to face, eyes closed, for several seconds. Ron could see Puck's lips moving as he spoke directly into Viola's mind, but Ron's frightened breathing was the only sound he could hear. He glanced around the kitchen to make sure no one else was watching.

In a few seconds it was over. Puck released Viola and Ron caught her in his arms as she swooned and slumped toward the floor. He guided her into a ratty chrome and vinyl chair in the dining area.

"She doesn't know anything," Puck said.

"You're sure?"

He leveled a withering glare at Ron. "De boy ain't in school. He ran off after Chief Wood was here Sunday night, and he ain't been home since."

"Maybe we should have a look around anyway," Ron suggested. He looked into Viola's glazed eyes. She couldn't yet focus.

"You're right," Puck said with a curt nod.

Ron said to Viola, "Do you mind if we have a little look around?"

"She won't mind," Puck said. He bustled through the kitchen, and Ron followed reluctantly.

Two little girls stood in the doorway that led upstairs from the living room. He knew them through Beth and his work with the

Founder's Day play. Sometimes they showed up, sometimes they didn't. They never knew their lines.

"Hi, Carlotta," Ron said to the big one. Disarmingly, he hoped.

"I'm Carla," she replied. "She's Carlotta."

"Sorry." Ron smiled down apologetically. "We need to look in the cellar for a second. Do you think you could show us the way?"

Without a word, Carla led Ron back through the kitchen, where her mother was standing at the sink now, staring blindly out the window. Viola didn't seem to hear the three of them pass through.

They looked around the basement briefly. There was nothing to see. They let themselves out the back door, then peeked into the garage and wandered through the barn.

They found nothing.

Puck stalked out of the barn toward the Bronco without looking back. Ron went back to the house and knocked hesitantly on the back door again. Viola came and glared at him suspiciously.

"When Greg comes home, could you give me a call? I can give you a phone number... This is very important. We need to talk to Greg."

"I'll let him know," she said, then slammed the door in Ron's face. He sighed and trudged back to the car.

"You can read minds?" Ron asked as he climbed in.

"I can sense thoughts," Puck answered.

"Another great trick," Ron said as they bounced the Bronco down the long driveway toward the road. "Are you going to teach me that one someday, too?"

Puck glared sullenly out the glassless side windows.

"What do we do now?" Ron asked.

"We gotta find Carl." He peered at the leaden sky. "Before nightfall."

"Damn right we do," Ron snapped. "He knows where I live!"

28

ALICE LOUISE heard voices coming up from a deep, dark well. Ghostly voices calling her name, and she recoiled, turning and turning, wanting to run, but there were bears in the woods, and dim, shapeless forms with long arms and hands that grasped at her and tried to pull her down into the darkness.

Beth was calling her name, shaking her.

"Al! Wake up!"

She pried her eyes open just enough to see her friend standing over her.

"What?" she asked stupidly, and tried to roll over, but pain exploded in her wrist and she came fully awake with a start. She sat up and took inventory. She was on her bed in Beth's house, still fully clothed, her aching wrist wrapped loosely in a sodden dish towel.

Watery daylight filtered through the thin shades.

"How long have I been out?" she asked, trying to get up.

"Oh, just about... *all freaking day*," Beth said, pushing her back down. "Take it easy, sis. You had a rough night."

"Tell me about it," Alice Louise muttered. She brushed Beth's hand away and gained her feet unsteadily. She glanced at the digital alarm clock.

Could it really be after four o'clock already?

"You tell me," Beth snapped. "I have no idea what you guys were into."

Alice Louise stumbled to the bathroom, where she found that Beth had bound her wrist with a bag of once-frozen peas in a towel.

"Peas?" Alice Louise demanded, holding up the sodden bag for Beth's inspection.

Beth was in the kitchen, making a fresh pot of coffee. "An old trick my grandmother taught me."

"Where's Ron?" Alice Louise demanded, alarmed at the sight of the empty couch. She rushed to the window and looked out. The trashed Bronco was nowhere to be seen.

Dammit!

"Don't know," Beth said. "Your guess would be a lot better than mine."

She sounded angry.

OK. Alice Louise, could understand that.

She grabbed the phone, but didn't know who to call.

"What's the number for the police department?"

"How would I know? They're not on my friends and family calling list."

Alice Louise grunted her impatience and found a pathetically thin phone directory under a pile of papers on the desk. A woman answered on the second ring.

"This is Michigan State Trooper A. L. Dubose," she said. "I need to speak to the Chief, please. *Now* would be good."

She only had a few seconds to compose her tale before the Chief was on the line.

"Chief, do you know... have you had any reports of Ron Blank driving around in your Bronco?"

There was a moment of silence. She hung her head and waited. Her wrist throbbed.

"Well, now. Dat's an interesting topic," Chief Woody said. He sounded a bit surly. "Yah, as a matter of fact, I got some reports. Seems dat some guy's been drivin' around in my car wid all de windows busted out and de doors and hood and everyt'ing smashed all to hell just a little bit. Muffler draggin' on de ground. Wheels a-wobblin'. Pre'ner totaled. Even been out south of town, harassin' some of Carl Rowley's family. You got any idea what dat's all about?"

Alice Louise hung her head. "Yes, unfortunately," she admitted. "I have some ideas about that. I do apologize, and I'll make it up to you."

For an instant panic seized her as she heard a familiar rumble. She remembered the Masticator bearing down on her, bellowing, its spinning teeth flashing in its gigantic maw, sending snow and ice flying for miles. She jumped up and looked out the window to see the battered Bronco pulling into Beth's driveway, Ron at the wheel.

A Cold Winter's Deathe

She covered the mouthpiece to muffle the rumble of the missing exhaust system. "Chief, something's come up. I'll have to get back to you on all this." He tried to interrupt, but she cut him off. "You'll have my report... in a day or two," she said, and hung up.

She met Ron at the door with Beth right behind her. Ron's face was hidden beneath a gray wool watch cap and dark sunglasses, an ice encrusted scarf covering his nose and mouth. Suddenly she wasn't even sure it was Ron. She snatched the sunglasses off and he winced and squeezed his eyes shut.

He stumbled as she grabbed him by the coat and yanked him into the cabin. She peered out the door past his shoulder. The Yooper kid was nowhere to be seen.

"Where the hell have you been?" she demanded, pulling off his hat and tossing it aside, then tugging the scarf down off his face. He squinted, as though the pale light of dusk filtering through the windows was still too bright for him.

"It's a long story," he said.

"Spill it."

Beth looked back and forth between them as Ron shucked out of his winter clothes. Ron nodded toward her and gave Alice Louise a significant roll of his eyes. Alice Louise looked at Beth looking at them. She made a snap decision.

"Spill it," she repeated. Then to Beth: "Take a seat. We gotta talk about some stuff that isn't going to make much sense, but it might be time you knew. Look outside," she said to Ron's expression of discomfort. "It's getting dark. Unless you have some really good news to report, I think we're headed for big trouble."

He confirmed what she already saw in his eyes. "We're in big trouble."

"We went back to the mausoleum," Ron said when they were seated around the table with coffee steaming in front of them.

Beth jerked and sat up straight.

"And?" Alice Louise prompted.

"He wasn't there."

"What?" she barked at the same instant Beth said, "Who?"

"Carl Rowley," Ron and Alice Louise said as one.

Beth slumped back in her chair and stared at them as if they were insane, which, Alice Louise realized, was a very real likelihood. "How?" Alice Louise demanded.

"Dragged away by someone. We checked a bunch of Rowleys and their shirttail relations out east of town, but Puck is convinced that no one knew anything about it. Then we drove around, looking for clues." He hung his head with embarrassment. "That worked about as well as you'd think it would. There must be hundreds of hiding places in Cavendish Township alone. Abandoned buildings, cabins, iron mines, copper mines. The list is endless. I'm pretty sure Greg is the key, but I don't know how to find him."

They'd broken into three unoccupied houses, he said. And several barns and garages, and searched everywhere for tracks running off on unused roads, drives, or logging trails. Panic and exhaustion had drained Ron's flagging energy. He ached in every inch of his body.

"You guys aren't making a whole lot of sense here," Beth muttered. She'd been listening in silence. Her eyes shifted back and forth between them. She looked as if she might bolt for the door in an instant.

"Now what do we do?" Alice Louise asked, ignoring her for the moment.

Ron sighed. "Hide?"

"And then what? What if he comes back tonight?"

"*Carl Rowley?*" Beth shouted. "Do you hear yourselves? *He's dead!*"

"He knows where I live," Ron said to Alice Louise with a voice of despair. "I mean, Puck said he's still little more than a zombie. He's not capable of intelligence. He probably doesn't even remember me. Yet," he added.

Beth's eyes were saucers, her mouth a tight line. "*Puck?*"

"Where is he?"

"Jumped out downtown and took off. Said he had plans of his own."

Ron looked around and Alice Louise followed his gaze. She knew what he was thinking. Beth's house was a log cabin, solid as a machine-gun bunker, with small, high windows and thick rough-sawn plank doors. Heavy steel locks and hinges. Thick shutters that could be closed, and latched from inside against the brutal winter storms.

"It's the best we've got. You think Carl might have known where you live?" he asked Beth.

She stared at him in disbelief, then gave a nearly imperceptible left-right shake of her head. Alice Louise wasn't sure if it meant he didn't, or she didn't know if he did.

A Cold Winter's Deathe

"If we're going to hole up here, I want to go home and get some things," Ron said.

BETH REFUSED to stay home alone. Actually, she drove, because the Bronco was probably on the Chief's most-wanted APB list by now, and it was obviously unsafe, blatantly illegal at any speed. They'd tucked it around behind Beth's camp and taken her Cherokee.

The last rays of sunlight reddened the clouds beyond the western ridge and the clearing at the end of the road just past Ruth's boarding house. Soon the streetlights would be flickering to life.

Ron urged Beth to stay in the Cherokee while he and Alice went in to talk to Ruth Kinderly. He introduced Alice to Ruth and asked about Julianna. He wanted to warn her somehow, but Ruth had not seen her in a couple of days.

"Who?" Alice Louise said.

"Um, a new neighbor," Ron hedged.

"I thought you would know where she is," Ruth said. "Her bed hasn't been slept in since she met you. She ruffles it up a little, but she doesn't sleep in it." Ruth threw him a significant look.

"Huh?" Ron and Alice said at the same minute.

Alice was looking at him strangely.

Ron shook his head with confusion, opening his mouth to protest his innocence. But then he thought better of it.

"If she comes home, keep her inside. Both of you stay inside, lock the doors and stay away from the windows. Please," he added.

Ron spun and headed toward his stairway with Alice on his heels. She'd discarded the sling so she could slip on her coat, but she still cradled her wrist protectively in her right hand.

"What was that all about?" Alice demanded.

"Nothing."

"It sure sounded like something."

They climbed the stairs and Ron unlocked his apartment. He walked in, but Alice froze in the doorway behind him.

"What the hell died in here?" She demanded. She backed out into the fresh air.

"What?"

She peeked in warily, her nose wrinkled in disgust. "I thought you'd said something about a mouse. Are you hiding a dead horse in here?"

Ron sniffed the air, but smelled nothing.

"Oh," he said. "Yah. I don't even notice it anymore."
"How can you *not* notice it?" Alice said. "It's getting worse."

She prowled the apartment with her hand over her nose and mouth, turning on lights and peering into corners as though she expected to find a carcass covered with maggots, or worse, while Ron stuffed an overnight bag. After collecting things out of the medicine cabinet, Ron stepped back into the living room.

Julianna was there, her back and hands pressed protectively against the closed door as though guarding it against their escape. She was staring darkly at Alice.

"Julianna!" Ron exclaimed. His heart leapt.

Alice looked at him, then turned to the door and saw Julianna. They appraised each other wordlessly.

Ron tossed his bag on the couch. Julianna sidled closer to Alice.

"Alice Louise Dubose, this is Julianna. Julianna, Alice Louise."

Julianna simply stared at her in open admiration. "Aren't you simply magnificent," she breathed. She gazed up and down at Alice's six-foot-plus frame, her eyes enormous and dark.

Alice paused. Wary. She thrust her hand out, as if to keep Julianna at arm's length.

Julianna looked down at Alice's hand without comprehension for a moment, then stepped forward, reached up, and took Alice's face in her hands. She rose up on her toes and somehow the waif was magically almost as tall as Alice. She leaned in as if to kiss Alice full on the mouth. Ron watched in astonishment.

"Hey!" Alice snapped. She stiffened. She swatted Julianna's hands aside, then took her by the shoulders as though to push her away. But somehow, to Ron's confusion, it seemed to be Alice who fell back, while Julianna stood solid as a pillar.

Julianna's expression switched from one of warm appreciation to confusion. Her eyes searched Alice's, as if Alice had just unexpectedly slapped her face.

Alice huffed and backed away, studying Julianna with suspicion.

Julianna stared at Alice for a moment, then turned to Ron, hesitated, then kissed him primly.

"Ron." Ignoring Alice now, she looked at his duffel bag on the sofa. "Are you going somewhere?"

"Uh..." He struggled to find his voice. Alice glared at the back of Julianna's head. He kept glancing back and forth between the two of

A Cold Winter's Deathe

them, wondering if Alice would spring up and cuff Julianna. "We're going to Beth's house for the night," he said.

"Beth?" Julianna pouted prettily. Then she glanced at Alice and her eyes flashed with mischief. "You have another one? Might I come too?"

"Um," Ron said hesitantly. "I... wish you would." He glanced at Alice for a sign, then ducked his head in a silent plea. He couldn't imagine Julianna unprotected with all that was going on in Deathe.

"Oh yeah," Alice said, her voice icy. She cut a lethal glare at Ron. "We insist."

Julianna beamed at Ron, her eyes glittering with secret pleasure. She turned to Alice and extended her hand. Alice made as if to swat it away. She brushed past Julianna and stalked out the door. With a mischievous glance over her shoulder at Ron, Julianna scampered along behind Alice. Seemingly unfazed by the bitter cold, she still wore the blood red dress she'd worn when Ron had first met her, with bare shoulders, head, and hands.

"Julianna! You need a coat!" he said, snagging an old barn coat from his closet.

He quickly gathered up his duffel bag, turned out the lights and followed them down into the gathering night, wondering what the hell he was getting into next.

29

THEY LOCKED themselves in for the night, shutters and all, then Beth set about fixing supper. Alice and Julianna sat at the kitchen table, Alice subdued and silent, shooting the occasional glare at Julianna, who watched Beth intently, much the way she had watched Ruth Kinderly the first night Ron had met her.

Her posture stirred an odd sense of deja vu in him. So much about her seemed vaguely familiar, as though he had known her a long time ago. He puzzled over it for a while, but no inspiration came.

Beth's initial meeting with Julianna hadn't been as dramatic as Alice's. Beth talked continuously while she cooked, about anything and everything. Julianna prompted her occasionally when Beth started to wind down, and she'd take off again, talking to fill the silence. The kitchen overflowed with rich aromas.

It crossed Ron's mind that Beth would make someone a great wife someday. Bill Trevarthan, her absentee boyfriend, rarely made it home to Deathe for a visit anymore. He couldn't know what he was missing or he would have quit his job with the State Police and moved back permanently.

Ron cruised the cabin, double- and triple-checking the latches on the windows and shutters, until he was convinced that nothing was going to get in, or out.

Beth had whipped together a Hungarian goulash. Ron was ravenous.

Julianna demurred. "I've just dined," she said.

They ate without her, Beth and Alice with enthusiasm. When Ron took one bite his stomach churned and threatened to reject it. It tasted a bit... rancid. He had to push it away and apologize.

A Cold Winter's Deathe

"I'm just not feeling so great right now," he said.

But yet he was still hungry.

Beth and Alice looked at him with concern in their eyes.

After supper they adjourned to the living room, which was of course only two steps to the left from the kitchen and dining area.

"Maps," Alice said, and a light came on. Beth brought out topographical maps of Baraga, Keweenaw and Houghton Counties. They poured over them for any indication of abandoned mines near Deathe. Julianna asked lots of questions, but they hedged their answers—trying to protect her from the awful truth. Ron didn't want to alarm her, and Beth and Alice went along without any discussion at all.

Eventually they found half a dozen good possibilities where a vampire could make a lair.

Yawns told Ron that the women were getting sleepy. Except Julianna, who was still bright-eyed and alert, listening and watching attentively. Alice had slept all day, but exhaustion was taking its toll, and Beth had to get up early to go to school again. Ron didn't care about work. He now felt energized by the quest.

He glanced over and saw that Alice was asleep sitting up.

"There's nothing more we can do tonight," he said. "I think we should all go to bed now, and find... our *friend*... in the morning." He didn't want to sully Julianna with Puck's name. They had been careful not to mention vampires that evening. He'd not spoken the word to Julianna since the night they'd first met. She was such a delicate flower, he didn't want to upset her. Or more likely, he had to admit, look ridiculous in her eyes with talk of vampires and vampire hunters.

"We'll get organized bright and early," he promised Alice.

Beth began to turn off the lights, then they all stood to go to bed, except Julianna, who sat watching them with faint amusement. Ron, Alice and Beth looked at Julianna. Ron looked at Alice. Alice looked at Beth, and Beth shrugged. Ron remembered hearing something once about the written word for *trouble* in the Philippine Tagalog language being a picture of two women under one roof.

Now he had three.

Alice rolled her eyes and sighed.

"Twin beds in my room. OK, yeah, I'll take her." She got up and stomped into the bedroom.

Julianna beamed. Beth slipped away into her bedroom and closed her door.

"I'm not sleepy," Julianna stated. Her turquoise eyes were bright and untroubled.

"Well," Ron said. "We are." Although at the moment he didn't feel exhausted. He still felt energized by the excitement of the hunt. "We're exhausted, and we have a lot to do tomorrow. Maybe you can just go in and lie down?" He felt like he was speaking to a child. "Try to sleep a little?"

"As you wish," she said, and kissed him primly.

She drifted into Alice's bedroom and closed the door. Ron did not want to think about the cold atmosphere that would permeate that room through the night.

Taking quick refuge in the bathroom, he undressed to his shorts and slipped into a loose sweatsuit. He examined the mysterious bruises that still marked his neck. Still sore, but at least they weren't getting any worse. He found a hand towel, tucked it into the collar of his sweatshirt, fluffing it up over the bruises. He turned off the last light, stretched out on the couch, and pulled up a blanket.

His eyes popped open almost instantly. Julianna was kneeling barely a foot from his face, staring at him intently. He could see her clearly, even in the darkness.

"Are you going to find them?" she asked in a low whisper.

"Find who?"

"The vampires. That's who you're looking for, isn't it?"

"Julianna, I never said–"

"Will *he* be with you?"

"Who?"

"The vampire hunter."

"I don't know. If we can find him, I hope so."

Julianna drifted back to Alice's room. Ron, nervous, alert, cruised the cabin, checking windows and doors, until he thought he cold lie down and close his eyes for just a moment.

Sirens woke him.

The house was dark. Ron knocked his watch off the end table as he grappled for it. Finally he found the table lamp and switched it on and squinted at the watch. It was just a little past nine.

The sirens died close by. Within two or three blocks, he guessed. Police sirens, not fire trucks. The old-fashioned siren of Chief Woody's Cherokee. Not good. Not good at all.

No one else stirred. A thousand dark thoughts passed through his mind. Police sirens were a rare occurrence in Deathe. He could only

A Cold Winter's Deathe

think of one reason for them now. He got up and padded to the doorway of Alice's bedroom.

"Alice?" He eased the door open. A shaft of light fell across the bed. Alice Louise lay sprawled gracelessly on her stomach, sound asleep, covered only by a thin sheet. He tip-toed to the other bedroom and cracked the door. "Beth?"

Beth made a sour face in her sleep, rolled away from the light and pulled the covers over her face.

He went back to the living room and sat and listened to the silence. Minutes passed like hours. His fears and curiosity wouldn't let him sleep. He debated on actually getting dressed and braving the night—walking around and trying to determine what was going on. But then an inspiration flashed.

Tino would know what was happening. He knew everything that went on in town.

Ron called the Buck Snort Saloon.

"Tino. Ron Blank. What's going on tonight? I heard sirens."

"Busy week for de cops," he said. "De fire out at Sid's. Carl twice. Now dis."

"Not Carl again," Ron breathed.

"No. De little Lopez girl's disappeared. One of Beth Atkins's, ain't she?"

Maria Lopez. Raúl's daughter.

"When?"

"Ain't been seen for a few hours, I guess."

"In this cold?" *Not good.* "What do they suspect?" Ron knew what *he* suspected.

"Too early to tell, but some folks are reporting some spooky kid in a big bomber hat hanging around her neighborhood earlier."

People can see him? This was new. Ron slammed down the phone and grabbed up his jeans and shirt.

"Alice!" he barked. He was pulling on his coat and boots before he realized that she hadn't answered. "Alice!"

He stomped to her bedroom and switched on the overhead light. She lay on her back with her hands folded. He sat down beside her and shook her gently, then more frantically. She came awake slowly, groggy and confused.

"What's happening?" she muttered. She lifted her head and pushed her hair off her forehead without opening her eyes. She sunk down and dug herself into the blankets to avoid the light, and squeezed her eyes closed.

"There's trouble in town. I'm going to go look into it."

"Huh? *Again?* What kind of trouble this time?" She propped herself up on one elbow and squinted at Ron in the bright light, now struggling to come fully awake. She still looked pretty beat up from the morning 's battle—worse than she'd looked during the day.

"There's been a kidnapping. Maybe," he hedged. "I'm going to go check it out." He hoped she would volunteer to come along.

She threw back the covers and sat up in her pink sweatpants and oversize Detroit Lions T-shirt, swinging her stockinged feet to the floor.

"Whoa," she said. She steadied herself with one hand on the nightstand, the other pressed to her temple. "Head rush," she muttered, squeezing her eyes closed, then blinking to clear them. She tried to stand up and sank back onto the bed, shielding her eyes from the ceiling light and squinting. "Where's Julianna?"

Ron looked at the other bed. Still made, barely mussed, and empty. He shook his head.

"I don't know. In the bathroom?" he said, growing impatient with Alice's lethargy. His body tingled with dread and anticipation. "I need to go. Now."

"Give me a minute," Alice snapped. She struggled to her feet.

Ron stood close to catch her if she toppled over. But he couldn't wait any longer. He pushed past her out of the bedroom.

"Alice, I'm going now. Catch up with me when you can."

"Wait," she said, but Ron grabbed his gloves and threw himself out the door into the winter night. He ran toward town, ignoring the Bronco and Beth's Cherokee, enjoying the cold, crisp air in his lungs, feeling the overpowering need to fly free, out of the house, running through the black, frigid night with the wind in his face.

30

ALICE LOUISE stumbled to the bathroom and leaned on the sink. She shrank back when pain erupted in her wrist. It ached like hell. Probing it with her fingertips, she massaged it gently, flexed it till the pain subsided.

The reflection in the mirror was not pretty, and she ached from head to toe. She pulled up her T-shirt and found fresh new bruises from her battle discoloring her flesh everywhere including her face and neck. Her hair was wild and unmanageable, so she grabbed a handful, gave it a twist, and tied it at the back of her head. Then she splashed cold water on her face, snagged her heaviest sweatshirt, and padded to Beth's room. She cracked the door. A sliver of light fell across Beth's face where she lay splayed across the bed.

Alice Louise turned on the light. Beth cringed, burrowing deeper into her blankets.

"Hey, sis. I gotta take a run downtown." Alice Louise tugged on her sweatshirt.

Beth moaned and pulled the bedspread over her head.

"Beth. I need to go. Make sure the doors are locked behind me. You hear me? Lock the freaking doors. And don't let anyone in except me or Ron."

"How will I know it's you?" Beth's voice was muffled under the blankets.

"I'll say, 'Beth. It's me. Alice Louise. Open the freaking door.' And then you open the freaking door. OK?"

"'K."

Alice Louise regarded the lump under the covers for a moment. Huffing with irritation, she turned out the light. The combination was hidden in the cookie jar. Alice Louise found it, read it, and dialed it into the combination lock of Beth's Liberty safe. She pulled out Siggy's lock box, unlocked it and set it on the coffee table. Favoring her wrist, she tugged on her wool socks, thermal long johns, and bundled up in Bill's snowmobile suit and pretty much every scrap of cold weather gear she owned. Finally she managed to pull her pink parka over everything.

Pressing her fingers to the bruises on her throat, she considered the painful effects of the frigid night air. She grabbed a long wool scarf and wound it around her neck three times.

Beth had left her Jeep keys on the kitchen counter, but now Alice Louise couldn't find them anywhere. She searched through the pockets of Beth's coats, and crept back into Beth's bedroom and rummaged through her nightstand. They were nowhere to be found.

Ron. Of course. She had a good mind to charge him with grand theft auto.

With a grunt of resignation, she snatched up the keys to Chief Wood's broken Bronco from her dresser. Turning off the lights, she headed out the door, carefully locking it behind her.

DEPUTY DONNIE'S old Cherokee and a couple other village trucks idled in front of Raúl Lopez's house, behind Chief Woody's Jeep Cherokee. Intense red and blue emergency lights strobed the night. All was silent but for the muffled exhaust notes. The Iron Bowl of Deathe and White Wolf Lake does not permit radio signals, even for cops.

Ron kept his distance, crouching behind some bushes, trying to gather a sense of what was going on. The cops were inside, taking statements. He could see figures moving past the windows—Raúl fretting and pacing, his wife, Alonza, sobbing violently, three of the other kids, and the cops, big, imposing, stoic.

He heard a throaty rumble in the distance. Not the Masticator. *Chief Woody's Bronco?* The racket grew louder as it came closer toward downtown. Ron eased out of his hiding place and jogged to intercept Alice before she could interfere.

He met her as the Bronco wallowed to a stop in front of the Buck Snort and died.

"Why on earth didn't you take Beth's car?" Ron hissed as he wrenched open the door. "You could hear this thing coming all the way to L'Anse."

"I thought you took it," Alice snapped. "I couldn't find the keys anywhere. Then I saw it was still there, but I'd locked myself out of the cabin and I couldn't raise Beth." She glared at him. "What the hell is going on here?"

"Well, maybe Beth stuck her keys in the cookie j–"

Alice bounded out of the car as quickly as she could, considering she was bundled up like a giant, mummified teddy bear.

"*Forget the keys!* What's going on *here*, now?"

He took a breath and filled her in.

Maria Lopez had gone missing a couple hours earlier. Now the fire department volunteers were all being called in to scour the neighborhood and try to find the girl.

Alice listened with growing horror. "Are you telling me she's been kidnapped?"

"Well, Tino said there were reports of some spooky-looking kid in a bomber hat lurking around town. Tino said something about a ghost, and then I remembered the kids at the school after Monday night's play rehearsal claimed they saw a ghost near the school parking lot." He hung his head. "And... I remember now that I saw footprints in the snow. What if it was Puck who'd been lurking–?"

"*You think Puck kidnapped this girl?*" Alice interrupted.

"He was looking at her funny Friday night in the bar. After the incident with Carl." The name Carl tasted metallic and bitter in his mouth. "I searched the room above the Buck Snort but the nest has been cleaned out."

"What about the footprints at the school?" Alice pressed her gloved fingers to her lips. "Small footprints? I've seen footprints too. At that burned out cabin Sunday and again Sunday night in the road where Carl was killed."

"You think it's just been Puck all along? Playing us for some reason?"

She shook her head. "I have no idea. Where do you think he is? If... if he's taken this girl?"

"I have a theory on that. We need to go to the cemetery."

"Somehow, I just knew this was going to end up there. *Hey! Wait for me!*"

31

ALICE LOUISE watched, stunned, as Ron jogged away from her, out of the timid glow of the streetlights, east into the frigid darkness.

She slumped back down behind the wheel of the Bronco, yanked on the door—twice—till it closed and latched, and reached for the keys. Stupid piece of crap. She'd probably wake up the whole town if she started it again. She reached down to the floor on the passenger's side and pulled up her metal lock box. Fumbling the keys out of her pocket, she unlocked the box, pulled out Siggy and laid him on the passenger seat.

Throwing caution to the wind, she started the Bronco and eased gently away from the saloon without touching the gas pedal. The damaged exhaust rumbled thunderously in the still, cold night.

RON CREPT UP behind Puck. The alleged vampire hunter crouched behind some evergreen shrubs, the stun gun clutched in his right hand, staring at the busted doors of the Fairview mausoleum. His tackle box sat in the snow at his feet.

The night was overcast and dark, yet Ron's vision was sharper than ever. He'd loped all the way to the cemetery without even breathing hard, clinging to the deep shadows, moving with silent stealth, feeling like a cat prowling the night for easy prey.

He could hear ice crystals fall from tree branches and hit the snow with a delicate, metallic ping. He heard Alice, three blocks away, as she opened her gun safe and pulled out her Sig Saur .40 caliber semi-automatic service weapon. The racket of the Bronco starting up was almost deafening.

Silently, Ron moved closer, until he was within arm's reach.

A Cold Winter's Deathe

"Expecting someone?" he whispered.

Puck lurched violently and spun on Ron, his ratty bomber hat bobbing on his head, stun gun at the ready. His eyes popped wide with alarm, and Ron felt a smug sense of satisfaction with himself.

"What are you doing here!" he snarled through clenched teeth.

"I could ask you the same question. Don't you know how dangerous this could be?"

"Go away!" Puck growled. "Get outta here and leave me alone!"

Ron turned and looked at the mausoleum.

"Now what would make you think Carl would come back here'" Ron asked with forced casualness. "Hmm? Seems that he's been moved out. Unless it's for the smell of..."

Once again, Puck looked stricken, like a little kid caught in a horrible lie.

Ron sniffed the air, smelling the metallic scent of fresh blood. He bolted across the road toward the cemetery, making no effort to conceal himself. He knew what he was expecting to find, and nothing else mattered. Puck stumbled to follow.

"Dude! You don't know what you're doing. We gotta go t'rough wit dis."

"No!" Ron said.

He stepped into the mausoleum. The stench of blood filled his nostrils and his head swam as he looked around the room. Even in the pitch darkness, he could make out every shape and form in the dark crypt. He saw no sign of Maria Lopez.

"Dude!" Puck huffed as Ron switched on the bare light bulbs. "What are you doing? You wanna get us killed?"

A pool of fresh, wet blood stained one of the cement vaults. The smell of it, thick and sweet, was almost... intoxicating. Ron ignored it, darting around the room, peering into the corners and behind the stone crypts.

"What de hell are you lookin' for?" Puck demanded.

"Maria Lopez! What did you do with her?"

"Who?"

Ron spun on Puck. "What do you mean, *who*? You mean you didn't kidnap...?"

"You mean dat little girl, de daughter of dat Mexican guy from de bar de udder night?" Puck asked, incredulous. "What kinda monster do you t'ink I am? Dis is just animal blood, man. I was hopin' to lure Carl back here and *cap him*."

Ron realized that suspecting Puck, as terrible as that had seemed, was actually the best, safest, most harmless, of all the theories he might have come up with.

A whole new level of dread descended upon him.

Puck glanced nervously over his shoulder, peering out across the dark cemetery, his eyes wide with fear. "You're screwin' up everyt'ing, man. We bedder get outta here."

In the distance, Ron could hear the Bronco heading their way. He switched off the lights and pushed Puck out of the mausoleum, then pushed the busted doors closed with surprising ease.

Puck stumbled through the cemetery toward the road, glancing around frantically. Ron followed, his footsteps light and sure. The cemetery lay before him and around him as if bathed in soft moonlight, although the night was moonless and overcast, and the nearest streetlight was at least a block away. He detected no furtive movements anywhere. He heard little save their muffled footsteps, and the approaching rumble of the Chief's Bronco.

They paused at the edge of the road. The Bronco wobbled drunkenly out of town toward them on bent rims and axles. Its one working headlight traced small, nervous circles just above the road, swinging its beam into the ditches and trees and back around again.

"What's our next move?" Puck asked, his head in constant motion, turning and spinning as he looked for vampires in all directions at once, left and right and back and forth, bobbing beneath the loose bowl of his mangy bomber hat.

Ron regarded the kid with alarm. "I was just going to ask you the same thing. I thought you knew what you were doing."

Puck avoided Ron's eyes. "I don't know where de hell you got dat idea," he muttered under his breath.

"*What?*" Ron cried in alarm. "You're supposed to be the professional vampire hunter here!"

"Well," Puck said. "About dat..."

The Bronco wheezed to a halt in front of them. Alice shouldered open the door with a resounding pop and got out. She regarded the pair across the roof with a worried scowl.

"What's going on?"

"Maria's not here," Ron said. "I thought... Well, it doesn't matter now what I thought."

"So where is she?"

"We were just discussing that," Ron growled, glaring at Puck.

"How de hell should I know? I ain't familiar wid dis area."

"OK," Ron said. He looked to Alice for support. "We went over all kinds of maps tonight. We found a few places where *we* think a vampire could hide out. We know the area, but we don't know vampires. Where would you think they might hide out? In caves? Under bridges? Abandoned mills?"

"Barns?" Alice added. "Mines?"

Puck appeared to give the suggestions serious consideration.

"Nah," he said. "I mean, if dey wuz desperate, maybe. But dey usually like a little touch of de old world luxury. You know, a stately old mansion or somet'ing."

Ron and Alice looked at each other.

"What?" Puck asked.

"Cavendish House!" Ron and Alice said in unison.

"I SHOULD HAVE thought of this sooner," Ron said as the Bronco waddled east, heading toward the old trestle.

Once again, Alice was driving, favoring her left wrist, peering squinty-eyed through the gaping hole of the busted out windshield. Ron rode shotgun, and Puck slumped in the back seat, unusually subdued.

"In fact," Ron went on, speaking loudly enough to be heard over the exhaust and the wind whistling through the cab. "I think I did. Sunday, at Sid's camp. You showed me those little footprints in the snow, and I saw them going off in the direction of Cavendish House. But it just didn't seem to register at the time. Now I can't believe I didn't remember it."

Alice glared over her shoulder at Puck. "Maybe that had something to do with people messing with our heads."

"Hey! Dat wasn't me!" Puck said, but then he ducked his head and looked a bit sheepish. "Or... maybe it was just an unexpected side effect. I really didn't mean it. Honest."

"You know we'll never get this thing anywhere close to Cavendish," Ron said, glancing around at the trashed Bronco. "Not with the side roads plugged the way they are."

"It's got four wheel drive," Alice said, glancing at the lever on the floor.

"Hell, it's barely got *four wheels!*" Ron said. "Besides, the bridge to Cavendish is laying in the bottom of the Stony Creek ravine."

"What's dat?" Puck yelped, thrusting his arm between them and pointing out through the nonexistent windshield.

They could see a white glow blazing in the sky up ahead.

"Not a fire," Ron said. "Too white and intense."

The light grew steadily brighter as they wobbled east toward the old railroad trestle, lighting up the low-hanging clouds, glittering in the snowy, crystalline trees of the dense surrounding forests somewhere on the far side. Alice wrestled the Bronco through the twist under the brick and stone arch As they emerged on the other side and the road straightened out, they could see some kind of a derelict hulk ahead of them, bathed in a backwash of brilliance.

The Bronco slowed to a wallowing crawl as Alice backed off the gas.

"It's the Masticator," Ron said.

He'd never seen it up close. The thing was huge. It loomed over them. Ugly. Angular. *Ridonkulous*. Hammered together from forged iron and rusty steel, randomly slathered in dull, depressing gray and beige colors, it looked like a scarred World War II battle tank.

It snored uneasily, shaking the ground and belching out clouds of angry steam that mingled with black exhaust fumes as it idled, unmoving, in the middle of the road.

Alice crept up on it cautiously, as if it might wake up and spin around to attack them.

"I t'ink it's asleep."

"Where's the driver?" Alice asked.

"I'll take a look," Ron said. He levered open the door and stepped out.

"Be careful!" Alice cautioned. "That thing nearly killed me!"

Ron looked at her with alarm. *Huh?* But there was no time to waste. Heart racing, he sidled to the driver's side of the Masticator. The ground vibrated through his boots.

There was something that looked like a ship's ladder bolted to the side of the beast. He grabbed on and put a foot on a ledge. He could swear he felt the thing's pulse through the cold steel. He paused there, half expecting it to wake up and shake him off. He hoisted himself up, scaling the side of the monster, until he could stretch his neck enough to see through the side window.

"It's empty!" he called down.

A Cold Winter's Deathe

Alice had her head stuck out the side window of the Ford. He couldn't fault her for not getting out.

Ron peered ahead of the Masticator. In the wash of brilliant headlights he saw a lump of rags a dozen yards up the road. He clambered down and ran around to Alice.

"I think that's the driver up the road a little ways," Ron said, and he turned and ran into the dazzle of the sleeping Masticator's floodlights.

ALICE LOUISE put her shoulder to the door until it popped open with a bang. Puck was right behind her, box and stun gun in hand, as she edged around the huge snowblower at a safe distance, and followed Ron into the deeper snow ahead of the beast.

Ron was kneeling by what looked like a lumpy old coat. She dropped down beside him, and together they gently turned it over. It was a man, of course. Unconscious. Barely alive. There was blood staining his collar, but not very much of it, Alice Louise was relieved to see. She pulled off a glove and dug her fingers into his collar to feel for a pulse. It was weak and thready, but still there.

"Help me roll him over."

With Ron's help, they did. He was a stubby guy, with a massive chest and arms under a ratty old barn coat. He had a broad, coarse face, with lots of beard stubble, and a less-than-full complement of teeth. Alice Louise titled his head so that the lights of the Masticator shined in his eyes.

"He's out cold," she said with hopeless resignation.

Puck stood behind them, nervously scanning the forest in all directions.

"What do we do with him?" Ron asked.

"We have to get him some help," she said. "Get him back to town somehow."

"We could stick him in the Bronco," Ron said. "I think there are some blankets in the back. Then we can take the Masticator the rest of the way. It's built like a battleship."

"We can't just leave him here. The Ford doesn't have any windows! He could die in there."

Animals will eat him, she thought. *Or worse.*

"Den let's load him in de Ford and just take him back to town ourselves," Puck said. "All of us. I'll drive!"

191

She thought furiously. "OK. One of us has to take him back to town in the Bronco. The others will have to go on to Cavendish House in that... *thing*."

They all looked at one another.

"I ain't drawin' de short straw on *dat!*" Puck mumbled.

Alice Louise and Ron looked at Puck and saw fear.

"I'll take him back to town," the kid said.

Ron was suddenly on his feet and in Puck's face.

"What is going on with you? I thought you were the fearless vampire killer. Are you turning into some kind of a wimp on us now?"

"OK. OK," Puck said, his eyes darting around their feet, avoiding Ron's glare. "OK. I, um, I ain't really a professional vampire hunter. I just, ya know, got sucked into dis business a few years back. So to speak. I, uh... I ain't never really killed an actual vampire or nuthin–"

Now Alice Louise was on her feet, standing side-by-side with Ron. Ron spat an oath and Puck cringed.

"Are you saying," Alice Louise demanded, "these *vampires* aren't real? Or what? You're just playing some kind of bizarre game? Because I saw Carl Rowley! I saw him dead by the side of the road, and I saw him attack us in that Bronco! He tried to carry me off to the mausoleum!"

"And *I* was the one who jumped on his back to try to get him off her!" Ron yelled, and then he stepped back, his eyes wide now not with rage, but with realization. "Nevermind," he said.

"What?" Alice Louise spun on him. "What do you mean, *nevermind?*"

"Look at him. He's scared half to death."

Alice Louise looked. The kid was terrified. Useless.

"Well hell," she said. Frustration and anger reddened her vision, but she wasn't ready to give up. "What do we do now? One way or another, I want this thing to end tonight. We have to try to get that little girl back."

"Assuming we actually find her," Ron said. "But it's still a good idea. We have to try. So we stick this guy in the Bronco, and Puck runs him back to town for help. You and I take the Masticator and plow our way to Cavendish. Or as close as we can get."

A Cold Winter's Deathe

32

THEY WATCHED the taillights of the Bronco wobble off toward Deathe, disappearing under and through the trestle.

Puck had left them with his tackle box full of tricks, and little else.

"You seen de movies," he'd told Ron. "You read de books. Just go wit' dat."

"The *Twilight* series?" Alice asked, disbelief straining her voice.

"*No!*" Puck snapped at Alice. "Don't be a dork. *Real* vampires don't sparkle! *Holy wah.* I mean de *primary* sources. *Dracula. Nosferatu.* Nunuhdat Ann Rice stuff, neither." He leveled a glare at Ron. "You might consider *Carmilla* for yerself. You shoulda done your homework."

So much for passing on the tricks of the trade. Then he was gone, with hardly a glance over his shoulder.

And good riddance to him.

"Well," Ron said, looking up at the enormous bulk of the Masticator, "at least we should be able to get as far as Stony Creek in this thing. That's farther than we could have ever gotten with the Bronco."

He scaled the side of the beast again, found an iron handle, and pulled the door open. Grinning triumphantly down at Alice, he squeezed in amongst the confusion of handles, levers, and gauges. He turned, braced himself, and reached down a hand to her.

Alice was already pulling herself up, hooking her arm around the steel ladder, still favoring her left wrist. She somehow lifted up

Puck's tackle box. Ron took it and stuffed it on the floor on the far side of the cab.

For such a ginormous machine, the cab was as cramped as an old Apollo space capsule, except without enough room for a third astronaut. Ron and Alice twisted themselves like pretzels to get Alice over Ron and into the right-hand seat. They finally untwisted, and came up for breath and to look around.

"Where's the steering wheel?" Alice asked.

Ron studied the forest of iron levers and handles, switches as big as pistol grips, small iron cranks sprouting from unlikely locations here and there, and knobs the size of his fist. Tubes and cloth-braided cables ran everywhere. The cab vibrated like an industrial strength massage chair. Needles jiggled wildly on the dials of platter-sized pressure gauges that looked like something from the Cold War era.

"How the hell do you drive this thing?"

Ron sure didn't know. But he didn't want Alice to worry.

"It's like an old steam locomotive."

"Well, I sure don't think it runs on rails."

"Or maybe more like a Cold War Soviet aircraft carrier," he hedged.

She gave him The Look and rolled her eyes.

"Let's try this." Ron squeezed a grip on one of the levers and pulled. The Masticator rocked and roared. Clumps of snow the size of V8 engines exploded out of the chute and sailed off into the forest.

"OK, I think we got the snowblower option on this cream-puff," Ron said, as he eased the lever home. He nodded at her thoughtfully. "We'll be needing that."

"What about this?" Alice twisted a handle that jutted out from the dashboard and they were plunged into total darkness. She wrenched it back, and the lights blazed again. There was fear and respect in her eyes. "OK, now we know what *that* does."

"More than we knew five seconds ago."

Together they tested all the levers and knobs and spun the iron wheels. Alice leaned out the window and reported to Ron what she saw—the massive snowblower lifting and lowering, the chute rotating, the front and rear tires angling left and right.

They avoided the handle marked "DO NOT TOUCH!!!" In red capital letters. With several exclamation marks. Circled and underlined.

It would take both of them, with all their strength and concentration, to drive the thing.

A Cold Winter's Deathe

"Ready?"

"As I'll ever be."

Ron wrenched up the idle speed, closely watching the torque indicator climb past VII to XXIV.

"Start the snowblower."

Alice squeezed the handle and eased the lever back. The Masticator bucked and strained as the wall of blades spun up to full speed.

"Well," Ron said. "Here goes nothing."

He released the brake lever and muscled the tiller—a big iron handle growing out of the space just above his feet—to the right as the beast dug in and lumbered out into the road. They soon hit a wall of snow. The blades bit in, blasting a torrent of snow and ice three dozen yards into the bush. The Masticator surged forward and bulled through the first drift, and forged on along the snow-clogged road.

They found the two-lane that led northwest, toward Cavendish Road and Cavendish House, and made their first turn. After a few close calls with the ditches and trees, Ron somehow managed to keep the Masticator close to the middle of the road and moving forward. Every slight curve required near Herculean effort.

Alice offered helpful advice like "Watch out!" and "You're too far to the right! Move left!"

They plunged ever forward, chewing up six- and eight-foot drifts like they were nothing, spewing the snow off into the darkness.

Chewing and spewing, chewing and spewing. It wasn't called the Masticator for nothing.

Their dead end on Cavendish Road took them by surprise. Ron yanked the tiller hard to the left. The tiller bucked back, and the Masticator threatened to plunge straight ahead. Alice leaned back and jammed her foot on the tiller, and together they mashed so far over that the beast lurched right suddenly. They bounded through the ditch. The stop sign vanished in a shower of splinters and metal fragments.

Ron regained control as the road narrowed.

Soon, off to the left, they spotted the sign in the wash of the Masticator's lights that said "Caution: Bottomless Pit—No Trespassing!" They knew they were nearing the driveway to Cavendish Manor.

"So," Alice said. "Just how deep is the Bottomless Pit?"

Ron grunted with irritation. "I told you last fall, it's bottomless."

"But seriously."

"Seriously. Deathe used it as a village dump for a hundred years, till the college started hiring all those do-gooder flatlanders, and they threatened to sic the EPA on us. Loggers and miners used it before that. The native Indian tribes used it forever. You would not believe the stuff they say is down there."

Alice rolled her eyes.

"Slow us down," Ron said, both hands with a death grip on the tiller. Alice pulled back on the throttle until the torque indicator quivered at IV.

The Masticator slowed to a crawl as they approached the stone pillars standing sentinel on either side of the private drive that led back to Cavendish Manor.

Ron muscled the tiller to the right, and Alice grabbed on and pulled with him. The beast balked. The tires jumped and chattered and slipped on the ice under the thick snow. Ron grabbed the small crank handle above his head that steered the aft tires, and spun it a dozen times. The back end slewed around. Alice held the tiller tight with her right hand while Ron worked the left and right brake handles. They squeezed between the pillars with inches to spare.

They entered a tight, low tunnel of cedars and thick pines. The Masticator-made blizzard blew back on them, coating the windshield and reflecting the dazzling floodlights back in their eyes. For a short time they drove nearly blind, steering only by glimpses of bare trees and evergreens through the side windows. The familiar two-track, which Ron had driven hundreds of times, seemed to take unexpected twists and turns.

"*Stop!*" Alice yelped, and they both grabbed the brake lever and pulled hard.

The Masticator shuddered to a halt. Alice throttled back and jammed home the lever that killed the spinning wall of blades.

The black, skeletal wreckage of the old iron bridge lay scattered before them like a loose pile of Pick-Up Sticks.

Ron and Alice sat in the beast, panting, hearts pounding, as they peered down into Stony Ravine. The barn-door-sized snowblower hung out over the abyss that yawned just inches from the front tires.

RON CLIMBED down.

Alice Louise crawled through the maze of levers, wheels, and cables onto the driver's seat, and dropped Puck's tackle box into Ron's waiting hands. She clambered down to join him. Her left wrist throbbed, aching as if filled with burning charcoal.

The beast snored and rumbled beside them, lighting up the woods beyond the ravine with about a million watts of high intensity candlepower.

Nothing like announcing your presence with authority, she thought.

"How do we get across?" she asked. It looked deep.

"It's not that far down. And the creek is frozen over."

He started down into the ravine. Alice Louise pulled Siggy out of her coat and checked him over. Safety. On. Check. Thirteen rounds in the magazine. Check. One round in the chamber.

"Should I have loaded some silver bullets?" she called down to the top of Ron's head.

His white face peered up at her from below. "How should I know? But I don't think we'll meet any werewolves."

"You sure about that?" she grumbled. She stuffed Siggy into her coat pocket and followed Ron down into the ravine, most of the way by sliding on her butt.

"On the other hand, I think silver works on vampires, too." He shot her an apologetic glance, as if remembering this fact earlier would have made buying silver .40 caliber bullets likely, or even possible.

They skated across a couple yards of solid ice and mounted the far side of the ravine.

The lights of the Masticator grew dimmer behind them as they trudged deeper into the woods. Alice Louise recognized the twists and turns in the drive, even though it had been three months–and a whole season—earlier that she'd passed down this driveway for what she'd hoped was the last time. She waded through knee-deep snow as Ron tripped lightly over it ahead of her.

As they rounded the last bend, she knew that Cavendish House would soon loom up out of the darkness in front of them, as big and solid as a black granite mountain.

And it did.

Dark as midnight, it seemed to regard them with blind eyes. *Glazed eyes.*

OK, glazed windows, which, when she thought about it, shouldn't be quite as ominous as it looked. But she'd been in the house. She'd slept there for several uneasy nights. And although Ron had told her, after she'd moved out, that the house had gone quiet, that was not the way *she* remembered it.

Cathy Cadaver had once lived and died there. And, to hear Ron Blank tell it, she was still in residence. But then again, he also insisted that the resident reprobate of Cavendish Junior College, Pud Ristimaki, was mouldering in a grave in Fairview Cemetery, too, so what the heck did he know?

All was quiet. As Alice Louise stumbled along in the darkness behind him, Ron strode up to the front door, and into the pitch black foyer. She heard the scraping of bricks, and a jangle of metal. A key. She heard the metallic snick of it sliding into the lock.

"You're not going straight in the front door?" Alice Louise protested through clenched teeth. Siggy was in her hands, held alongside her thigh, ready for anything. Well, almost anything.

"Um..." Ron said. "Maybe? OK. On second thought, maybe not."

Jingle-scrape. He returned the key into a cubbyhole and slid the brick over it. No fumbling. Amazing night vision.

"I suppose we could go around to the back."

"You know this place better than I do. What other ideas do you have?"

"Well, I guess if we have a vampire infestation, I'd expect them to be living... er, sleeping... in the cellars. But the place is pretty well sealed up. The drapes are heavy, they could probably wander around the downstairs all day without getting fried. But if it was me, I'd be in the cellars."

"What time is it?" She wanted to get to her watch. It would light up if she could find it—and the light button—under her gloves and coat and sweatshirt sleeves and underalls. But she didn't want to release her two-handed grip on Siggy. She winced with the pain in her wrist.

"Half past four. You really think that gun will work on Carl?"

"A forty cal. Thirteen rounds. It'll bring down a bull. How long till dawn?" She had a vague idea that they might be able to despoil any lair Carl, and whatever other vampire there was, had made, and catch them in some kind of crossfire as they came home to roost..

Ron brushed past her into the murky, marginally less-dark darkness outside the foyer. She could barely see the white outline of his face as he scanned the sky beyond the skeletal trees.

"A couple of hours. Maybe less."

A Cold Winter's Deathe

She closed her eyes to center herself. Then she took a breath and laid out her plan. It wasn't much of a plan, but he didn't challenge it. He even added a few worthwhile suggestions. Until she got to the end.

"*Arrest* them?" he barked.

"Well, yeah! At least until we know exactly what we're dealing with here."

"But... you *did* see Carl Rowley trying to chew his way through the Bronco to kill us all, didn't you? I mean, *he almost made it!*"

"Lead on," she growled. "Be ready. I might change my mind and just shoot anything that moves, and deal with the fallout later."

"OK, yah. But just to be clear," he said, "I'm moving now. Don't shoot me. OK?"

She gave him a shove.

He moved like a gazelle, quick and sure-footed in the darkness and thick snow. She was a moose, stumbling blindly along behind; kicking gracelessly through knee-deep drifts; stumbling into unexpected holes; tripping over buried branches, rocks, ice mounds, and her own stupid feet. The were at the back of the house. It was even darker than at the front of the house, impossible as that seemed.

"This is it," Ron said, gazing down at what he'd told her used to be the old coal chute. It was now a half dozen narrow concrete steps, leading down to a small cellar door. Ron waded down into the little stairwell. "I have a key on the mantel," he said, reaching for it. "But it's not here."

Alice Louise felt an icy electric current course down her spine.

"The door's unlocked," he said, and she brought Siggy up to shoulder level.

She heard the door creak open, and the ghostly phantom that was Ron vanished into the darkness beyond the doorway.

33

ALICE LOUISE descended the stairs, ducked under the door, and she was in the cellar. Every nerve in her body tingled. Her eyes strained against the impenetrable darkness. She heard Ron set Puck's box on the floor, the rustle of his clothes as he knelt over it, and the clunk and clatter of its contents as he rummaged through it. A spark of light poured out from under the lid as Ron drew out a flashlight.

He crouched by the box and stabbed the beam around the room. Light and shadows leaped and darted. Alice Louise saw movement everywhere. Snapping off the safety, she fell back against the wall, jerking the Sig Sauer and her head in all directions at once, eyes wide.

"Shh!" he said, and they both froze and held their breath. The silence was total, engulfing them like the vacuum of the universe. Their eyes met.

"Follow me," Ron whispered.

He led her through a yawning cave. Everything was as she'd imagined it might be in a 150-year-old cellar beneath a decaying mansion. Only worse. Deep warrens, like crypts, pocketed the crumbling walls. Tiny rooms angled off into darkness in every direction, lined with rotting shelves, stacked high with moldy jars and bottles, dusty barrels, and detritus she couldn't identify. The boiler, cold and rusting, as big as the Masticator, looked like two steam locomotives crushed together, with pipes and valves and iron grates everywhere.

"Here," Ron said, and the beam of the flashlight fell upon two wooden, oblong boxes sitting on sawhorses.

The familiar stench of death rolled over Alice Louise. It smelled just like Sid's Francis' root cellar, and... Ron's apartment.

A Cold Winter's Deathe

Cringing, she buried her nose in the crook of her arm. She stared at the back of Ron's head. He seemed blissfully unfazed.

"Um, Ron? Do you not smell that?"

"Smell what?" he asked, giving her a quizzical look over his shoulder.

OK. Excellent night vision, but apparently his olfactory senses were toast.

"What do we do now?" Her "plan," such as it was, had vanished from her head.

He set down the tackle box and dug out a small glass bottle.

"Puck's holy water," he said. "At least I think it is. It might be moonshine, but I'm not going to taste it to find out." He held the light up to it and studied the bottle, turning it in his hand. Alice Louise could see that it had an amber tint and it was crystallized.

"Damn," he said. "It's freezing. The little weasel hasn't been drinking enough booze."

"OK, I have no idea what you're talking about—and I'm not sure I want to."

"It means we need to move fast. Unless you want to hold this in your armpit and warm it up." She didn't. "I'm going to try to spread some of this in these boxes to evict the vampires."

A guttural growl exploded from somewhere *in the room with them.*

Ron jerked around and stabbed the flashlight beam into the corners. Alice Louise saw movement in the darkness. Her heart hammered in her chest. She drew down on it with a straight-armed, two-fisted grip, as she thumbed off the safety.

"*Police!* Stop where you are and show me your hands!"

Ron cast the wavering beam on a ragged corpse of a thing shambling toward them with outstretched arms. Gnarled fingers clutched at the air. Red eyes darted from Ron to Alice Louise, glaring out from a white, doughy face.

"*State Police! Stop or I'll shoot!*"

Her finger tightened on the trigger.

"*Alice! No!*" Ron barked. He held the beam steady on the hideous face, and the figure paused. "Ron?" Ron said.

"Huh?" Alice Louise glanced wide-eyed from the walking corpse to Ron and back, her finger still a fraction of an ounce light of firing the .40 cal Sig.

"I think it's my neighbor. Ron? Is that you?"

The creature paused. It looked confused.

"Mr. Blank?" it said. "I... I can't let you do dat. I got my orders. I'm sorry."

It lurched toward Ron. Alice Louise opened her mouth to shout a last warning as her finger squeezed tighter. There was a flash and *snap!* The creature jerked, went suddenly rigid, and toppled over to the dirt floor.

A thin thread of smoke drifted up from the stun gun in Ron's hand. He knelt down and poked at the limp body. Alice Louise eased up on the trigger and pointed Siggy aside.

"Yah. It's my neighbor, Ron Borke." Ron admired the stun gun in his hand, then looked up at Alice Louise. "Holy man. This thing has some wicked sting." He waved away a trail of smoke that rose from the creature's shabby jacket, dead center of the chest. "I thought Ron had the flu. He's been in pretty bad shape for the past few days. Now it looks more like he was–"

"Under a spell," Alice Louise finished for him. A black sense of dread descended upon her. "He said *they* wouldn't let him. Who, or *what*, are *they?*"

"Vampires, I imagine."

"We've met Carl. Who else?"

"I don't know. Something we haven't seen yet." He looked his neighbor over. "I think he's down for a while. We'd better serve our eviction notice on these boxes here, and get out before they come back. I think I have an idea for laying a trap."

Alice Louise held the flashlight while Ron shook his "holy water" out of the bottle in dribbles and chunks. It added a whole new dimension of *ambiance* to the fetid stench of the coffin-like boxes. The dirt in the boxes sizzled with each drop. White vapors rose up and oozed over the edges, cascading slowly and silently to the floor.

"Hurry it up," Alice Louise said. "We need to search this place for that little girl."

Everything that had happened tonight—no, the whole damned weekend—had her losing her focus.

"Are you thinking what I'm thinking?"

"Yes," Ron said.

"I mean, just to be clear, are we sure that–"

"Yes, we are," Ron said, leading Alice Louise out of the coffin room.

A Cold Winter's Deathe

She stopped and put a hand on his chest. "That Ron Borke snatched Maria and brought her here. It was Ron. Borke. Right?"

Ron sighed. "She's here somewhere. Ron is our kidnapper. Happy now?"

They closed the battered, rough-sawn oak door of the coffin room and stuck a bolt in the hasp, leaving Ron Borke trapped inside for later disposition.

With the cellar secured, they moved up to the main floor and began a search of all the many and various rooms there. The electricity was on, Ron had told her, but they agreed that they should leave the lights off and tiptoe through the house in darkness. Alice Louise was still familiar with the layout, from the cavernous living room, to the kitchen, the dining room, library, parlour, the multiple foyers, and the disintegrating conservatory. Ron had snagged a barely-functional flashlight from a junk drawer for her. She had to thump it every few seconds to keep it working.

"We need to get organized," she whispered to Ron as she followed him through the narrow passage of the butler's pantry. Once again, she imagined scowling faces in each of the ornate dinner plates lurking behind the deformed glass. "There are dozens of rooms to go through."

Ron stopped dead.

"I have an idea."

He darted ahead of her and disappeared out of the pantry, the glow of his flashlight flickering and vanishing beyond the corners and doorways.

"Hey!" she hissed, as she ran to keep up, slapping the flickering flashlight in her palm, as he darted through the entry foyer and spun toward the grand staircase that led up to the second floor. The bouncing glow of his light grew dimmer as he padded up the stairs, two at time, with Alice Louise following as fast as she could.

They ran down the long corridor of closed bedroom doors, past the one where Alice Louise had spent several sleepless, uneasy, long, dark nights.

And she suddenly knew where they were going.

Ron's light went suddenly dark. Alice Louise froze and waited.

She heard Ron round the corner to the left—a dead-end hall— stopping before one door.

Miss Catherine Cavendish's bedroom. The Cathy Cadaver of U.P. legend.

Alice Louise had actually been inside the room once. The door had been locked on her first night, then, a night or two later, and for no apparent reason that Ron could explain, she had found it ajar. The bedroom had been gorgeous, a soft, feminine refuge of luxury and grace. Inviting.

Alice Louise cupped her hand over the lens of her flashlight, only allowing a feeble sliver of light to leak out between her fingers. She inhaled, held her breath, and edged around the corner behind Ron.

The door was once again ajar—just barely an inch.

Ron silently set down Puck's box and pulled out the stun gun. Alice Louise thumbed off her flashlight, holding Siggy and the light together in a two-handed grip. Just like you see on TV, she thought with a wince. The moon must have been up, because as her eyes adjusted to the darkness she became aware of Ron, and the walls, and the floor, and the door, all barely visible in a dim glow filtering through the small window at the end of the hallway.

With the stun gun in his right hand and his flashlight held over his head like a club, Ron eased the door open with his shoulder.

Alice Louise heard a muffled squeak.

Ron flicked on his light and shadows jumped into the corners and twitched in the palsy of his unsteady hands..

A child cowered in the immense canopy bed, bound and gagged, and tied to the bedposts.

Alice Louise pocketed Siggy and the flashlight and raced to her, unbound her arms, freed her feet and pulled the gag out of her mouth.

The girl flung herself into Alice Louise's arms and clung to her neck, sobbing.

"It's OK, baby," Alice Louise cooed. Cradling her head, she buried her face in the girl's soft curls. "We have you now. You're safe with us."

"Well maybe," Ron mumbled from the doorway. "We gotta get out of here first."

Alice Louise shushed him, horrified that he'd be saying such things out loud in front of the girl. But she realized he was right. It was still pitch dark, and the kidnappers—including, she remembered, a terrifying beast that might have once been Carl Rowley—were still at large.

She pried Maria loose from her neck. Flicking on her flashlight, she held the child at arm's length, checking her over quickly. Pale. Red-rimmed eyes. Cooing gentle reassurances, she pulled at the flesh under one eye and peered in. Shocked at the lack of color, she pushed back the girl's lips and looked at her gums. Almost white. Bloodless. There was bruising on her throat. Looking closer, Alice Louise could see several punctures just over the girl's jugular.

"I'm sleepy," Maria whimpered.

Alice Louise scooped the child into her arms, wrapped her in a blanket, and carried her to Ron, who still waited by the door.

He ducked into the hallway ahead of her and peeked around the corner, down the long, dark corridor.

"What now?" she whispered. "She's beyond anemic. We have got to get her out of here."

"Ron Borke's here, so he must have come on his snowmobile. I'm betting it's in the carriage house. We'll go there."

"OK, genius, so where are the..." In consideration for the small ears pressed to her throat, she rejected the urge to say *vampires*. "Where are the other kidnappers?"

Ron winced and sighed. "Oh, probably just lying in wait for us somewhere."

34

RON LED the way down the corridor, past his bedroom and Alice's, and down the stairs. He paused occasionally, stretching out his senses beyond their immediate surroundings, beyond the rooms and the walls into the forest. He heard nothing. Felt nothing.

The house was empty of spirits. Miss Catherine had fled.

Still, his nerves jangled in anticipation of the inevitable.

Alice followed behind him, carrying Maria. Teeth chattering, stumbling over her own feet. Louder than a scurry of squirrels brawling and crashing through endless piles of dry leaves.

Deafening.

"Slow down!" she hissed. "I can't see!"

He paused and stopped himself from hammering the wall in frustration. What was wrong with her? He could see just fine. He'd realized it as soon as he'd turned off his flashlight outside Miss Catherine's suite. Not quite as well as in broad daylight, or even an overcast November day, but everything stood out clear and distinct now in an even, silvery glow.

And he felt damned good. Like he could run all the way back to Deathe carrying Maria and Alice on his shoulders. Who needed a snowmobile?

They crept out the back door and angled toward the carriage house, an immense barn with five stalls, stables in the back, and a loft that ran from wall to wall. It stood a dozen yards behind the manor. Ron peeked through the old windows into the first stall, looking for Borke's snowmobile, and a collection of garden tools he knew were out there somewhere. Hoes, shovels, hopefully even a scythe. Anything that might be useful in a fight with the undead. He finally had to relent and

A Cold Winter's Deathe

shine his light inside to see. The snowmobile was in the fourth stall, hidden under a tarp. He slipped the hasp and pulled open the doors.

"You go. Get her back to town," he told Alice.

He grabbed the bar on the back of the machine and steeled himself to wrestle it around 180 degrees, to aim it out the door. It proved to be remarkably light. He spun it with ease.

"What are you going to do?"

"It'll be getting light soon. I'll stay here and wait for sunrise. Then we'll see. Send back help." He didn't know how that was going to work out for her. Who would she send? Chief Woody? Professor Van Helsing? The Ghostbusters? What would she tell them? Ron Blank is single-handedly holding off a horde of vampires at his haunted house out in the bush?

He pulled the tarp off the machine. He was pleased to see it was the Arctic Cat, not the ratty old Ski-Doo.

He was not pleased to see it was a high performance model, with seating for barely more than the driver. Worse yet, he saw the empty hole where the key should be.

"How the hell do I get there?" she whispered. "I've never driven one of these before. I can't get this thing across the ravine. And I sure as hell can't drive the Masticator by myself!"

He flicked on his flashlight and shined it around on the snowy ground outside the carriage stall.

"See these snowmobile tracks? Follow them back toward town. Ron must have come by deer trails. It'll be shorter and quicker anyway." He lifted up the seat and rummaged around in the small cargo space. "Ah ha!" He came up with a key and dangled it in front of Alice. "You know anything at all about these things?"

"No."

"Swell. I'll start it, you just get on. I'll show you the basics." Which was the limits of his own knowledge of snowmobiles. "Steer with the handlebars," he said helpfully.

"I know how, Mr. Blank," Maria peeped from Alice's throat.

"Good girl!" Ron said. "We'll put you in charge. Keep Trooper Dubose safe, OK?"

She nodded. He ruffled her dark hair.

Sticking his head out the carriage house door, Ron scanned the area for signs of danger. Nothing moved in the darkness. All was silent, beyond Maria's and Alice's shallow breathing. At Ron's urging, Alice straddled the seat, and took the handlebars in a death grip. Maria tucked in behind her and locked her arms around Alice's waist. Ron guided Alice's feet into the stirrups, then showed her the throttle under her right thumb, and the brake handle on the left. Maria's head flopped, limp and loose, as she drifted on the edge of consciousness. Ron took her head in his hand and pressed her cheek to Alice's back.

"Here goes nothing," he whispered.

"Hang on, baby," Alice said. To Maria, Ron assumed.

He set the parking brake and choke, pulled up the stop switch, and gave the key a twist. The starter ground and the engine caught and revved, making a deafening racket, then it settled down to a sputtering, jangling idle. So much for trying to be quiet.

"This is insane," Alice said suddenly. "I can't just leave you here!"

"You said yourself you have to get her back to town."

He flicked a switch and the headlight flooded the snow-covered grounds behind Cavendish Manor, lighting up the night with dazzling white brilliance.

"Now go!" Ron commanded. He stepped back.

Alice Louise sat frozen on the snow machine, staring straight ahead. Ron spun to see what she was looking at.

Carl Rowley stood in front of the carriage house, blocking their escape.

ALICE LOUISE let go of the handlebars and ripped off her gloves. Her right hand took on a life of its own. It dove into her coat pocket and whipped out Siggy, flicking the safety off as it brought the weapon up and leveled it at Carl Rowley's chest. Her left hand sprung to assist and she held the Sig in a classic two-fisted grip before she had time to think about it.

Carl stood rooted before her like a redwood, his misshapen face white with blind fury, his black hair wild.

Ron was suddenly a blur of motion, diving directly into the line of fire.

Carl bolted forward and they crashed together. Ron bounced back as if hitting a brick wall, but not before his stun gun popped like a flashbulb, snapping so loud she could hear it over the idling snow machine. Carl lifted up, his back arching like a bow pulled taut, and dropped to his knees. Ron tumbled to the ground and rolled up on his feet, crouched and ready to spring, as Carl drooped, but stayed upright.

A Cold Winter's Deathe

Alice Louise stood up on the Arctic Cat and drew down on Carl. Head shot? Much smaller target than that massive chest, but it seemed like the safest bet.

Maria tumbled off the machine behind her. She glanced over her shoulder at the child, still and motionless on the dirt floor, and her heart broke. She turned back to Carl. Only her years of training and experience stopped her from pulling the trigger. Carl swayed on his knees, his dead eyes cast downward, unfocused.

"Down on the ground," she said, but her voice cracked, and it came out as barely more than a whisper. No one could hear it over the snowmobile's engine. She cleared her throat for a second try.

Ron circled around Carl, stun gun at the ready.

Carl got one knee up and planted a foot on the ground.

"Carl Rowley!" she shouted.

Hearing his name, he turned his head her way. His glazed eyes tried to focus on her.

Alice Louise's mind raced. To shoot, or not to shoot. Their lives, and her career, hung in the balance. And what was her life without her career? What would she be?

Ron crept up behind Carl, poked the stun gun in the back of his neck, and pulled the trigger. *Snap!* Carl went down on his face. Alice Louise breathed a little easier. Holding Siggy aside, she jumped off the Cat, reaching down to comfort Maria with her left hand.

Carl rolled over and struggled to get up.

Ron moved in again, but Carl's hand shot out and swatted Ron away like a pesky insect. Again, Ron tumbled away through the snow. This time he stayed down.

Alice Louise grabbed up a handful of blanket and pulled Maria onto the seat.

Carl was already on his hands and knees. She raised the gun again.

Ron gained his feet. He waved his arms at Alice Louise, trying to wave her off. He reached into his coat and pulled out the glass bottle. Unscrewing the cap, he turned the bottle upside down over Carl and sprinkled him.

Nothing happened. Carl didn't react. Oblivious, he struggled to get his feet under him.

Ron scowled at the bottle. Sniffed it. Tasted it. Made a face. He shrugged at Alice Louise and tossed the rest off it down his throat.

Throwing the empty bottle aside, he dug into his jacket again. He pulled out another bottle, uncapped it, and poured it on Carl.

Carl screamed. He buried his face in his hands. Wisps of smoke escaped between his fingers, and for an instant Alice Louise thought he would melt into the ground, wailing, "O what a world, what a world."

But Carl shot to his feet and spun on Ron, smoke now billowing from his head and hands.

"*Go!*" Ron shouted to Alice Louise. "*Now!*"

He turned and ran into the forest with Carl lumbering close behind him, howling with pain and rage.

Alice Louise watched, stunned, as they vanished into the darkness. Maria moaned. Stuffing Siggy into her pocket, Alice Louise dropped onto the Cat's seat, reached around and pulled Maria upright and tight against her back. She tugged the limp girl's arms around her waist and locked her hands together.

"Hang on tight!" Alice Louise commanded in her most official State Police voice. She patted the girl's hands, and said softly, "Stay with me, sweetie. Do *not* let go."

She thumbed the throttle and the Cat lurched out of the carriage house.

35

RON RAN west for all he was worth.

Carl hung close behind, crashing through the underbrush, snarling and spitting guttural grunts that were not human, but almost like an alien language—Klingon, maybe—and sounding suspiciously like deadly threats to Ron's life and limb.

Which was only to be expected.

At least Carl didn't have a shotgun this time.

Hurdling an iron fence, Ron flew across the snowy landscape. Racing through the Cavendish family cemetery behind the manor, he darted between century-old tombstones and black marble spires and monuments. He could hear Carl stumbling over grave markers behind him, pinballing off trees and headstones, falling behind. Ron vaulted the low stone wall on the far side of the cemetery and continued on, flying, the wind in his face, his breath coming free and easy, his arms and legs singing with joy.

Pausing a dozens yards further on, Ron turned and saw Carl still shambling in his direction, trailing wisps of smoke. He turned and jogged on, feeling good, not letting himself get too far ahead..

He missed seeing the signs.

Suddenly he was plunging headlong down a steep incline, arms flailing.

His toe caught a snow-covered tree root, and his heart caught in his throat as he fell toward the abyss. He reached out and hooked a sapling in the crook of his arm, slamming him to a halt. Momentum flung his feet out over the edge as he spun around and dropped hard, still clinging to the tree, his legs kicking in free air. Heart pounding, he clawed his way up the tree, digging his toes into the exposed roots, until he could finally stand. Leaning against the tree, breathing hard, he looked back.

Carl was stumbling around aimlessly, peering this way and that, lost and confused.

"*Carl! This way!*"

Carl stopped. Sniffing the air, he peered at Ron through the forest.

With a steadying hand on his tree, Ron stepped into full view.

"Come on, ya big, ugly bully!" Ron shouted. "Come and get me!"

With a howl of rage, Carl charged.

At the last instant, Ron simply stepped aside.

ALICE LOUISE leaned over the handlebars, teeth chattering with cold and fear, peering at the confusion of marks and gouges in the snow ahead of her. She saw snowmobile tracks in the flood of the Cat's headlight, but she had no idea whether they were coming or going. She angled to the left, changed her mind and pulled back to the right. Maria was a limp rag behind her. She thumbed the throttle and the Cat jumped forward, nearly throwing the girl off the back.

Fear and concern blackened her vision as she stopped to pull the girl upright. Maria's head lolled. She shivered violently. Alice Louise stripped off her down-filled parka, pulled Maria out of the blanket, zipped her into the parka, arms and all, and cocooned her in the blanket again. Unwinding the wool scarf from around her neck, she got back on the snow machine and somehow managed to pull Maria close behind her. She looped the scarf around them both to bind the girl tight to her back, safely tucked out of the frigid headwind.

She could hardly see the trail before her for her constant worry about Ron, back there at Cavendish House, dealing with Carl. She should have stayed. She should have shot Carl in the head, putting him down once and for all. But would that have worked? Her extensive police training, her emergency medical training, her life experience, her numerous forced marches into the morgues of southeast Michigan to view the corpses of perps and victims of violent crimes... all this was telling her a shot to the head should have worked.

Her gut told her that tonight, with Carl, it wouldn't have.

Reassured by the press of Maria against her back, she pulled the scarf snug and knotted it tight at her belly with shaking hands.

A Cold Winter's Deathe

She pressed her thumb to the throttle, but paused. She thought she heard a high-pitched whine. There was no way she would kill the engine to listen, out here in the forest, in the dark, with monsters not nearly far enough behind them. She pulled her chuke off her ears and strained to hear. Somewhere far off to the west she thought she saw lights flickering among the trees. They soon vanished.

"You OK, baby?" she whispered to the limp girl at her back.

Maria mumbled something vaguely affirmative.

With a quick glance over her shoulder, Alice Louise thumbed the throttle and the Cat leaped forward.

RON MADE his way back to Cavendish Manor.

Unfinished business awaited him. He no longer had Puck's tackle box. Nor the stun gun, Ron realized with a sudden jolt of panic. He patted every pocket and fold of his clothes. Nothing. No weapons at all. Black despair descended upon him. He had no idea what he would be facing, but he was sure it couldn't be any less frightening or dangerous than the undead Carl Rowley.

In the distance he heard the whine of a snowmobile. Alice Louise with Maria, safe and on their way to Deathe.

Then he saw lights moving somewhere near White Wolf Lake. Farther to the west than he would have expected. Was she lost? Pausing to look, he realized the sputtering whine of the snowmobile was actually getting louder, and closer, rather than farther away. The lights, too.

Holy wah. She'd gotten turned around and she was coming back to Cavendish House!

He picked up his feet and ran to meet her.

Darting through the Cavendish family plot, he jogged past the carriage house and the dark glass walls of the conservatory and around to the front of the house, just as the snowmobile clattered to a stop near the foyer. It wheezed and sputtered, its headlight shining directly into the recess of the front foyer. Ron stopped in his tracks.

Something was horribly wrong here. He sidled closer, only to see a figure in a mangy bomber hat clamber off Ron Borke's junkie Ski-Doo.

"Puck?" Ron asked, not believing his senses.

"Dude," the kid said. "I couldn't just leave you here. I felt really bad about dat. So I took de troll back to town–"

"*Troll?*"

"Well, I'm pretty sure he wasn't an *elf!* Though he might be a dwarf, I dunno. But not a real dwarf. More like one o' doze in dat *Lorda de Rings* t'ing, ya know? Anyways, I dropped him off at de police station, den I had a kinda attack of conscience or somthin'. I didn't recognize it at first!"

"I can't believe I'm saying this," Ron said, "but I'm really glad to see you."

"Oh yah?" He looked around, wary. "Where's.... you know? De vampires?"

"Carl's gone. I led him into the Bottomless Pit."

"Really? Bottomless pit, eh? Cool!" He scrunched up his face. "How deep is it?"

"It's *bottomless*. OK?"

He looked Ron up and down. "Where's my tackle box?"

"I don't know," Ron admitted. "I think I dropped it out back, by the carriage house."

"De stun gun, too? We might really kinda need doze, ya know." His head suddenly jerked toward the foyer, the bomber hat bobbing. He stiffened, yet seemed to physically shrink before Ron's eyes. "Like... *right now.*"

Over the sputtering idle of the Ski-Doo, Ron heard the front door creak open. He turned to look. In the light of the Ski-Doo's headlamp he saw a figure emerge from the house.

An angel. Incandescent. Glowing from within, so radiant, so dazzling and beautiful, it pained Ron's eyes, but he couldn't turn away.

"Julianna?" he said.

Her bare feet trailed beneath the lacy hem of her white gown as she floated across the snow-covered yard toward Ron, not leaving a trace of her passing. Her eyes were pure love. She opened her arms to him. Inviting him in. Welcoming him with unconditional love and acceptance. He wanted to melt into her embrace. He yearned for her to enfold him in the warmth of her pure, eternal love. Rising up off the ground, weightless, he floated toward Julianna. Mesmerized. Hypnotized.

"*No!*" Puck breathed.

Ron drifted closer to Julianna. She filled his vision.

"*Look away!*"

Julianna shielded her eyes from the glare of the snowmobile's headlight and squinted at Puck.

"Connie?" she said.

A Cold Winter's Deathe

Ron jerked to a halt.

Connie?

The fog that had nearly engulfed him cleared just a little. He twisted around to see Puck, The kid looked just as dazed as Ron felt.

"*Connie?*" Ron asked.

"Um. Yah. Dat's kinda short for Conrad. It's a long story Remember, dat's my name. Conrad. It ain't really Puck." Unable to meet Ron's eyes, he looked away. "Um. Mr. Blank? Um. Dis is my mudder."

Ron's jaw dropped with an audible clack.

Julianna? Puck's *mother?* She was barely out of her teens! And what the hell was she doing *here*, of all places?

"*How can this possibly be?*" Ron hissed to Puck.

"Well, she's a lot older den she looks to you right now. So am I. She got bit and died about eighty years ago. When I was nine or ten."

Ron stood dumbfounded, spluttering wordlessly.

"Den when I was seventeen," Puck said, "she came home and bit me an' dad. But we didn't die!" he protested. "I ain't a vampire! But now I don't age so much anymore. And better yet, I inherited some neat powers, eh? I been lookin' for her pretty much ever since."

"What the hell other secrets are you keeping from me?" Ron whispered.

"Well... I ain't really a Yooper–"

"So that's probably not the worst thing you could have said."

"We're Canadian."

"Now you're getting close."

"French Canadian."

"OK. You're there."

"Connie, Connie, Connie." Julianna heaved a sigh of resignation. "I had no idea *you* were the one pursuing me." She shook her head and clucked with profound disappointment. "Whatever were you thinking?"

"Well, I gotta do what I gotta do, eh?"

"And so must I. Ron? Kill Connie, please," she said sweetly.

Forces beyond Ron's control seized his body. Puzzled by the bloody scream emitting from his own mouth, he spun and charged at Puck. The kid stood his ground. Ron dove, swinging, but the kid ducked aside. Ron sailed past him, his fist connecting with nothing but empty air.

At the last instant, Puck's hand reached out of the red fog, fingers splayed, toward Ron's face. A fingertip brushed his cheek, and Ron collapsed to the ground in agony.

Black despair flooded over him. His life flashed before his eyes, past, present, and future. He saw that now he was worthless and unloved. A liar and fraud. Heartless. His life, his entire existence, lay bare before him. Wasted. He was a blight on the face of the earth. Grief filled his soul and he wanted only to sit in the snow forever and freeze solid. He sobbed for all the misery he had caused in his pathetic life.

He heard Puck's voice, hollow with distance. "Sorry, dude. You gotta get up. I need you."

He needs me? Ron felt a tiny glimmer of hope. No one had ever needed him in his life. Had they? He saw Puck reach a hand down to him.

"It ain't real, dude! You gotta get up now. I ... I can't stake my own mudder, ya know! I mean, dat would be just plain *wrong*."

"Ron!" Julianna's voice snapped like a stun gun inside his head. "You're an idiot. Now get up and kill Connie."

Ron scowled with irritation. Yes, he was an idiot. But he didn't appreciate being reminded of it. Even by Julianna. Puck gripped his hand and pulled him to his feet.

"Look at her," he said. "Look really good."

"Get away from him," Julianna commanded.

"Empty your mind," Puck whispered. "Get her out of it. Den look again. You got de power to see t'ings as dey really are. So? Now see dat t'ing as it really is."

"Don't listen to him," Julianna snarled. "He's playing you for a fool. *Look at me!* I am yours. Forever. See?" She tugged the folds of her white gown and fanned it, pirouetting for him. "This is my wedding dress. For you, Ron. Just for you." Her bare feet hovered inches above the snow as she turned. She smiled at him over her shoulder.

Ron shook his head to clear it. Like clearing the screen of an Etch-A-Sketch, the image of Julianna, young and beautiful, faded. Wiped away. To be replaced by....

A desiccated corpse, floating before him in filthy rags. Looking at him with a rictus grin.

He turned away. "Tell me you're not doing this to me!" he said, but Puck was no longer at his side. The kid was moving away from him, angling around toward the corner of the house.

A Cold Winter's Deathe

Julianna saw Ron's eyes following him. Her face jerked toward Puck.

She screamed. It pierced the night. Ron covered his ears. Puck bolted around the corner with Julianna flying after him, leaving Ron alone with the idling Ski-Doo. He hopped aboard and gunned the engine, shooting off after them.

36

ALICE LOUISE blasted through town with Maria still strapped to her back. Dawn was a vague promise in the east, but right now Deathe was deserted. She slowed and looked around. No sign of life anywhere. The village hall was dark, the police station abandoned. She had no idea where Maria lived, or Chief Woody, or anyone else, for that matter, except Beth and Ron. No clue where she might find any help at all.

Twisting the Cat's handlebars, she thumbed the throttle and rocketed toward Beth's.

The Cat chattered down Beth's street, blasted through the hardened snow piles at the end of Beth's driveway, and caught air. Alice Louise was already squeezing the brake with all her might when it hit the ground and slammed to a halt. She reached around and pulled Maria under her arm, carrying her on her hip to Beth's door.

She pounded and pounded on the door until a light finally came on.

"Who is it?" Beth asked, her voice muffled behind the thick oak.

"It's me! Alice Louise! *Open the freaking door!*"

"Good thing you remembered the password," Beth said as she pulled the door open. "Good Lord!" Beth breathed. Her eyes flew wide at the sight of the little girl, bundled in a blanket, as Alice Louise charged past her into the humid warmth of the cabin.

"Get her some liquids," Alice Louise barked as she laid Maria out on the couch. "Hot liquids. Milk. Apple juice. Tea with honey. Anything. She's freezing." She stuffed a pillow under the girl's feet, and took her face in her hands. "Beth! You have any hot water bottles?"

"No," Beth called from the kitchen. "I have a heating pad. And my electric blanket."

"Get them!"

"How about a shot of whiskey?" Beth called from her room as she stripped her bed.

Alice Louise paused in her assessment of the girl. "For her, or for me?"

"Yah."

"Do you think it would help?"

"It couldn't hoit," Beth said. "Could it?"

Alice Louise pulled off the girl's boots and rubbed her tiny, frozen feet. No sign of frostbite.

"How should I know? Bring it. And one for me. And get Chief Woody on the phone. I'll be glad to get *him* out of bed for a change," she added.

"Aye aye, Captain!"

"Draw a warm bath. And where's that heating pad?"

RON LEANED into the turn. The Ski-Doo's headlight lit up the carriage house and the yard behind the manor as he rounded the corner. Puck was on the ground, on his back. Not moving. Julianna stood over him, her face rigid and unreadable. Puck's tackle box lay a dozen feet beyond them, but the stun gun was nowhere in sight.

Ron braked to a stop.

Julianna turned toward Ron. From a dozen yards away, she reached out and yanked him off the snowmobile and threw him across the ground. He landed in a tumble of arms and legs, and before he could gather himself up she was on top of him, holding him down. Her desiccated face was inches from his; her filthy, matted hair hung over him like rotting curtains, brushing his cheeks.

She threw back her head and shrieked, then looked around expectantly. Ron glanced at Puck. He saw no sign of life.

"What have you done with my children?" Julianna hissed, her mouth pressed close to Ron's ear. Her breath smelled of carrion. "Where is my precious Carl? My protector. My defender. And my good boy? The other Ron. My good and faithful servant. He's been most helpful to me."

"Ron Borke?" Ron breathed. Something clicked in his brain. "He's your *personal assistant*?"

She lifted her head and gazed across the yard. *"Do not* tell me you have brought harm to them."

Ron gulped.

"I took care of 'em," Puck called to her, as he painfully levered himself up onto one elbow. "I t'rew Carl in de Bottomless Pit."

"The Bottomless Pit," Julianna echoed, seriously amused. Her dead eyes searched Ron's. "How deep is that?"

"Geez." Ron said, struggling helplessly under her surprising strength. "What part of *bottomless* can't anybody understand?"

From the corner of his eye, he saw Puck standing over Julianna's shoulder. He heard a zipper.

Julianna screamed with pain. In an instant she was halfway across the yard by the Ski-Doo. Smoke billowed from her hair and back.

"Uh oh. I got some of my holy water on ya," Puck said to Ron as he zipped up his jacket. "I manufactured a new batch a while ago," he said, showing Ron a beer bottle.

"That is just plain *sick*, man" Ron spat.

In a fit of rage, Julianna picked up the snowmobile and flung it twenty feet. It rolled over and over, the yellow fiberglass shell shattering and shredding across the yard.

"Don't worry, dude. I got it under control." Puck showed Ron the stun gun clutched close to his chest. But his voice and the fear in his eyes betrayed him.

And then he was gone. Carried away, as Julianna launched herself across the yard and body-slammed him into the carriage house. The stun gun lay at Ron's side. He picked it up.

Julianna and Puck tumbled through the snow. Ron struggled to his feet, stun gun in hand, and circled them as they flailed. Julianna clawed and bit, but Puck held his own. She screamed obscenities. Ron thrust the stun gun at her and pulled the trigger. It snapped, but she'd spun away. She swatted him, and pain exploded in his head as he fell to the ground.

The stun gun vanished into the darkness.

Ron crawled to the Ski-Doo. He rolled up onto its track and skids. Straddling the seat, he pulled out the kill switch and yanked the starter cord. The engine sputtered, but didn't fire. He pulled again. And again. And again.

The sky was lightening. Morning was a soft, even glow, blanketing the forest.

A Cold Winter's Deathe

Julianna stood over Puck. She glanced at Ron, pulling the starter cord for all he was worth, then her eyes returned to Puck, limp at her feet.

The Ski-Doo's engine caught and sputtered to life.

Julianna rolled her eyes at Ron, dismissing him. Her gaze returned to Puck. With a sigh of sad resignation, she said, "I'm sorry, Connie. I guess I'll just have to get back to you later."

She picked him up and threw him into the forest.

Ron stabbed the throttle with his thumb, and the Ski-Doo jerked forward and accelerated.

"Where are you going, Ron? You can't get away from me, you know."

He glanced back over his shoulder to see her loping along easily, her head thrown back, laughing at him. Enjoying the chase, a cat after a mouse. Her bare feet hardly touched the snow. She flew over it.

Through the trees he could see beyond White Wolf Lake, glittering white at the edges, ominous black in the middle. And the lights of Deathe beyond. He aimed for them.

Black tree trunks shot out of the darkness at him. He dodged them, hurtling over exposed roots. Low branches slapped him in the face. The Ski-Doo shot over a ridge, slammed down onto the snow covered beach. Ron cranked the throttle and shot out onto the lake.

ALICE LOUISE breathed a sigh of relief. Chief Woody was on his way with some of the volunteer fire department paramedics. Maria looked good, all things considered. She was out of danger as far as frostbite and hypothermia were concerned. The bite marks on her neck were not as severe as she'd first thought. More like nibbles. But Alice Louise was convinced she'd need a blood transfusion.

Alice Louise cupped a mug of hot chocolate in her hands, luxuriating in it.

"Where's Ron?" Beth asked, pulling Alice Louise out of her reverie.

Holy crap. She hadn't forgotten about him... exactly. Now fresh fear gripped her heart.

"I left him at Cavendish House," she said.

"What's he doing there?"

Fighting vampires, she thought. Maybe. She remembered that Cavendish House was somewhere to the northeast, beyond White Wolf Lake. She padded over to the window, brushed the shades aside, unlatched and threw open the storm shutters. The sky was dull gray with the promise of a clear new dawn. Stars faded in the soft glow of imminent sunrise.

No phone. No radios. If only there was some way he could let her know what was happening.

"I have to get back there," Alice Louise said. "Help me saddle up."

She zipped up her snowmobile suit and pulled on her gloves as she charged out the door.

Beth slipped into her coat and stumbled after Alice Louise, hopping on one foot as she tugged on her boots, to where the Arctic Cat sat, silent, in the frigid predawn.

Alice Louise heard the wail of a village police cruiser's siren. Very close. Then headlights flashed and Chief Woody's Cherokee slid into the driveway, closely followed by two SUVs belonging to the volunteer firefighters.

"Inside!" Alice Louise called to them, waving them toward the door.

She straddled the Cat and reached for the starter. Looking out across the expanse of the lake, she saw a light flickering in the distance.

She called to Beth. "What's that?"

Beth ambled to her side. She followed Alice Louise's gaze.

"Looks like some idiot is trying to ride a snowmobile across the lake."

JULIANNA SCREAMED. The thrill of the chase, he thought, had suddenly turned challenging for her. He glanced back. She was still coming— furious, desperate.

With no shell and no windshield, the icy wind shrieked in his face. The battered machine shook like a cement mixer. Ron saw the thin, white ice racing beneath the vibrating runners in a blur. The speedometer glowed a soft green—45 miles per, but not climbing.

He wrenched the broken mirror so he could look back. Julianna was gaining ground, her tattered, dingy wedding gown streaming out behind her, bright red in the glow of the taillight. He thumbed the throttle harder, but the Ski-Doo had no more to give.

The ice turned dark. Freezing spray stung his face like a million needles. Water gushed out under the runners and shot high behind the spinning track. Julianna ignored it. In the cracked mirror, he could see

A Cold Winter's Deathe

her reaching, her fingers outstretched, clutching, grasping, just a few feet behind.

Alice Louise hit the starter. She cranked the handlebars toward the lake and pressed her thumb on the throttle. Beth suddenly grabbed her collar and pulled hard.

"*What the hell?*"

"You *cannot* go out on the lake!" Beth shouted over the rumble of the engine. "It's not frozen over! You'll go straight to the bottom!"

Alice Louise stared out at the figures—*figures?*—racing toward the lake's dark center.

"So will Ron! We've got to do something!" She pressed the throttle. The engine revved.

"Wait!" Beth barked. She looked around wildly. "I'll get the ladder."

Ladder?

Beth dashed to the side of her shed where a short extension ladder hung on two hooks. She pulled it off and carted it back to the Cat. Alice Louise ducked as Beth swung it around and aligned it with the machine. She stuck her arm through the rungs and held it tight.

Taking a deep breath, Beth snapped, "What are you waiting for? *Give her tarpaper!*"

Alice Louise hit the throttle and the Cat shot toward the lake.

RON HEARD the ice cracking, even over the scream of the engine and the roar of the spray. The rear of the machine dipped, and the spray of water and ice shot a huge rooster-tail back over Julianna. She howled with rage. The ice vanished completely and he was fishtailing on open water. Then the skis caught a chunk of solid ice and he was thrown into the handlebars.

He stopped dead in the middle of the lake.

Julianna shrieked and plunged into the icy waters close behind.

The tail of the Ski-Doo dropped. The headlight shined up into the sky, then blinked off as the engine sputtered and died, and Ron was in near-darkness, in silence, and in freezing water.

The machine was sinking, pulling Ron under. Freezing waters enveloped him, driving the breath from his lungs, burning his flesh like fire.

He kicked free of the handlebars and the Ski-Doo was gone to the bottom.

Thrashing to hold his head above water, he fought against shock and the burning, fiery cold.

Julianna flailed close by.

"Ron!" she called. "Come to me. Help me."

He stole a glance over his shoulder. She was just a few yards away, her honey-blond hair plastered to her head. She reached out to him. Her face was beautiful again. Angelic.

God help him, he wanted to save her. But first he had to save himself.

Kicking, grasping, he managed to hold onto a thin sheet of ice. He pulled himself forward. It broke off and he went under. He came up spitting and gagging.

Hearing the whine of a snowmobile engine, Ron's heart leapt. It died somewhere in the distance, and his hopes died with it. But then he heard another voice, coming from the direction of Deathe. A light shined out across the ice, and in it he saw dark figures running across the ice toward him.

Alice Louise Dubose. And Beth. But how could that be? Why were they carrying a *ladder?* He was in the water, freezing, not high up somewhere, looking down on them.

Not yet.

"Go back!" he tried to say, but his voice cracked and nothing came out. He grasped at the thin ice. It flaked away in his hands.

"Help me, Ron," Julianna pleaded. "My love. Save me."

Alice dropped to her hands and knees, then splayed out flat on her belly and inched forward, pushing the ladder ahead of her across the ice toward him.

"Grab the ladder!" she screamed. Beth was behind Alice, on her hands and knees, clutching Alice's pantleg.

His inner fire was burning out. Numbness replaced the pain in his arms and legs. He stopped kicking and sank instantly. Ice water closed over his face and mouth. He kicked again, once, and came up sputtering for breath.

He couldn't reach it. Alice pushed the ladder closer.

"Go back," Ron breathed. *Save yourself.*

Alice shook free from Beth's grasp and crawled on top of the ladder. She inched closer to Ron, reaching out her hand.

"O-*ree*-un Clemens Blankenship, *damn you!* Take my hand! *Now!*"

A Cold Winter's Deathe

He stretched out and she caught his fingers. She hung on to a rung of the ladder with her other hand, dug in her toes, and crushed Ron's hand in hers. Beth scrabbled backwards, flat on the ice now, tugging at the ladder for all she was worth, with Alice and Ron clinging for life. He tried to pull himself up onto the ice. It kept breaking off in his hands.

He heard Julianna behind him, gurgling. Sinking.

"Ron," she said. "I love you. Save me."

He looked over his shoulder in time to see her slip beneath the black surface.

With a last effort, Ron managed to throw his arm up and over the top rung of the ladder. Alice stretched out, grabbed his collar and held on. He heard other voices now. More people were running across the ice toward him. Someone lumbered up behind Beth with a rope.

Chief Woody?

The burning cold was gone now. He could no longer feel his arms or legs.

He went limp, but Alice held fast. He was suddenly feeling quite warm. Deliciously warm.

White light filled his vision. He felt himself pulled toward it. But suddenly it went dark, and he saw a beautiful face hovering over him in its place, looking down with affection and deep concern... crying, sobbing with terror and joy and pain and relief.

He reached up with a frozen glove and patted Alice's cheek, then fell into darkness.

37

FROM HIS cushy nest on Beth's couch, Ron could see the full length of White Wolf Lake through the window. He squinted against the midday sunlight, trying to make out the hole in the center, or even a dark spot on the ice. The place where he had almost died. He couldn't see it. The lake had healed over. Flash frozen.

Alice sat hunched over Beth's desk, thumbing through a notebook.

"Catching up on paperwork?" Ron croaked.

"Ron! You're awake!" She popped up from her chair and rushed to perch on the couch at his side. She pressed her hand to his forehead and ignored his feeble attempt to brush it away.

"I'll have to file some kind of report eventually, you know. I have no idea what it'll say. This is Puck's journal." She thumbed the ancient notebook. "I found it near the carriage house."

"When?"

"Yesterday. You've really been out of it for the past thirty hours or so. I went back with Woody and the boys, and we searched the house and grounds. They're still trying to sort out what was going on out there. I, um... haven't been too helpful on that just yet." She looked away. "I told them we had an anonymous tip that Maria had been taken there. We found her and I brought her back. How are you feeling?"

"Bad. Hung over. It must have been some party."

"It was," Alice groaned. "A real killer."

"Puck had a journal?"

"No one knows about this journal yet. It's... interesting. If you can believe any of it. Did you know he wasn't even a Yooper?"

"I think he mentioned he was French Canadian."

A Cold Winter's Deathe

"True enough. I guess. He was born in Quebec. He claims to have chased vampires all up and down the St. Lawrence River. For decades. Apparently never actually killed one, though. He talks about his mind trick, learning to use it, learning its limitations. Other stuff. Like that 'holy water' of his you used. You do know it wasn't really holy water, right?"

"Um, yah. That I do know."

"Yes. Just some kind of liquid with silver nitrate mixed in. Apparently the old legend about vampires not tolerating silver is true."

Ron sighed with relief. One mystery explained. Although he was loathe to tell Alice exactly what the liquid was. "Refined" beer? That might lead her to ask questions she didn't want answered.

"Did you find him?" Ron asked.

"No. No sign of him. Or Carl Rowley's body."

"We're safe on that count," Ron said.

Regardless of everyone's skepticism about the Bottomless Pit, there was no chance Carl would ever be seen again.

"Well, it's still an ongoing investigation, but no one knows he was out at Cavendish House last night, walking around, trying to kill us after he was dead. And I am *not* about to tell anyone *that*. Ron Borke is recovering at home. He's under house arrest—B &E, petty theft and the like. But Chief Woody cites extenuating circumstances. Drugs and alcohol, mostly. They found him passed out in Miss Catherine's bed, surrounded by all that expensive liquor you left behind. Well, the empties, anyway."

Ron groaned, thinking not only of his collection, but of Ron Borke defiling Miss Catherine's bed and bedchamber. He had not felt even a hint of her presence in the house when they'd been searching for Puck's vampires. She'd probably been chased away—to wherever gentle spirits go when they're offended.

"How did he break out of the cellar? We had him locked in pretty securely."

"No idea. He has no memory of anything past last Friday."

"What about the coffins?"

"Nothing left of them but ash and charcoal. No scorch marks anywhere in the room. No one has any idea what burned there. Or how."

"Maria?" Ron asked.

"She'll be OK. They choppered her to the big hospital up in Hankock. But her parents are way beyond overjoyed. They want to throw you and me a party."

His eyes felt heavy.

"Ron? Do you want to talk about all this?"

"Just to say… we're not really going to tell anyone about any of this, are we? Ever?"

"Who could I tell? I don't even know myself what happened. I'm having trouble believing it now. Hell, I'm having trouble remembering it." She scowled at the floor with frustration, then shook her head as if surrendering to the fact that some vagrant thought had permanently eluded her.

His mind was perfectly clear, even though he was feeling as if he was coming down off a three-day drunk. Or maybe some kind of hallucinogenic drug overdose.

"So," Alice ventured. "Where was this prime vampire that Puck was chasing? I mean, who, or what, made Carl like he was?" She shivered. "Did you see it? I don't understand any of this.

"And by the way, whatever became of your… *girlfriend?*" she spat. Ron peered at her, curious about her irritation, not believing that he detected a note of jealousy in her voice. "*Julianna* or whatever her name is. She seems to have just disappeared the other night."

"I really can't say," he said.

Alice seemed to accept that as a declaration of ignorance. She shook her head and thumbed through the yellowed pages of Puck's journal, lost in thought.

Ron turned to stare out over the lake.

The sky was clear—a pure, intense blue-white that dazzled his eyes. The air temperature was in the single digits and still dropping.

The lake would probably now be frozen nearly solid till spring.

And come spring, when the lake warmed, and the ice broke and melted away, and boats were launched, and fishermen trolled the shallows for record bass and bluegills... the busybodies at Cavendish Junior College would probably call the DNR and the EPA and insist that someone must try to retrieve Ron Borke's snowmobile from the lake bottom.

Ron Blank wanted to be there for it.

Julianna was still waiting for him somewhere down there.

Sleeping.

A Cold Winter's Deathe

Visit

www.yoopernaturalmysteries.com

for news of upcoming releases.